DEC 20 1984			
JAN 7 1985			

RECOVERY

RECOVERY

Steven L. Thompson

WARNER BOOKS

A Warner Communications Company

Warner Books Edition
Copyright © 1980 by Steven L. Thompson
All rights reserved.
Warner Books, Inc., 75 Rockefeller Plaza, New York, N.Y. 10019

 A Warner Communications Company

Map by Paul J. Pugliese, GCI
Distributed in the United States by Random House, Inc., and
in Canada by Random House of Canada, Ltd.
Printed in the United States of America
First Printing: October 1980
10 9 8 7 6 5 4 3 2 1

Library of Congress Cataloging in Publication Data

Thompson, Steven L
  Recovery.

  I. Title.
PZ4.T4762Re   [PS3570.H6437]   813'.54   80-12706
ISBN 0-446-51207-9

Book design by Helen Roberts

For Merry,
who started it all

Author's Note

This is a work of fiction, in which the characters and events spring entirely from the author's imagination. However, some fundamental details of the story are based on facts, many of which were classified until recently. For instance, it wasn't until the declassification of an Arms Control and Disarmament Agency report on September 9, 1975, that the origins and functions of the United States Military Liaison Mission in Potsdam, East Germany, were brought to full public disclosure. Moreover, the Air Force's interest in biocybernetic research and development, which was used as the basis for the Jesus Box and which aims to link man and machine in a combat aircraft, was first reported in depth in the January 29, 1979, edition of *Aviation Week & Space Technology*. And only five months before, on September 3, 1978, Fairchild Republic issued a press release officially acknowledging its intention to build an all-weather, electronically advanced A-10 Thunderbolt II in an attempt to make the already deadly ground-attack aircraft even deadlier.

Acknowledgments

Without the knowledge, experience, and insight of its two technical advisers, *Recovery* could not have been written. Lieutenant Colonel F. Clifton Berry, Jr. (USA, Ret.), and Major Herbert O. Hester (USAF, Ret.) worked endlessly to ensure that the story is as accurate as fiction can be. The results speak for themselves.

Besides official help, this novel was supported by others whose aid was invaluable. Among those, David Abrahamson, Leon Mandel, Michael Jordan, and Ted West form the vanguard, and under this heading also belongs the name of Jacques de Spoelberch, a friend and literary agent who won't let the craziness or laziness of a writer keep a story from being written.

Additional assistance came from so many that recognition in these pages would consume too much time and type. Suffice it to say that I am grateful to all those who pushed, cajoled, typed, phoned, researched, tested, and just read *Recovery* into life. Only the reader can know if their efforts were justified, but I can never thank them enough.

STEVEN L. THOMPSON

San Pedro, California
March 18, 1979

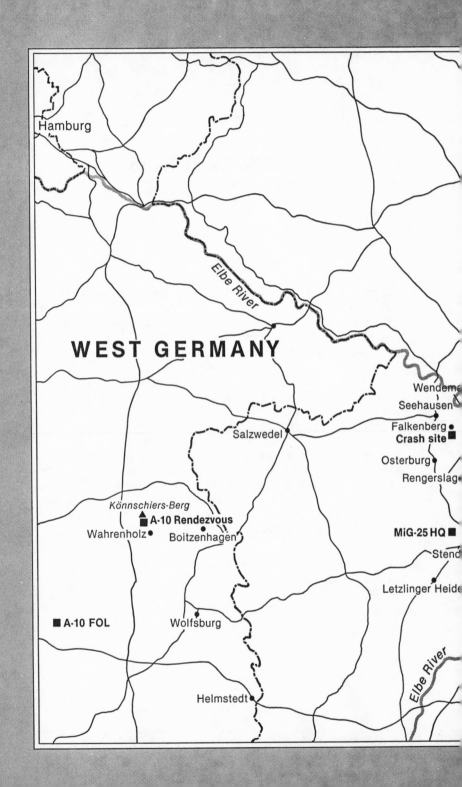

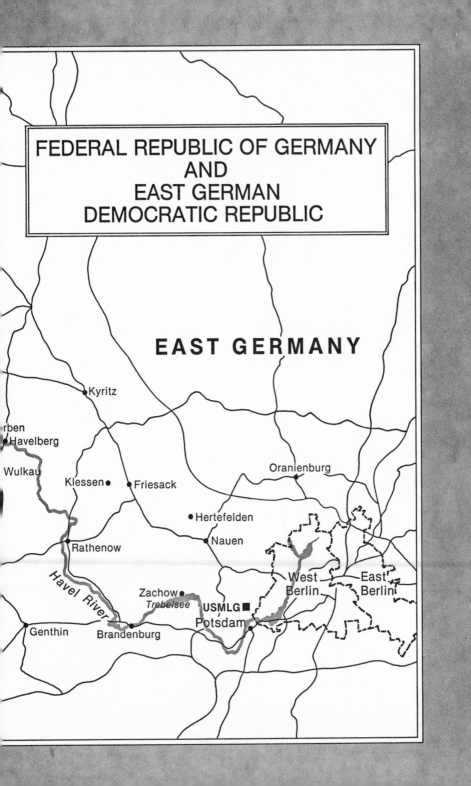

PROLOGUE

1963

THE COLD AND THE ROAD TO NEHRINGEN FINAL-
ly stopped him. An icy wind came out of the lowering sky
and probed his wound, forcing him to halt his headlong
flight. He crouched, panting, on the weed-covered bank,
the pain in his leg growing worse as the temperature
dropped.

Only his ruthless training prevented him from pitching forward on the deserted road. His mind was fogged
with pain, his body numbed with cold. He wanted desperately to rest. But the years of intense training drove him
on.

After a few moments he slowed his hoarse breathing
and lurched to his feet. Unsteadily, he began to hobble
along the little country road. His gaze was fixed in front of
his stumbling feet.

He collected rocks. Stooping stiffly from the waist in
order to avoid bending his left leg, he collected round
rocks, oblong rocks, square rocks. They were all about the
same size. Egg-size. When he had an armful, he looked
both ways along the twilit road. To the west, Nehringen.
To the east, Nossendorf. Two remote East German farm
villages, linked by the narrow, iron-hard road.

It stood on a levee, like a Dutch farm road. To the
north was the edge of the dense forest through which he'd
emerged. It ran all the way to the Baltic Sea, thirty miles

3

away. To the south, past the canal and the frozen, stubbled fields, the whole of East Germany. He could go no farther.

He swayed as the pain bit hard. After a moment his heart slowed down and he looked carefully at the roadside. About ten feet away, a culvert undercut the raised roadway. Around the mouth of its rusted corrugations stood a clump of stumpy trees and undergrowth. He strained to see through the growing darkness. The little trees were the only cover near the road for a quarter of a mile either way. And a quarter of a mile was the limit of his endurance.

He limped slowly to the road's shoulder above the culvert. He dropped his precious load of stones. The little avalanche rang like a burst of machine-gun fire, but nothing moved in the winter silence.

Biting his lip against the waves of pain from his slashed leg, he lowered himself to the ground next to the scattered stones. He looked at the wound once he sat down. The cannon shell had torn through the fleshy part of his calf. He'd bound it with parachute cord and nylon, but it was still bleeding.

He pushed the red haze back and began stacking the rocks. It took all his fading concentration. The marker had to be about a foot high, they'd said, and conical in shape. His fingers had long since lost their feeling, so the cone was slow in forming. The rocks would stack neatly to a point, then he'd watch helplessly as they tumbled down. As he worked it grew colder and darker.

He knew the stakes, so he kept piling the little stones up. The cold of the road sucked the warmth through the flimsy nylon of his dirty flight suit. His legs and buttocks were completely numb when he carefully placed the last rock on the little pyramid. Holding his breath, he willed his shaking hand to make it stay. He drew his hand away, and the rock slid into place. It didn't move.

He stared, exhausted, at the marker. It took all his strength to crawl away from it. He moved slowly, straining to keep his frozen limbs away from the rocks. He cleared his legs and lay on his side, gasping.

4

Concealment. He had to have cover. The thought pounded through his brain. There was only the little clump of trees by the culvert mouth. They'd have to do.

He rolled over on his stomach and inched to the edge of the road. He would have to slide down the levee bank. He couldn't walk. He reached out with his left hand and pulled himself sideways over the edge.

The bank was steeper than he'd thought. He couldn't brake his momentum. He slid down lengthwise in a miniature landslide of dirt and pebbles. His left leg hit a buried rock and the jolt sent a shock through him. He gasped in agony and nearly fainted. Then he was lying, limbs akimbo, at the bottom, wedged against the wiry tree roots. Some dirt continued falling, coating him with a rime of earth. He rested his head where it had landed among the roots, panting.

He could manage only to turn over. His strength was completely gone, and he knew it. He could feel his body only in moments of acute pain. He struggled and brought himself to a reasonably comfortable position.

He lay faceup, his legs along the edge of the levee, aimed back toward Nossendorf. He was defenseless, save for his revolver. He had no more options. He struggled to bring his hand up and finally jerked the .38 out of the shoulder holster. Its stubby outline was little enough reassurance, but it was all he had, aside from the marker above.

He reviewed what they'd told him. The memories came sluggishly, as if his mind, too, were freezing. Ask for a Russian officer, they'd said. Don't talk to the East Germans at all. Give them nothing but name, rank, and serial number. Just like Korea. And the Pacific. His eyelids drooped. It seemed strange, he thought drowsily, that he should have survived hot wars completely unscathed to lie dying in a cold one. To avoid the flak and fighters only to buy a piece in a border incident.

For a moment he almost grinned. It was crazy, maybe, but no crazier than any other way to die with an airplane. Better this than burning up in a flaming dive. Getting lured across the East German coast by a phony TACAN

5

beacon and mixing it up with a bunch of MiG-15s had it all over burning up. And after all, he'd gotten three of the bastards with the tail 20-mm before they'd chopped off his port wing.

He thought of their reactions back at the base when they heard how he got it. Back at Sculthorpe, they'd know, somehow, that he'd gotten a few. And that he'd held on like a madman while the crew bailed out. They'd know, whatever happened to him in the frozen ditch. Thinking about that made him feel better. He dozed off.

When he jerked awake, it was deeper night. The stars cast a faint, creamy glow over the barren landscape. He twisted his neck to see if his little marker was still above on the road. From where he lay he could just make out the tip of the irregular pyramid. Nobody had gone by. Any marked vibration and the stones would have tumbled down. A self-erasing marker.

But would anyone on his side come along to see it? He forced his stiff fingers from the grip of the revolver and looked at his watch. He'd been on the ground five hours. How could he have been missed? By now the German Volkspolizei must surely have his scent. They couldn't be that clumsy. And if they were, then the Russian specialists they'd told him about in Intelligence most certainly would not be.

The only explanation was that because the crew bailed out in the low cloud only seconds before the bomber blew up, their trails were confused. There'd been a hell of an impressive fireball. And he hadn't seen or heard anything on his way to the Nehringen road. Winter in East Germany obviously wasn't a time for travel.

He felt for the little radio in his flight-suit pocket. It was continuously transmitting a Mayday signal. Why hadn't his people—the search-and-rescue types who were supposed to live just for little cones by the road—why hadn't they showed up? The Intelligence people had drilled them endlessly on crash procedures in East Germany, always centering their training on the search-and-rescue teams. If the transmitter didn't bring them, Intelligence had said, the marker would.

6

So far neither had worked. The only company he had was the cold. Thinking about it made him shiver. The pain in his calf flamed. He gasped and cried out. Then he felt as if a giant fist clenched his leg and he passed out.

He regained consciousness slowly. He focused his eyes and saw that it was still night. The stars had not moved much. He had been out for only a short time.

Everything below his chest was numb. He stared at his feet and tried to make them move, but he couldn't. He blinked and ice fell from his eyelashes. Ice rimmed his lips. Staring at the coagulated blood that had seeped through the parachute cord, he willed his leg to hurt again. But he felt nothing. He tried again, concentrating his last energy on the long wound. And almost missed the faint drone of the motor.

It was a low vibration in the earth at first. He felt it as a tingle through his body. Then, seconds later, he heard the faraway sound of a car engine. Even then its meaning escaped his fuddled mind.

By the time the headlights made the frigid air glow he had made the connection.

They were coming.

But who? Vopos or Americans?

The drone got louder. He strained to identify it. But the pain and cold had stolen his senses. His thoughts were mired in molasses.

He looked at the gun still gripped by his numbed hand. Name, rank, and serial number, they'd said. Talk only to Russian officers.

The drone grew louder still. It became a roaring drumroll. Toward his feet, the headlights lit up half the sky.

Russians only. Name, rank, and serial number.

I got three of you bastards.

He hefted the gun unsteadily. Above him, a large car thundered past. The dazzling glare of its headlights was instantly replaced by the red glow of its taillights. It was moving very fast. The little pile of stones shivered.

He hadn't time to realize they'd passed before there was a change in the sound of the engine. It dropped in

7

key. Became less urgent. The drumroll slowed. Then stopped. There was a distant squeal of tires.

They backed up. He recognized the whine of a reverse gear. It seemed to take a long time before they stopped directly above him.

Russians only. Name, rank, and serial number . . .

A door opened, then slammed shut. Gravel crunched under heavy feet. The pilot craned his neck painfully to stare up into the glare above. A man was silhouetted against the light. The pilot saw him reach into his pocket and withdraw something bulky. He pointed it down into the ditch.

The pilot raised his .38. His arms shook and the gun weaved erratically. He groaned and struggled to lift the gun toward the figure above. He squinted against the glare and aimed unsteadily. He had the man in the sight, but he wouldn't stay put. He wobbled around. The pilot shut his eyes and squeezed the trigger.

Nothing happened. He opened his eyes and squeezed again, desperately. But his strength was gone, drained into the hard, cold dirt of East Germany. He let his arms drop and stared hopelessly up at the man above.

A beam of light stabbed out from the object in the man's hand. It blinded the pilot. He tried to aim the gun up the bank at them again and screamed.

The scream came out a croak.

"Russians only, you bastards. I got three. Come on—"

Then they had him. Strong hands pulled the gun out of his frozen fist. He slumped, helpless. They began to haul him up the slope, and he mumbled, "Name, rank, serial number. Russians only, officers only, name, rank—"

A laugh boomed out from the man carrying his legs. The pilot opened his eyes and watched him as he spoke.

"Hell, Captain, you don't have to go through that. We know who you are. We've got your navigator and bombardier in this here Ford. You're as good as home right now."

They lifted him onto the road and he saw the speaker in the headlights. He wore U.S. Army sergeant's chevrons.

Before the pilot could say anything, they had him in their arms again. Anxious hands—his crewmen's hands—

8

reached out of the back seat of the Ford to help. They pulled him into the warm car and he found himself looking up into the concerned face of his navigator. A door slammed, then another. He felt the car *thunk* into gear. They began to move forward.

He struggled for speech against unconsciousness.

"Who . . . who are . . . they?"

The navigator grinned down at him. The car gathered speed.

"It's just like they told us in Intelligence, Cap'n. When you get into trouble over here, just dial *R* for these guys." He inclined his head toward the two men in the front seat.

The pilot's vision was becoming clouded. He frowned through the haze.

"*R?* What's . . . "

The navigator grinned wider.

"You know, Cap. *R* for 'Recovery.' "

The pilot smiled. Then his eyes closed as the Ford started them on their long journey home.

1982

1

HORNAK SWEATED. THE CLAMMY FOG CHILLED him to the bone, but still he sweated.

Perhaps it's only natural, he thought as he looked again at the brightly lit entrance to Operations. Perhaps one has a right to be nervous when one hasn't been activated for so many years.

Except for the fluorescent glow from the Ops building's foyer, it was dark. Silent as a tomb in the cold English mist. At the flight-direction center for a fighter base whose aircraft were grounded by bad weather and darkness, it could hardly be otherwise.

But still Hornak sweated. He stood like a sentry across from the deserted parking lot in front of the old brick building, and the cold perspiration trickled slowly down his back.

He knew he had nothing to fear. In all his years among the Americans he had learned many things about them. Things that, to his surprise, he found he liked, but more things that proved the truth of what he had been taught in Hungary and Moscow. He had discovered much, but most of all, he had discovered that Americans were never prepared. So, he told himself, he had nothing to fear. His plan would not fail because it was unexpected.

He looked at his watch. Three-forty-five. After hours of empty duty the two men inside would be dulled and listless. Ready for companionship.

He took a deep breath and strode quickly across the wet asphalt. Entering the foyer, he carefully wiped his feet on the mat, then turned left down a long corridor. At the end stood a steel door, flanked by a TV camera high in the corner and a small black computer-lock keyboard set flush into the wall. A small speaker grille was mounted above the keyboard, along with a push button and a notice: ATTENTION VISITORS TO THE COMMAND CENTER: PUSH RED BUTTON AND HOLD UNTIL SPEAKER ACTIVATION.

He slowed his erratic breathing, composed his features, and pushed the button.

Behind the steel door a light glowed on the duty officer's command console. Asleep on a cot in the small anteroom behind the display boards, he didn't see it. But the persistent drone of the buzzer awoke the man dozing at the next console. Technical Sergeant Joe Kearny glanced at the light, then tried to focus on the monitor in his console. Blinking, he made out, through the distortion of the wide-angle lens, the close-cropped gray hair, lantern jaw, and big nose of a man wearing an Air Force fatigue uniform with master sergeant's chevrons on each sleeve. Even without straining to read the name tape sewn on the man's fatigue jacket, Kearny knew who it was.

He flipped up a toggle and spoke into the microphone in his console. "For Chrissake, Gus, what the hell are you doing over here at this time of night?"

Master Sergeant Gustav Hornak, supervisor of the RAF Bentwaters Flight-Line Life-Support Unit, smiled up at the camera. "Me and the boys had a late night with the new rafts. Figured what the hell, might as well drop by to see you, Joe. And to, well"—Hornak held up a bundle to the camera—"see if this would do the job for you." He said the last words with a slow wink.

Kearny chuckled. Good old Gus. The only supply dude you could count on. "Sure thing, Gus," he said. "Bring your butt on in."

The door buzzed and Hornak walked into the com-

14

mand post. He blinked away the sweat and forced a smile.

Kearny swiveled his chair and held a finger up to his lips. "Shhh—the duty officer's on the rack."

Hornak followed Kearny's nod and saw a pair of combat boots hanging over the end of a cot behind the map boards. He smiled. "Not much going on tonight, huh?"

Kearny rolled his eyes. "Whole damn country's socked in tighter than hell. Nothing going on over on the Continent, either." He swept his hand across the console. "Just dead air, thanks to the fog."

Hornak settled heavily into a nearby chair. He held out his small bundle to Kearny, whose eyes lit up like a small child's at Christmas.

"Got it for me, huh?" Kearny took the green package from Hornak and placed it on the console desk. He untied the knot on top, unfolded the cloth, and revealed a brand-new Air Force cold-weather flight jacket. He peered at the label inside.

"As usual, Gus gets it," he said. "Right size, on the mark." He turned back to Hornak, who had put his feet up on a desk and folded his hands over his considerable paunch. Kearny grinned and said, "Thanks, Gus. This'll really do the job on cold nights."

Hornak grinned back, his leathery face wrinkling. "Yah. No sweat, GI. Anytime you need something, ol' Gus'll get it."

"Sure, Gus. Listen, if there's anything—"

Hornak waved a hand. "No need, Joe. I need something, don't worry. I'll let you know. Right now what I could use is some coffee."

Kearny got up quickly. "Hey, good idea. I think the pot's still warm." He brushed past Hornak and placed a palm against the side of a battered chrome urn. "Yup. How do you like it?"

"Black," Hornak answered. While Kearny was pouring the coffee Hornak looked at his watch. Nearly four. Time to get going.

"Hey, Joe," he said to Kearny, who was stirring sugar into his own coffee, "where's the can around here?"

Kearny jerked a thumb toward the door. "Out the hall

15

to the left—across from the Ops Room. Can't miss it."

Hornak sighed heavily and lurched to his feet. "Okay. Keep the joe warm, Joe."

Kearny did not smile as Hornak went up the stairs to the door. He'd heard the same words a million times. But, he thought as he punched the button that released the lock on the door just as Hornak got to it, old Gus was a guy who always came through with the goods. That made up for a lot.

Hornak didn't walk too quickly down the corridor; he was sweating again. He came to the junction of hallways, turned left, and saw the latrine to the right. He walked up to it, stopped, and slowly looked down both empty hallways. Nothing moved.

He pivoted quickly and faced the Ops Room door. Gently, he tried the doorknob. It was locked. He looked at his watch. He had about five minutes—no more than seven at the outside—before even Kearny would get curious. And if the DO woke up and needed to relieve himself . . .

Hornak forced himself to begin. He withdrew a picklock from his left trouser pocket and inserted it into the old English latch lock. It took only a few seconds, even with his lack of practice, for the worn latch to click open.

Looking both ways again, he opened the door into the Operations Room and silently closed it again. He knew the room was unguarded by any kind of electronic alarms, but still he dared not switch on the light; the space under the door would allow a big chink of light through.

From his breast pocket he took a penlight. Its beam was small but bright, and with it he quickly made his way to the file cabinets behind the map table. Holding the penlight in his mouth, he slipped on a pair of thin silk flying gloves.

The file for flight plans was in the first cabinet. A standard Air Force combination lock hung from the steel rings, tightly securing the drawer he wanted to open. He smiled. Just as the makers claimed, nobody had ever succeeded in picking this type of lock. But Hornak had been taught well in Karl-Marx-Stadt how to deal with one.

16

A small plastic-tipped hammer came out of his right trouser pocket. Still holding the light in his mouth, he pulled the lock body down with his left hand and tapped sharply with the hammer right at the point where the lock ring entered the lock body. Nothing happened. He frowned. Had they changed the locks after all these years?

A second tap, slightly lower on the lock body, freed the pin and the heavy chrome lock snapped open. The simultaneous clack was loud in the stuffy room.

He knew only the operation name, and his instructions had been simple: Photograph the entire contents of any folder with that name on it.

He opened the drawer and flipped through the file folders. His was near the back. TOM AND JERRY/SECRET NOFORN read the folder flag. Marking its place, he withdrew the red-bordered folder. It was fat with papers and maps.

After he set the folder on the operations officer's desk, he looked at his watch. Three minutes left. But the sweating had stopped. Action was always better than waiting.

He slipped off his watch. An expensive, gaudy digital type, it had a large screen that could display the day, date, minutes, seconds, elapsed time, and even phone numbers. But it was also a camera, a feature its Japanese manufacturers had not given it. That had come from a small workshop in Leningrad.

He pushed the button that altered the screen and set the camera. It was self-focusing and self-adjusting, but needed a preset flash strobe. This had been built into his penlight. He connected the watch and the light with a thin, flexible wire tipped with male and female sockets. They were now in phase.

He opened the folder, positioned the first piece of paper, and aimed the camera. Squeezing the timer button with his left hand, he aimed the strobe with his right. It popped softly and the tiny reel in the camera whirred.

He repeated the process until the contents of the folder had been photographed. When at last he came to the back of the folder, he was sweating again.

17

Disconnecting the strobe, he snapped his watch back on and carefully arranged the folder as it had been in the file cabinet. After he had closed the drawer and snapped the lock back together, he had only one minute left of his allotted seven.

He picked his way across the dark office to the door. Switching off his penlight, he listened. There was nothing.

He released the latch and stepped out, swinging the door swiftly back into place. The latch set with a loud click.

Stepping across the hall, he went into the latrine and pulled down a toilet handle. As it flushed he steadied his breathing and began to whistle tunelessly. He wet his hands and dried them with towels, making as much noise as possible. He looked at his watch. Thirty seconds to go.

He had hardly pushed the buzzer before Kearny had the door lock released. When Hornak was back in the command post, Kearny looked up.

"Have fun?"

Hornak grinned. "Sure. She was a doll."

Kearny laughed low. "Hope she was good enough to be worth cold coffee."

Hornak sat down and reached for his cup, smiling.

"Nope. But, then, this isn't cold, either." He must not appear nervous.

Kearny nodded. "Sometimes I think this stuff is better cold than hot anyway."

Hornak said nothing, sipping his thick black coffee slowly. He could not rush. Kearny must have no reason to remember his visit—or at least none other than the two-hundred-dollar jacket, which, Hornak noticed, had already been put out of sight. He needed to make small talk, something he had not grown skilled in despite twenty-five years of living as an American. He set his cup down.

"That's good, cold or not. Anything going on over there?"

Kearny followed his gaze at the map boards. He shook his head. "Nah, nothing much. Got some kind of activity down near the Czech-Hungary border, though, according to USAFE. Twix came in a few minutes ago."

Kearny took a long swallow of coffee, his eyes still wandering over the huge map of Europe. Thinking of something, he turned back to Hornak.

"Say, Gus, you're from down there somewhere, aren't you? I mean originally?"

Hornak made himself smile. "Yah, that's right—from Hungary. Budapest, for sure." Kearny was looking at him curiously. Perhaps too curiously? "Left in '56. You remember—when the Reds came in and knocked hell out of us? Well, maybe you was too young."

Kearny shook his head. "Nah—I remember that all right. I was always pissed off that we didn't go in and help. You must feel the same way, huh?"

"Well, you got to remember, Joe, we thought the Amis—the Americans—were our friends. Figured they'd help us get the Reds out. But"—he sighed heavily—"I guess I'll never go home again now. That's why I joined up in '57. I hate Reds. Always."

Kearny looked at Hornak in surprise. "Jeez, Gus," he said, "I never knew—"

Kearny was cut off by a loud Klaxon. Simultaneously a red light began flashing on the console. "Shit," said Kearny. "Wouldn't you know it? Just like those bastards to schedule an alert in my shift." He reached over and punched the button that stopped the siren, although the red light kept flashing. "How 'bout waking up the DO, Gus? This looks like somebody else's show, but we'll have to monitor it."

Gustav Hornak, carefully planted mole for the Soviet GRU, Revolutionary Hero of the Hungarian Communist Party, smiled his assent. He heaved himself to his feet, and by the time the big speaker above the map boards began to crackle with coded alert messages for some base in the European command, he was gently shaking the officer's shoulder.

The fortyish officer sat up slowly, muttering. "Yeah, yeah, what the hell is it this time, Kearny?" He stopped when he saw Hornak. "Hornak? What's—"

"Just an alert, Captain. Joe said you'd need to be up."

19

Cursing softly, the officer sat up. "Yeah, he's right. Jesus, I hate these damn night shifts."

"Know what you mean, Cap'n. Was just getting off myself when I stopped by to see Joe."

The captain's reply was drowned out by the speaker crackling into life.

"Attention Red Fox. This is Sally Prime, repeat, this is Sally Prime. Code seven, repeat, code seven. Five groups. First group . . ."

"Better go home, Gus," grunted the captain. "This one isn't for us, but we'll be busy for about an hour and you might as well get some sack time even if we can't." He grimaced at the last word.

They walked back to the console, where Kearny was entering the code groups into the log.

Hornak walked up the stairs to the door and turned around, waiting for the lock to be released. Kearny was absorbed in writing, but the captain, still standing, punched the lock button. The door buzzer went off, and the DO called to Hornak, "Hey, Gus, what about that Nomex flight suit?"

Hornak paused halfway out the door, sweating in his haste to be gone. "Uh—sure thing, Captain. You'll have it sometime next week."

The door slammed shut and the noise was once again bottled up in the command post. Hornak took a deep breath and started down the hall.

And, he thought as he stepped back into the darkness outside the building, someone else will have what he wants by next week, too. If his blind drop in London worked as well as it usually did, whoever it was who needed to know what was in that mission folder would have it within days.

Touching his watch, he smiled grimly. It wasn't as glamorous a life as they'd promised when they'd picked him from his Komsomol class to be a defector, but at times like these it wasn't bad.

Tom and Jerry was no longer secret.

2

THE ROOM STANK. A HISSING COAL FIRE CAST A red glow over the two men slumped deep in ancient armchairs. Beer bottles carpeted the floor, reflecting the dull fire in tiny brown highlights. There was no other light and no sound but the muttering of the fire. A thin, bitter haze made up of beer mist mixed with coal and marijuana smoke blurred the edges of the room.

Max Moss lifted his eyes from the bottle of Double Diamond his big hands cradled protectively in his lap. He stared at the man sitting opposite. Lou Devault was apparently dead to the world, resting his feet on the stained coffee table between them, his body enfolded by the overstuffed old chair. His eyes were closed, but Moss knew he couldn't be asleep. His beer was still held upright in his lap.

"What," he croaked, his throat seared by too much drink and smoke, "what time is it, Lou?"

Devault didn't move.

Moss lifted the big bottle to his lips and swallowed some of the warm stout. It tasted terrible.

"Hey, Lou, what the hell time is it?"

Devault still didn't move.

"Dammit, Lou, *wieviel Uhr ist es? Kotory teper chass?* How—"

Tech Sergeant Louis Devault, USAF, held up one hand, his eyes still closed.

"Shut up, Max. Who cares what time it is?"

Moss frowned. The pressure on the back of his eyeballs worsened. He stopped frowning.

"Listen. It's my party, so I'll care if I want to. To coin a phrase."

Devault slowly opened his eyes. Moss came into focus. His body was sunk into the faded baize of the armchair. His long legs were splayed across the table. On one foot he wore a combat boot; on the other, a dirty white Adidas marathon shoe. His fatigue pants were filthy with spilled beer and cracker crumbs. A once-respectable velvet smoking jacket, purchased at a London Salvation Army thrift store, was twisted up around his body. Its faded scarlet splendor clashed violently with the yellow Yamaha racing-team T-shirt beneath. Below the brim of an almost unrecognizable blue-and-white Goodyear baseball cap, Moss's features were completely relaxed. Devault studied the face he had seen almost daily for the last two years. Long, straight nose. Wide-set eyes set deep under a high brow. Eyes too startlingly green to belong to a man with jet-black hair and pale skin. Thinnish lips that could stretch wide in easy mockery, and often did. And a jutting, aggressive chin with a tiny slantwise scar where a normal cleft would be. In repose, an almost handsome face. But one that became slightly unnerving when the restless green eyes were open.

Under Lou's steady gaze, Max opened his eyes now. He brushed aside an unruly lock of black hair.

"Well?" Max made the word a taunt.

Devault sighed. He carefully set his half-full bottle down on the table. He moved slowly, trying not to make the boiler factory start up in his head again. Moss followed his moves with interest, his green eyes hooded.

"It is," said Devault as he studied the watch glowing on his left wrist, "exactly four-nineteen in the morning. Or, for you GIs, oh-four-nineteen, twenty-seven October, 1982. Of course, that's only here in beautiful Barton Mills,

England. If you were in the out-processing station at McGuire Air Force Base right now, why, it'd be—"

Moss saluted Devault with his beer. "Thank you, Sergeant Devault, but as one who will soon be in that very processing station, I have already made the calculation myself. In fact, it may surprise you to learn that even as we sit I have applied the theories taught me at great expense by the United States Air Force and—"

Devault sank back into his chair and took up Moss's familiar chant of the last two months.

"—the countdown now rests at thirty days, nine hours, and—"

"—fifteen minutes." Moss scowled. "How the hell did you know?"

Lou Devault smiled, his eyes still closed. "I've heard it twenty-seven times tonight. Besides what you're not going to do when you get out, you haven't talked about anything else all night."

Moss swallowed some more Double Diamond. It still tasted terrible.

"Isn't that what discharge parties are all about?"

Devault didn't answer.

Max scowled. "I mean," he said with an exaggerated British accent, "I wouldn't want to be accused of not following the *form,* don't you see? Not good for morale, what? Not good at all."

Devault looked irritated. "Dammit, Max, don't you ever stop with that mimic shit? This time of night it's just not very goddamn funny, you know?"

Moss staggered to his feet, swept his cap off the floor, and bowed. He wobbled as he looked up again, his eyes glinting mischievously in the firelight. *"Ach! Aber entschuldigen Sie mir, mein lieber Herr. Es ist nicht unmöglich—"*

"Ah, shit." Devault looked disgusted. "I'm going to the crapper." He stood up, shouldered unsteadily past the surprised Moss, and opened the door to the hall. A cold draft rushed in as he left the room.

Max stared after Devault. The whole night had been like this. One not very amusing scene after another. He sat down slowly. The cold air began to flush the stinking haze from the room. His head began to clear. And to hurt worse.

For the first time, Moss began to realize what a mess the little living room was in. It wasn't the first party they'd had in the place, and it wouldn't be the last. The house had been leased to successive waves of American enlisted men since sometime in the fifties. Its ideal location—only five miles from RAF Mildenhall, the giant transport base where Moss worked as a line maintenance man and Devault as a personnel NCO—was unequaled for the purposes of young American servicemen because of its seclusion, size, and layout. There were four widely separated bedrooms upstairs, as well as two large bathrooms. And the whole downstairs area was perfect for entertaining. With a living room, large den, and formal dining room, three separate parties could go on all night.

Looking around in the bright wedge of light from the open door, Moss knew for the first time that he'd actually miss the place. He'd agreed two years ago to join in the co-op lease with Devault and two other guys just to get out of the NCO barracks; he was the ranking staff sergeant, and he wanted no part of the responsibility that entailed. So he had been glad enough to settle into Barton Mills. But he hadn't realized how comfortable the cheery fires, flowered wallpaper, ancient furniture, and creaking floors would seem until he was this close to leaving them.

Devault returned, breaking into Moss's bemused contemplation of the room. He was clearly still irritated. He switched on a wall lamp and scowled at the scattered party debris.

Picking up a trash can, he began filling it with bottles. "Come on, Max. The party's over. The sooner we get this garbage cleaned up, the sooner we can get to bed. Maggie the Maid won't be here for two days, and I'm not going to put up with crap all over the place."

Moss got to his feet, subdued. "Sure thing, Lou. Say, listen, I—"

"Never mind, Max. Guy's got a right to be fucked up

at his own short-timer party. Sorry I got pissed off. Too much smoke, I guess."

Together they collected beer bottles, paper plates, cigarette butts. All the stale paraphernalia of the celebration went into the trash.

When they'd collected everything, they crammed it all into three thirty-gallon garbage bags and dragged them to the trash-collection point near the house gate. Even at five in the morning the darkness was damp and impenetrable.

A few moments later, they sat across from each other at the kitchen table. Devault nursed a steaming mug of black coffee while Moss sipped at a cup of pale tea.

Neither spoke for a long time. Finally Devault looked up at Moss.

"On the level, Max. What are you going to do when you get out?"

Moss stared into his tea.

"I really don't know, Lou. Thought I might have a little vacation at first. You know. Grow some hair, lie around until noon, draw my unemployment. Be just Max Moss instead of Staff Sergeant Moss, transient-aircraft maintenance technician."

Devault nodded. "Yeah. Sounds reasonable. But what then?"

Moss looked at Devault. There seemed to be a curious intensity in his question. He snorted.

"Well, not my old man's factory in Silicon Valley, that's for sure. If I never so much as *see* another microchip it'll be just fine with me." His gaze drifted from Devault. "Or my old man, either, for that matter."

Devault studied Moss's face. Moss had the ability to withdraw suddenly from contact, transforming his face into a stone mask.

"Your father . . . was a general, wasn't he?"

The faraway look left Moss's face. It was replaced by a twisted smile that had no humor in it.

"A major general, to be precise. Friend of kings, presidents, senators, and other Very Important People. I wasn't one of them."

The booze and the hour were making Moss more open about his past than Devault had ever known him to be. "If you don't mind my asking, why was that?"

Moss shrugged. "Don't mind at all. It's simple. I was never as good as I was supposed to be. And you can be a lot of things as far as my father's concerned, but you can't be a failure."

"A failure? I thought you graduated from Berkeley at the top of your class. How—"

Moss looked up sharply. "Where'd you find that out?"

Devault grinned. "Personnel guy, remember? Don't forget that I'm in charge of out-processing you. That means I have to check on a lot of things . . . among them, how much education you've got. And your records make it pretty clear. Which reminds me"—Devault leaned against the back of his chair—"why did you lie on your enlistment papers?"

Startled, Max spilled some tea. "What?"

"Under 'education' you wrote 'high-school graduate'—and nothing else. Why?"

Moss downed his tea in a single swallow. He carefully placed the cup on the table and stared into it while he spoke. "I just didn't want anybody trying to get me to take a commission."

"All officers are assholes, huh? Funny—I wouldn't have thought a guy with your background would feel that way."

Moss's eyes narrowed. "That's because you don't know a goddamn thing about my background. And maybe it ought to stay that way, eh?" He lurched to his feet to fill his cup again.

Devault smiled at Moss's back. "Too late, Max. I also know that you were a stock-car racer, and not a bad one at—"

Moss swung around. His face was suffused with blood, his mouth stretched into a tight line. His hands were shaking.

"What the hell is this, Lou? Who gave you the right to check up on me? And how did you find out about *that?*"

"Like I said, Max. I have to know. Actually, I was impressed. Seems like in just two years you got pretty good."

Moss sat down and slumped against the chair. "Damn good. Good enought to lead the Sportsman Three Hundred at Daytona. Hell, I had sponsorship from the factory. If that motor hadn't blown on the last lap . . . Well, anyway, it's all over now." His face was a mask again.

Devault pressed on, leaning over the table. "Why'd you quit?"

Moss twisted his face into a sardonic smile. "Thought you knew everything, Lou. Well, your files missed some important facts. See, when I got out of school, it was just naturally *expected* that I'd take a job in the factory. Lowest job there was, of course. And then, just like in the stories, why, I'd work at each one for a while until I was ready to work directly under my old man." His eyes were slits, his hands clamped so tightly around the teacup the knuckles stood out whitely. "Trouble was, see, my old man never asked me what *I* thought of the deal. Not once. Not all my life. So during my senior year at Berkeley, when I met this guy who raced once in a while, I started hanging around the track with him. It was a lot more interesting than Russian courses or cramming for a lab experiment in electro-optical engineering, right? So when I finally tried racing— and it turned out I was pretty good—I was hooked. No way was I going to work for my old man. So"—he shrugged—"I didn't."

When Moss saw Devault's look of surprise, he said, "Hey—did you think all rich kids turned into Teddy Kennedys? This is a common story, man. The only thing is, usually in the story the hero checks out and his old man finally leaves him alone." His hands tightened again. "Didn't happen that way with me. He found out what name I was racing under and somehow managed to apply some old-boy leverage on my most important sponsors. So much for Maxwell Taylor Moss, future champion race driver."

Devault looked confused. "But why join the Air Force?"

Moss grinned, and this time there was some humor in it. "He was Army. Always hated the fly-boys. I knew that if

27

I enlisted in the Air Force and refused a commission, he'd finally get the point. Since I haven't heard from him in four years, looks like I was right."

Devault shook his head. "Jesus. I'm sure glad my family isn't like yours. Which reminds me. What about your mother? What did she have to say about all this?"

Moss went blank again. "Never knew my mother. She died when I was young."

"But your records show a Mrs. Eric Moss—"

"He remarried about ten years ago. To a real knockout—fifteen years younger than him, beauty queen, the whole bit. Nice girl, but dumb."

Outside, a dog started barking. It was still dark, but another working morning had begun in England.

Moss was suddenly impatient with the discussion. He finished his cup of cold tea, slammed it down, and stood up. "Listen, Lou, about this stuff. I guess it's all right if you know about it, but don't spread it around, okay? I only have a month left with these guys, and I don't want any more problems than I've already got."

Devault stood up, too. "Sure, Max. Sorry if it bugged you, but it's my job, you know. And you really shouldn't have lied on your papers. The Air Force could have taken it the wrong way."

"Yeah, yeah, I know. But thirty days from now it won't matter. In fact, it doesn't matter now. So if you don't mind, I'll hit the sack. It's been a long night. And I don't have the duty tomorrow, so don't wake me. Check?"

"Check, Max. Good night."

Upstairs in his room, Max Moss peeled off his tattered smoking jacket and tossed it onto the bed. Damn Devault, anyway. Why did he have to dredge up memories that were best buried? Nobody had been as curious about him during the whole four years he'd spent in the Air Force.

He sighed and sat on the bed to take off his mismatched shoes. He was just as happy, of course, that nobody had cared. The harmless machismo, the endless drinking and boasting about imagined conquests, the whole two-dimensional life was just what he needed. A

28

perfect antidote to the confused years that had gone before. And that now might return.

The thought was unsettling. He knew that nothing would really be solved by burying himself in the anonymity of service life—had known, really, since the day he stopped at that North Carolina recruiter's office on the way back from Daytona. He lay back on the bed and closed his eyes.

Images flashed across his mind like scenes from a movie. The day he'd won his first race in Arkansas. The day he'd met Christie in Cambridge. The day, a month ago, when he'd left her. The day he'd stood numb in the phone booth while his father coldly detailed the prospects of his wasted life. The day his father . . .

That was the trouble. No matter what he did, behind everything was his father. If it hadn't been happening to him, it would have been almost comical. A barely plausible plot for a bad play. A play that would get scathing reviews from critics who were sure that such relationships simply didn't exist anymore.

He could write the reviews himself. He knew the failings of the plot well enough, as well as he knew the weaknesses of the characters.

He thought of himself. Not from inside, but as someone he might see on a stage, performing the acts of his life. Not a bad actor, certainly; twenty-eight years old, a fine body, slightly above middle height, well toned and fit. Say 160 pounds soaking wet. And that coal-black hair above those sharp features would attract women. He thought of Christie again. She had certainly been attracted, anyway.

He listened to himself onstage. A little pompous at times, but good delivery. A nice low tenor voice with good projection. Nobody would ever misunderstand what he said. And a fine sense, he must admit, of the language. Perhaps even a natural-born linguist. He had taken to German and Russian quite easily in school, after all. And for an amateur, his impersonations were not bad.

In all, a decent actor. Not great, admittedly. Certainly

worth considering for character roles and second lead. The lead itself would go to a different kind of man. Someone like . . .

Someone like his father.

Lou Devault paused at Moss's closed bedroom door. He leaned close. Max was tossing and turning, his breathing loud and irregular. But he was asleep. Lou nodded and walked quietly downstairs.

Even before Max had gone to bed, Lou had known that today was the day. After a quick shower and shave he'd pulled on his uniform and prepared to go to the base.

The little red Mini was covered with dew. He slid inside and cranked it over, keeping the engine running slowly on half choke. When it was finally warm enough to drive, he switched on the headlights and backed out the narrow driveway. There was little traffic at six-thirty in the morning.

The mist cleared a bit after he drove through the little town of Mildenhall. By the time he was rounding the curve at the end of the main runway of the base, light was appearing in the east. Another gray dawn in a bleak English winter. As usual, his heater had begun to work only by the time he parked in front of the two-story brick building that housed Personnel.

It was barely seven o'clock. The building was still locked. Cursing, he fumbled out his office keys and let himself in. He switched on the main lights and the long fluorescent tubes popped and sputtered in the cold while he climbed the stairs to Room 201. His office.

Devault sat down at his desk. Unlocking his top drawer, he withdrew a small card file. He flipped through to a red-bordered card and set it by the telephone.

The number had eleven digits. It took almost two minutes for the scrambler circuit to verify his line and connect him. When the double rings stopped, a voice said, "Potsdam."

Devault said, "Mildenhall here. Is Colonel Martin available?"

"Stand by," said the tinny voice. Devault waited. His breath condensed in clouds in the cold office.

"Colonel Martin here."

"Devault, sir. I think he's ready. Shall I proceed?"

There was a brief silence.

"How certain are you? We'll only get one chance before he's out."

Devault didn't hesitate. "Frankly, sir, I'm not certain at all. He's very confused. But I think we ought to go ahead."

Martin's voice, badly distorted by the scrambler and static, came after only a moment.

"Okay. Start today. I'll inform Intelligence."

"Yes, sir," said Devault, and hung up.

He rested his hand on the receiver for a few seconds, gazing into space, ordering his thoughts. He had been through this three times before, but each had required different handling. He decided to start with the bulletin.

Unbuttoning his blue greatcoat, he pulled a copy stencil out of his desk and rolled it into his electric typewriter. Switching it on, he began to type, slowly and precisely. Within a few minutes his fingers warmed up.

Devault finished in fifteen minutes. He reread the words carefully, then attached the print-order sheet and switched off his typewriter.

Nobody was in the printing shop in the Personnel building. It was still too early. Devault unlocked the door to the big office with the three Chief offset printing machines and shuffled through the bulletin material in the office's IN basket. He stuck a priority notice on his stencil, placed it on the top of the file, and walked back down the long, echoing corridor to his office.

Now, he thought, now it's all up to you, Max.

And five miles away, Max Moss writhed in uneasy sleep, fighting demons who all wore Major General Eric Moss's angry face.

3

PATIENCE DID NOT COME EASILY TO KARL
Stachel. Throughout the long and bitter struggle to his
present position he had forced himself to practice it, but
the effort was always enormous. Especially in dealing with
the Russians. And even more especially when dealing with
Yuri Andreyevich Koshka.

He had been sitting in Koshka's reception office for
more than three hours. And that after a terse phone message from Colonel Koshka had sent him scrambling into
his departmental helicopter in Berlin to fly to Koshka's secluded portion of the huge Soviet Air Force field at Finow.
The pilot had been worse than a truck driver, jinking the
big Mi-8 chopper through the towering thunderheads and
nearly bringing Stachel's breakfast up. Then the breath-
less drive across the windblown airfield with that lunatic
Ukrainian Koshka insisted on using as his personal driver.
The man had nearly killed them both and destroyed a
parked MiG-25 in his haste to deliver Stachel to Koshka's
headquarters. And now, three hours—no, *over* three
hours—later, he, Karl Stachel, director of the Military Intelligence Liaison Division of the East German Democratic
Republic's proud Volkspolizei, was still cooling his heels
on Koshka's lavish carpet and warming Koshka's decidedly
unlavish visitors' bench.

He had had enough.

He stood and carefully adjusted his silk tie, at the same time stubbing out the last of the Marlboros he had with him. Setting his face into its coldest glare, he clasped his hands behind his back and harrumphed loudly.

Twenty feet away, Koshka's chief aide looked up from his work. Unlike other Soviet staff officers, Koshka did not use his privileges to procure pretty women for any of his personal staff positions. His aide was a frontal-aviation ensign whose relative youth was offset by obvious toughness. He was a crack fighter pilot, a superb driver, and a dead shot—and knew exactly where his colonel's interests lay. That was why he had been selected, and that was why he had ignored the officious rumblings of the overdressed and overbearing director of the Vopos' Military Intelligence Liaison Division. Like his superior, the ensign considered most Germans to be highly unreliable, suspiciously prone to Western influences, and, although loud in their protestations of Marxist faith, not to be trusted politically. He did not place Karl Stachel outside this category.

"Ah, Herr Stachel. Is there something?"

Stachel knew the tactic well. Intimidation of a superior by denied access to another superior. But he would not be brushed aside.

"Comrade Ensign, I have been sitting in this room for three hours. During that time I have observed that you have neither announced me nor in any other manner communicated the fact of my presence to Comrade Colonel Koshka. Do you have an explanation?"

The Russian returned his look impassively. Stachel was a huge man, full of loud bluster to cow the naturally timid. His heavy, slablike face hung on a great cannonball of a head, with reddish-blond, swept-back hair above and a ferocious Lenin-style goatee below. A beak nose jutted forward aggressively between bushy brows and deep-set, slate-colored eyes, through which, with lids half closed, Karl Stachel examined the world as though it were a slovenly recruit and he a disgusted drill sergeant. Those eyes would often open wide in fury, Kolyachin knew, just as his

33

lips would curl in anger, as they did now. A couple of birthmarks disfigured his neck and temple, which Stachel tried hard to compensate for with his swaggering manner and expensive Western clothes. For most people the effect was exactly as imposing as Stachel hoped. But not for Koshka's aide. He gazed back at Stachel and said, in his cold, perfect German, "He knows, Comrade Director."

Like a crumbling building, Stachel's patience fell away. His face grew livid as he fought for control of his normally high-pitched voice.

"Then why, Comrade Ensign, am I still waiting? One does not summon the director of a German Democratic—"

Before Stachel could continue, the large steel double doors leading to Koshka's office abruptly opened.

A general of Intelligence—Stachel thought it must be Malakov—emerged, walking with Koshka. Both men were smiling. Outside the doors, the general turned to Koshka and spoke rapidly in Russian. Stachel strained to understand, but it was a dialect unfamiliar to him. The general then strode from the office.

Koshka turned to Stachel and, before the German could speak, said, "Please excuse me, Herr Stachel. This operation will be unusually delicate, and I required clearance from above. Please come in."

Stachel silently obeyed. He had never gotten used to the sheer power of Yuri Koshka's presence. No mean master of the tricks of command himself, he was awed by the subtle intensity Koshka could bring to bear in making others do his will. Physically unimpressive, the Russian colonel had a body that was slender to the point of thinness, with ferretlike features: mouse-brown hair; pale, high forehead; thin, tight lips; bladelike nose; sharp-edged jaw; protruding Adam's apple. But his eyes were those of a natural commander. They were deep hazel, set slightly too closely together; they protruded, too, and were almost hypnotic. He was of only medium height, but Koshka carried the colonel's stars on his midnight-blue Air Force uniform like a Hannibal. When he cared to, Koshka could make anyone do anything.

And right now he wanted Stachel to help on an operation. It was the first time in over six months.

Stachel lowered his bulk into the straight-backed chair standing in front of Koshka's modern steel desk. Koshka closed the doors and Stachel saw that only one item rested on the polished desktop. A buff Special Operations file folder.

Koshka sat down and fixed Stachel with an appraising stare.

"So. How have you been, Herr Stachel? We were very impressed with your handling of the Meyerlitz case."

Stachel flushed, and was furious with himself. No one but Koshka could bring color to his face, even for a compliment.

"Thank you, Colonel. Naturally, a great deal of the success was due to your own organization."

The eyes held him a moment longer, then dropped to the folder. "Yes. So I am told." Was there a hint of a smile on that monk's face? Stachel squirmed.

Koshka flipped open the file.

"Herr Stachel, it is once again required that we mount an operation to capture an American aircraft. We will use a new variation on our standard joint plan Felix. We will do this within absolute conditions of security, and we will do it on November first. Is your department prepared for such an operation?"

Stachel was dumbfounded, and his mind raced. November first? That was only three days away, and a Felix operation usually required at least two weeks to pool the necessary drivers and service the cars. Not to mention—

"Herr Stachel?"

"Of course, Comrade Colonel. But isn't this unusually short notice for such an operation? There are substantial personnel requirements that must be seen to, and the equipment—"

Koshka cut him short. "I know, Comrade Director. But there is no time. After you have heard the *rest* of the briefing, you will know why." The edge of his sarcasm bit into Stachel like a knife.

"Of course. Please go on." Dark rings began appearing under the arms of Stachel's modish Western suit.

Selecting three minifilm print enlargements, Koshka pushed them across the desk to Stachel.

"The top photo is of a standard U.S. Air Force flight planning form. You will see that it is stamped SECRET and carries the operation title Tom and Jerry. The second photo shows the route and location of the flight, along with marks for the ground forces involved in some kind of exercise. This exercise is a routine NATO joint-forces maneuver of a week's duration. We have been properly notified by SHAPE headquarters in Brussels about the maneuvers—code-named Mickey Mouse—but Tom and Jerry, which is obviously a part of the exercise, was not part of our briefing. Of course, as you no doubt know, even that is not so unusual; NATO countries often schedule secret small-scale operations to coincide with the planned maneuvers. The larger action acts as camouflage. But in this case we have a vital interest in that secret operation. You will see it in the third photograph."

Stachel shuffled the prints. The third photo was a telephoto-lens picture, very unclear. Obviously taken at great distance and under difficult conditions, it showed a three-quarter view of an American Air Force aircraft. Stachel finally identified it as an A-10, a twin-engine ground-attack plane developed in 1972 to counter the Warsaw Pact's tanks.

"Wrong," said Koshka. "It is not simply an A-10. The photo you have was taken at a remote American testing base in New England. That aircraft is a very special variant of the A-10. Our sources in America tell us that it is called the A-10F. As you will know if you've kept up on American aircraft, the current deployed version of this airplane is an A-10C. However, there is a greater difference between the C and F than two letters in the alphabet. This airplane, Comrade Director, is a greater threat to the security of the Warsaw Pact alliance than anything you have ever imagined."

Stachel stared at the blurry photo. The airplane looked identical to all the others he had seen. Single-seat cockpit, long, straight wings, a host of "hard points" under the wings and fuselage to mount weapons, a mottled-gray Luftwaffe-style camouflage pattern. He was puzzled.

"I'm sorry, Comrade Colonel. I do not see—"

"And you will not see it, either. What makes this aircraft so threatening does not lie in view of the camera, Herr Stachel. It is in the cockpit." Koshka got out of his chair and began pacing, back and forth, behind his desk.

"It is no secret that the Americans still have a long lead on the socialist peoples in development of what is termed electronic countermeasures. In fact, so superior is the worldwide socialist military deterrent that it is only by way of extensive use of clever electronics that the United States maintains any parity with the USSR at all.

"But this single ground-support airplane has taken that lead and, at least theoretically, extended it far beyond anything previously known. The balance of forces is therefore tipped dramatically in favor of the NATO alliance. In short, Herr Stachel, we must have this aircraft. There can be no delay, and no failure. Too much is at stake." He sat down.

"We have been given the task of procuring one. Our first—and perhaps only, if we bungle it—chance will be three days hence. We must not fail."

Stachel suddenly realized that Koshka was sweating. Tiny beads of perspiration stood out on his pale forehead. *My God,* thought Stachel, *the man's worried.*

It was an alarming thought. In the five years he had known Koshka, the Russian had never so much as looked flustered. Not even at the moment the helicopter he and Stachel had been flying in suddenly lost power over the Elbe River that night they had been chasing the pilot of the Luftwaffe Tornado they'd succeeded in luring across the border. When the chopper pilot had panicked, Koshka had calmly unbuckled his seat belt, squeezed through the tiny bulkhead door to the cockpit, taken the controls away from the terrified copilot, and restarted the turbines. All while the helicopter fell like a thirty-ton rock.

In fact, everything Stachel knew about Koshka suggested that the man had no nerves at all. The secret dos-

37

sier he had kept ever since Koshka had been assigned to the command of the shadowy liaison office had slowly accumulated facts to support the view. At forty-two, Koshka had already done things not more than half a dozen other Soviet Air Force officers had matched. After entering the Moscow Academy, Koshka had raced past his contemporaries to emerge in 1961 with a doctorate in aeronautical sciences. Party member the same year, Air Force commission the same year, and accelerated training in advanced fighters followed. Unconfirmed reports that he had flown unmarked MiGs in Vietnam were matched by recorded action in the Middle East. Squadron commander during the Czech affair, liaison in London for two years, a posting as lieutenant colonel in Technical Intelligence at Plesetsk, a two-year stint deep in the Kremlin, and now, a line of communication to the very chief of the GRU. And nobody, in Karl Stachel's fifteen years of experience in the Volkspolizei, had ever managed to link himself directly to the head of the Chief Intelligence Directorate of the Soviet General Staff. But Yuri Andreyevich Koshka had.

And now Koshka was worried.

"Well, Herr Stachel? I trust I have not lost you?"

Fumbling with the photos, Stachel composed his thoughts. There were opportunities here beyond mere promotion within the Volkspolizei. If Koshka were worried as badly as he looked, it was possible that the cause of German nationalism, of German Marxism, of a genuinely German socialist future, could be advanced. If only slightly.

Stachel cleared his throat. "Yes, Comrade Colonel. If there is indeed something that can make this aircraft proof against our defenses, no efforts will be spared in its procurement. You say the aircraft itself is of no importance— just something in its cockpit?"

Koshka picked up another enlargement and studied it. "Details are extremely sketchy. Security around this aircraft has been far greater than anything we have encountered before from the Americans. All we are sure of is that there is an electronic component or components located near the pilot which enable the aircraft to completely nullify the most sophisticated antiaircraft measures the Americans have. And since our own antiaircraft technology isn't, in all honesty, all that much better than the Americans', that is cause for the gravest concern."

"What are the chances we could use plan Viktor and achieve the desired results?"

Koshka shook his head. "Simply knocking down the aircraft will not do; we must know how the electronics interconnects with the airframe itself. Besides, if our information is correct, using surface-to-air missiles would have little effect on the aircraft, since that threat is precisely what it has been built to evade. No, we must proceed with Felix, suitably altered to fit this target's capabilities."

He stood up. "For this we will need the Area One map." He pushed a hidden button under the edge of his desk and the wall to Stachel's left hummed. He turned and saw the wood paneling being replaced by a large white screen, which was being lowered from a reel at the top of the wall. It was typical of Koshka that he would not simply have paper maps.

Koshka walked to the wall opposite the screen and pushed the fourth button down in a vertical row of ten. A projector, hidden by an elaborate piece of woodwork, threw out a bright light. Seconds later, a map appeared on the opposite wall. It showed a square piece of central Germany. The East-West border split the map from top to bottom almost through the center.

"Here," said Koshka, "is Wolfsburg. Mickey Mouse, the NATO maneuver, will take place about thirty kilometers north, near the village of Boitzenhagen. NATO says that two divisions will be engaged here, both backed up by heavy armored units. Our intelligence supports that."

He pointed to a spot farther from the border. "Here is Edemissen, about seventy kilometers west of Wolfsburg. According to the plan for Tom and Jerry, the grass airstrip at Edemissen will be used as a forward operating location for the aircraft that will engage in the joint operations. There will be three squadrons of A-10s from the U.S. Air Force base at RAF Bentwaters in Suffolk, England. Among those three squadrons will be four A-10Fs. The group flight plan specifies some aspects of those aircraft's missions, but not all. Unfortunately, our agent did not know that the detailed plan for that A-10 would not be with the group plan, so we have only a few clues. Luckily, they're all we should need."

Stachel was studying the map intently, trying to piece together the complex action Koshka was explaining. It was true that the Americans sometimes held a covert operation as part of an overt one, but seldom was there such a dearth of information for the Russians to work with.

"Although we have only a little information as to the deployment of the four special aircraft, we do know that their flight leader—we'll call him Mishka—is instructed to orbit a small hill at a specified time. At fifteen hundred hours he is scheduled to be in position above an eighty-meter hill called the Könnschiers-Berg, about fifteen kilometers west of Boitzenhagen. He is to orbit it at less than twenty-five hundred feet—that's less than one thousand meters—until his flight has formed up with him. Then they are to return to their forward operating location." Koshka's eyes were glowing.

"It's when he's arrived at his orbit point that we'll bring in the Felix flight. Kolyachin will lead them, and he will have them in readiness at the Stendal airfield. When our man on the ground signals, we will implement maximum jamming along the border area. To this end I will strengthen the radio troops along the border." He saw the astonished look on Stachel's face. "Don't worry. I know we cannot hope to completely jam their systems for long. The jamming need continue only long enough to allow Felix flight over the border and behind Mishka. The flight will then fan out and drive him to the border."

"What if he fights back?" Stachel asked.

Koshka smiled thinly. "He may try. But this is only a ground-attack airplane, not a fighter, and I am sending Kolyachin with the special MiG-25s. Besides, our information is that the Americans will use their new laser scoring system in their maneuvers, only simulating live ammunition. So there is a good chance he will not even be armed. And that means he will have no option but to run in front of Kolyachin—and then to land on command." Koshka's thin smile became a look of unbridled ferocity. "And then he will be on our side of the border. On our territory. We will have Mishka and his special electronics where we want him."

Stachel pondered the plan for a moment. Felix was usually employed against low-risk targets. Transports, civilian aircraft, anything that wouldn't shoot back. The reasons were obvious; an engagement over the other side would be tantamount to a declaration of war. True, they had launched their MiGs across the border many times before. It was perfectly safe as long as they were over and back within about ten minutes, and as long as they flew below the radar net. But there were still serious questions.

Stachel nervously ran a hand along his tie.

"A splendid plan, Comrade Colonel. But won't the NATO people be suspicious when we mount a sudden jamming effort? And won't the Airborne Warning and Control aircraft they always have at fifteen-thousand meters detect our move?"

Koshka's fixed smile disappeared.

"As to the jamming, it is a risk we'll have to take. But you can be certain that the NATO command will use the opportunity not to protest but to try their equipment against ours. They will know, after all, that we have no units on alert and no ground forces close to the border there. They will take it as simply an exercise on our part—our testing of their electronic defenses."

Stachel shifted uneasily.

"But the advanced radars on the AWACS plane—"

"Not so, Herr Stachel." Koshka shook his head. "Don't forget that our satellite forecast predicts an increase in the foul weather we have had. In such weather, who can blame aircraft for losing their way and crossing the border? Besides, they will be flying outside the range of the local ground radars of the exercise troops and well below the range of the fixed stations behind the border. No one will ever know. In fact, when we have Mishka, we will be able to complain about *NATO* overflights." He laughed harshly.

41

Karl Stachel had seen the countryside around the proposed operations zone. He knew the truth of what Koshka said about the weather—the forests would be wind-whipped and miserable, the air frigid, the rain like a solid sheet—but the plan required exquisite timing and flawless execution. Still, something held his objections back. Not the power of the man, nor even the power of his office. No, on the razor's edge of success or failure for Koshka's modifications of the standard Felix operation, there lay potential. Both for the advancement of Germany and for Karl Stachel. So he merely smiled and nodded.

"And then, Comrade Colonel, the disposition of the ground-chase units?"

Koshka returned to the map. "We will place greatest emphasis on the military restricted zones fifteen and sixteen—at Letzlinger Heide and Rathenow. The Felix pilots will try to force the A-10 down well inside one of them so that we will not have to face even the remote possibility of interference from our friends in Potsdam." Koshka grimaced slightly as he said the last word.

Stachel knew what he meant. It was a never-ending source of irritation that the Potsdam people continued to wrest two prizes in three from him and Koshka. Stachel felt some pride even in that ratio of success; his predecessors had managed to lose almost all of their captures. All he could hope for was that the MiG leader would be good enough to do as Koshka planned. If the American came down outside a permanent restricted area, it became a race between the Americans at Potsdam and his people. And he didn't relish that idea.

"What about ground support, Comrade Colonel? Can our drivers expect any help from your organization?"

Koshka frowned and looked out the window at the gray day. "Unfortunately no, Comrade Director. My entire cadre of skilled drivers has been requisitioned by Moscow for a special assignment at the China border. This happened some days ago. If we had known . . . well, as it is, there is only your group, the military police, and myself. I have requested more drivers, but as General Malakov said, although the Soviet soldier is a fine fighter, he is not necessarily a good driver. It will take some time to replace my men." The grim set of Koshka's sharp jaw told Stachel much about the heated exchanges that were sure to have taken place when Koshka's elite chase drivers had been transferred.

"One more thing, Colonel. Will we have better jamming of the Potsdam position than was the case last time? You will recall that we lost our quarry when we were only a few kilometers away because of the sophisticated—"

"Yes, yes, I remember, Stachel. This time we will have a special team set up across the lake. They will have the latest equipment. The only thing they will not be able to jam will be electro-optical communications. And I doubt if even the Americans can punch a hole through five thousand meters of clouds with a laser."

A buzzer sounded within Koshka's desk. He picked up his telephone receiver and said in clear Russian, "Yes, Kolyachin? What is it?"

Stachel couldn't hear the reply, but Koshka's features twisted into irritation.

"No, Ensign, I will see him. Deputy ministers are not to be kept waiting. Send him in, please. And"—he glanced at Stachel—"send for Vanya and tell him to take Comrade Director Stachel back to his helicopter." He hung up and came from behind the desk.

"You have everything, Herr Stachel?"

Stachel inclined his head. Koshka had kept him waiting three hours, spent fifteen minutes briefing him, and was not even going to offer lunch. Typically Russian. Typical of Koshka.

"Of course, Comrade Colonel. I will telephone you when everything is in order."

"Excellent." Koshka had already dismissed him, preparing himself for dealing with the deputy minister, who was entering as they spoke. Stachel turned to leave and saw that it was Alexei Grezhin of the Central Committee. Koshka suddenly became obsequious.

"Ah, Comrade Grezhin! It has been a long time, no? How is little Natasha—"

The rest was lost when the ensign shut the doors. It

43

was ever thus with the Russians. Brothers in socialism, but don't ever forget who's the big brother, dear Germans.

Stachel grimaced as the huge Ukrainian sergeant came in. The man saluted and boomed in awful German, "Is the comrade director ready?"

Stachel gathered his hat and greatcoat from the rack. He nodded to Vanya.

"Yes, Vanya. The director is ready. But first, is there a place to have lunch?"

The massive Russian's head swung back and forth.

"I'm sorry, Comrade Director. I have orders to take you directly to your helicopter. Perhaps the comrade colonel can—"

"No, Vanya." Stachel sighed. "That won't be necessary. It's only another forty-five minutes to my restaurant in Berlin anyway. Let's go, shall we?"

Expressionless, the Russian spun on his heel and held the door open for Stachel, who squeezed through the doorway with as much arrogance as he could muster.

The drive back to the helicopter and the ensuing flight were as bad as those he'd endured in the morning. Could none of the Russians operate machinery properly?

As he sat thinking in the wildly heaving helicoper, Stachel realized it was this incompetence that most bothered him about the scheme to capture the A-10. Impelled by an overwhelming national sense of inferiority, the Russians had by sheer brute force driven themselves to the top of the world with their military machine. But it, like everything else they built, was massive only because it was poorly designed and as poorly operated. And in that lay the flaw in Koshka's plan.

Bucking back and forth in the big helicopter, Stachel snorted. Mishka, indeed. The pilot of the special American aircraft was not likely to be a "mouse" no matter what else he might be. Fifteen years of chasing them across East Germany had taught Stachel respect for his American opponents. He despised their ideology, hated their fascist regime, but could easily admit his admiration for their bravery and skill. It was one thing to point at a projected map and draw pretty plans. It would be another thing entirely to make them happen.

Especially, thought Stachel, if the American pilot did not do as Comrade Yuri Andreyevich Koshka wanted.

The thought of someone defying Koshka made Stachel smile until the helicopter encountered a sudden downdraft. And then all he could thing about was his empty, churning stomach.

4

MAX AWOKE SLOWLY, DRIFTING IN AND OUT OF consciousness. The unconscious parts were best. Every time he came up through full sleep and only-dozing to almost-awake, someone started to squeeze his head in a vice. He also noticed that it was cold.

Finally he could stave off awareness no longer. He forced his gummy eyelids open and felt the blood pound through his chilled body. It was excruciating. Each beat expanded his head a little more against the vise. He lay still a few moments, not even thinking.

The world began to focus in bits and pieces. It was cold because he'd forgotten to switch on the little electric heater in his bedroom before he'd crashed into bed. And since his door was closed, none of the heat from the rest of the house would take the chill out of the air. He sighed. Life in England had its drawbacks. Like a national disdain for central heating.

It was murky and gray outside. The early-morning fog had given way to rain. It clattered sporadically against his windows, blown by a restless wind that also shook the trees in the lane.

He carefully turned his head to see what time it was.

The green-lit digital clock on his dresser displayed the time in numbers almost three inches high, but it took him thirty seconds to focus his eyes on them. Just past two o'clock. In the afternoon.

He lay a little while longer, watching his breath condense in small clouds above him. He deliberately kept his thoughts simple.

Had it been a good party? If the consumption of cases of beer and boxes of joints made a party good, yes. And if having ten guys take part, yes again. But, fun? He closed his eyes. Even after four years he couldn't describe the attempt to get hysterically high with a bunch of desperately lonely men as fun.

They must all have sensed his own disgust with himself. Nothing kills a party like someone who hates himself for being there. That must have been why they had all left by midnight, leaving him and Lou to finish out the night. It would have been different with women there—even Christie—but Lou had wanted to keep the party stag.

Lou. Why had *he* stayed up? In the two years they'd lived in this house he and Lou—for that matter, he and any of the other three who co-opped—had gotten together in the same party only four times. And even those times only because of a common sense of diplomacy.

His head began to pound again. Too much thinking, he told himself. Concentrate on blankness.

But he couldn't shake the nagging thought that Lou had been after more than just booze and grass last night. Certainly it hadn't been friendship; he and Max had never been anything more than distantly polite with each other before last night. In fact, it had been Lou who first suggested that Max hold a short-timer's party. And that he hold it downstairs.

Moss shook his head. The vise went away, to be replaced with the entire Ford Motor Company assembly plant going at full blast. He felt as though his head would split down the middle like an overripe melon.

Groaning, he realized that getting up was the only solution to his misery. He readied himself, then gritted his teeth—even that hurt—and jerked back the covers. The

47

cold air hit him like the icy North Atlantic. He shivered in spasms and rolled sideways. He fell on the floor.

The floor was even colder than his bed. But it did awaken him enough so he could ignore his headache. He stood slowly, holding the bedframe, and gathered his strength for the dash to the bathroom. The dash turned out to be a shuffle. He lurched over to the door, wrenched it open, and staggered the ten feet to the bathroom. The heater in the wall was still on—a serious infraction of the house rules. He blessed whoever had screwed up and left him a warm room. He slammed the ill-fitting door closed and leaned over the chipped porcelain sink.

He looked up into the mirror. A concentration-camp inmate who had broken into the schnapps warehouse looked back. His black hair hung limp and lank across his forehead. His too-green eyes were now too red. Hard black stubble covered his face from his cheeks down to his Adam's apple. His lips were drawn and white, his nostrils enlarged and red. Two red spots highlighted his prominent cheekbones. The rest of his face was fish-belly white.

Suddenly it all came up. He fell toward the toilet and for five minutes puked until there was nothing left. As usual, he felt better at the end than he had at the beginning. His head was now cleared of some of the relentless pain.

The shower worked perfectly for once. Clouds of hot steam and needles of hot water brought him back. When he stepped out, it was possible to imagine life beyond the next breath.

He toweled himself dry and noticed that the big bulletin board they'd put in the bathroom for communal messages held a new paper tacked in the middle. As he rubbed his scalp he stepped closer to read it.

It was today's daily bulletin, the official base news organ. Printed on cheap bond paper, it was not intended as a newspaper; it simply disseminated official statements to the four thousand people who worked at RAF Mildenhall. He usually ignored it. But his eye was caught by the last item on the first page. It had been circled in red.

7. *Driver/linguist:* A requirement exists for a driver/lin-

guist meeting the following prerequisites: TSgt. or below; excellent physical condition; able to speak fluent German and Russian; experienced in auto racing and repair. Individual must be a volunteer. Further details will be furnished upon identification of candidate. For further information, contact TSgt. Devault/SSgt. Harrison, ext. 2158. (DPMCA/2158)

When he saw Devault's name, Max grinned. So that was why Lou had pumped him so hard last night; all for a fake daily bulletin item. He plugged in his blow dryer and chuckled. So much for a personnel guy's sense of humor. Anyone getting out had to expect a lot of practical joking—fake orders, fake promotions, the whole routine—but only Lou Devault, dedicated lifer and personnel geek, would think of faking a daily bulletin. Moss was relieved. At least now he knew why that strange scene had been acted out in the kitchen. Grinning again, he switched on the hair dryer.

But the bulletin item kept returning to his mind through the next hour. He sat at the kitchen table, munching an old butter scone and sipping some of the strong Chinese tea the others hated, and thought about it. It didn't seem like Lou to pull such a stunt. He took his job entirely too seriously for that. When he'd admonished Moss the night before about lying to the Air Force, he'd meant it. Devault was a third-term man; despite his slow ascension up the promotion ladder, he loved the service. Max had noticed that he joined in the normal GI bitching hesitantly, if at all. In fact, the more Max thought about it, the less plausible it seemed that Devault would caricature something he took very seriously.

Moss put down his cup and pursed his lips. But that meant that the item in the bulletin could be for real. Sure. Maybe Devault had known about it yesterday—maybe he was simply trying to see if Max were a likely candidate, just out of ordinary curiosity. After all, Devault and Frank Harrison had the task of handling applicants. It sounded reasonable.

The job itself, though, didn't sound so reasonable. Who the hell needed a driver who could speak two lan-

49

guages, race and repair a car? Since the late seventies, all staff cars driven in Europe had been chauffeured by drivers from the armed services of the local nation, as specified when the new NATO status-of-forces agreement had been ratified. Moss had even known some ex-Air Force chauffeurs who made no secret of their anger at losing a soft job. So chauffeuring in Germany or even Moscow was out. What was left?

The yellow tea grew cold while Max thought hard. There just didn't seem to be any way that those particular requirements would add up to any service job he knew about. Perhaps an embassy needed help, or . . .

Nuts. The easiest way was simply to call Lou. He looked at his watch. Three-fifteen. Lou would be in his office.

He dialed the base and asked for extension 2158. Devault picked up the receiver on the first ring.

"Personnel, Sergeant Devault speaking. May I—"

"Hey, Lou. Listen, this is Max. What the hell is that item in the deebee all about? Who needs a guy who can—"

"Are you calling from the house, Max?"

"Yeah. I—"

"Then don't say any more. Are you interested?"

"Well . . . sure. I guess. I mean, after you grilled me last night—"

"Good. I've been expecting your call. If you want to know some more, come on down. If not, forget it."

Moss frowned.

"Why not just tell me tonight?"

"Sorry, Max. This is classified. If you want to know, you'll have to be briefed here. Okay?"

Max was silent for a moment. When Devault said the magic word "classified," he believed it. He was one of the few people below the rank of general who did, but that was a measure of how devout he was in the faith of the United States Air Force. It drove Moss crazy, but Devault was a stubborn man. Max gave in.

"Sure, okay. I'll see you in fifteen minutes."

"Fine. Wear your uniform."

"What? Listen, what is this, Lou? I'm on my day off."

"Wear it or don't bother. See you—and don't forget to turn off the heater in the bathroom."

The line went dead.

For a moment Max thought seriously about ignoring the whole thing. After all, in a month he'd be a civilian again. No cares except making the unemployment line and nobody to tell him that his hair was too long. Or to drag him out of bed to fix a landing-gear strut some asshole of a pilot had managed to break at two o'clock in the morning.

But what the hell. The day was shot anyway. Maybe he could catch a movie after seeing Devault. He went upstairs and dressed in his blues, just to mock Lou a little. Besides, the wool shirt worn with a tie was warmer than his fatigues.

The constant rain had slowed traffic to a crawl. The engine in Moss's Lotus was highly modified, and didn't like sitting behind trucks at fifteen miles an hour. But the snail's pace gave him some more time to think about what the job that the bulletin referred to so teasingly could be. Half an hour's worth of driving and thinking later, he pulled up in front of the big brick building in Mildenhall's old central area and still had no more answers than when he'd started. Well, he soon would have.

Devault looked up as Max entered the 201 office. Harrison was gone. There were no other people in the room. Without speaking, Max pulled a chair over to Devault's desk, sat down, and leaned across, dripping rainwater onto Lou's papers.

"*Psst.* I'm agent X-24. What's happening?"

Devault looked at him calmly. The flying glasses Lou wore framed his perpetually steady eyes and made him look scholarly. He said nothing but got up and hung a CLASSIFIED BRIEFING IN PROGRESS sign on his door and locked it. Moss followed his movements with curiosity.

"Jesus, Lou. Is all this necessary?"

Still Devault said nothing. He sat down, reached into his top drawer, and pulled out a folder. It carried the red border of a secret document. Moss saw to his amazement that his name and serial number were on the folder flag.

Devault took out three pieces of paper, each a partially filled-in form, and arranged them right side up in front of Moss.

"Sign each of those next to the X."

Moss was suddenly angry.

"The hell I will. Dammit, Lou, this is like a scene from some low-grade spy movie. Why ... "

Devault did not smile. He pointed to the papers.

"I'm sorry, Max. But if you want to know any more, you'll just have to sign those secrecy agreements."

Still angry, Max grabbed the black government ballpoint out of Devault's hand. He scribbled his name and the date furiously on each paper. Then threw the pen down.

"There, *mein Führer*. Now, cut the shit and give me some facts." His pale green eyes were glittering.

Devault scooped up the papers impassively.

"Here's the deal. There's an outfit in the Berlin area that needs people occasionally to drive cars in East Germany. The cars sometimes have to be driven very fast and very well. And sometimes the guys have to talk to East Germans and Russians. The drivers sign up for four years and get a bump in grade. If you're interested, you can find out more at Intelligence." He sat back and studied Moss.

Moss was incredulous.

"*East* Germany? What are American guys—"

"Can't tell you, Max. The papers you signed give you access only to what I've told you. You can get more from Captain Brown. Do you want to?"

Moss didn't hesitate. He had no interest in doing the job Devault had sketched, but he was angry enough to make them tell him about it.

"Damn straight I'm interested."

Devault picked up his phone and dialed a four-digit number.

"Captain Brown, please. This is Sergeant Devault."

There was a pause.

"Captain? Devault here, sir. I have Sergeant Moss in my office. He would like the second briefing. Yes, sir. He'll be right over." He replaced the receiver.

"Max, Captain Brown will tell you a lot more. Probably all you want to know. He's in building four-fifty-one, down by the main hangar."

Moss stood up and jammed his cap on his head. He turned to go, but Devault stopped him.

"Here are your papers, Max." He was holding out a fat manila envelope. "If you take the job, you'll need them over there, and you won't have to out-process." Max took the envelope without comment, his face a mask.

Devault stood up and held out his hand.

"Good luck, Max. I hope you get it." Max looked at him. Devault was obviously speaking the truth.

Max shook his proffered hand. He was puzzled.

"Thanks, Lou. But why?"

Devault smiled ruefully.

"It's perfect for you, Max. And if you don't take it, you'll never forgive yourself."

Moss dropped his hand and smiled a twisted smile.

"Oh, yes? You ought to know better by now, Lou. I can forgive myself anything—especially when it means getting out. I've played this game long enough. It's time for me to get back to living."

Devault said nothing. He unlocked the door.

Moss stepped out of the room and said, "Come off it, Lou. You know I never volunteer for anything. I'll be home by six, ready for the TV dinner that you're going to stick in the oven for me."

Devault watched Moss walk down the hall.

"Maybe," he said, and closed the door.

Max climbed into his yellow Lotus and switched on the engine. While it was warming up he thought about what Devault had said. What could lead Lou—who certainly knew him well enough to know his aversion to put-me-in,-Coach antics—to believe that this mysterious deal in Germany would hook him? So far it sounded like some kind of delivery service for the brass. And, thought Max grimly, I've had just about all the brass kissing I can take.

He parked his car in a space marked NCOIC INTEL just for the hell of it. It was raining even harder and the small act of defiance suited his mood. He was being jerked

53

around again, and it was beginning to wear down his well-developed sense of distance from such daily humiliations.

The Intelligence building was an old World War II temporary Quonset hut that had been added to and rebuilt as the years went by. He had been there once before, a year or so ago, to take some mandatory courses in espionage and sabotage detection. They had seemed pointless then and he'd found the sense of privileged secrecy in the warrenlike corridors of the building irritating. It was irritating still.

He was immediately scrutinized by the wiry little tech sergeant who sat at the reception desk.

Before Moss could speak, the man said, "Moss? Stand by." He picked up a yellow phone receiver and spoke softly into it. He didn't look up again. Moss stood there and dripped rainwater onto the ancient linoleum.

A door opened behind the sergeant. A young captain stepped out and looked at Moss. Max noticed that his blouse held three rows of decorations, pilot's wings, and jump wings. The man looked too young to have all these.

He spoke in a pleasant baritone.

"Sergeant Moss, I'm Captain Brown. Please come this way." He motioned to Max, and they walked down a corridor. Posters of Soviet aircraft, ships, tanks, and uniforms lined the walls. Outside, the rain hammered away at the corrugated metal of the exterior. It sounded like machine-gun fire.

Brown led Max into a small briefing room. A blackboard filled one wall, map boards with security masks covered another, and a row of file cabinets a third. A projector screen was set up in front of the blackboard. Max sat down at the little table in the center of the room. The officer closed the door and did not sit down. He went to a file cabinet and pulled out two sheets of paper. He put them in front of Moss.

"I'm sure Devault hasn't told you everything you want to know about all this, Moss. I'm pretty sure I can. But you'll have to sign these secrecy agreements first because this briefing will be classified top secret."

Moss stared at the forms on the table. He hadn't actually read the ones Devault had given him, but he studied

these carefully. In the space for description of the classified matter, only five letters were typed: USMLG. He
shrugged. Why not? He was getting curious. He scrawled
his name on the bottom of each form and the officer
picked up the papers. He turned and switched off the
lights. A projector hummed into life behind Max. On the
screen appeared the words POTSDAM AGREEMENT.

"You know about the Potsdam Conference, Moss.
The one in which Truman, Stalin, and Churchill met to
decide the shape of postwar Europe. The provisions of the
agreement that emerged from their talks are well known.
Not so well known is the communiqué which was issued to
the joint staffs at the meeting. It resulted in another Potsdam Agreement. This one."

The projector whirred and a shield appeared, showing an image of the American flag—with only forty-eight
stars—in front of a sword. Above them were the words
UNITED STATES MILITARY LIAISON GROUP and a curved banner of gold inset with the single word POTSDAM. A banner
of red, white, and blue duplicated the curve of the large
gold one. Above the shield, ceramic letters spelled out
HUEBNER-MALININ AGREEMENT. 5 APRIL 1947.

Brown went on. "Lieutenant General Huebner—an
American at European Command Headquarters who reported directly to General Lucius Clay, who ran American-
occupied Germany at the time—and Colonel General Malinin of the Soviet Army signed a joint agreement as a
result of that Potsdam conference. It established liaison
missions in each country's zone of control. Malinin also
signed agreements with the French and the British for the
same purposes.

"Originally, those purposes had to do most with legal
questions arising out of the reestablishing of order within
Germany. Repatriation of prisoners, protection of travelers, even reuniting German families in which husbands
had been Allied prisoners of war. Gradually, however,
through the Berlin Crisis of 1948 and then of 1961, the
American mission grew in importance in an altogether different way.

"As it was clearer and clearer that we'd have to face

55

off with the Soviets, our liaison group began acting as an intelligence outpost. The provisions of the agreement gave absolute right of extraterritoriality to the grounds and buildings of the mission, along with guaranteed freedom of travel for its members within any part of Germany."

Moss was fascinated. What this captain was telling him was that the military machines of both the Soviets and the Americans had established a secret deal to allow themselves freedom in the cold-war zone of Germany. If Tail Gunner Joe McCarthy had known about this, thought Moss, he would have gone berserk and arrested the whole damned Army.

Brown continued in the measured tones of one who is used to making a complicated subject easy to absorb.

"Naturally, neither side was particularly happy with the snooping of the other side's mission. So permanent restricted areas were set up in both East and West Germany, which neither side could enter without escort and permission. The Russians, predictably, carved out huge chunks of Germany for this purpose"—he flicked to a slide that showed a map of East Germany, in which the zones were giant red areas—"thus cutting down the usefulness of the mission as an intelligence center.

"However, our mission, which is located on the outskirts of Potsdam"—he flashed another slide, and a four-story mansion appeared, fronted by a circular drive and flagstaff flying the American flag—"found ways around this problem." He changed the picture to a photograph of a car. A late-model Ford Fairmont, painted dark blue. Moss, with trained eyes, immediately spotted the telltale hump in the hood, the huge tires, internal rollover cage, and heavy suspension pieces of a highly tuned automobile.

"This," said Brown, "was one of them. Because the agreement limits the personnel at our mission to twenty officers and enlisted men, they had to have a method of quick travel. Originally, the idea of fast cars was for this purpose. But after 1955 they were used for something entirely different. And that's why you're here."

Moss nodded, his suspicions confirmed. Chauffeurs for the brass. Just as he'd figured.

Brown switched slides again. At first Max couldn't make out what it was; it seemed to be a junkyard. Then he saw the tail section of an old bomber—it looked like a B-66—and realized he was looking at the scene of a crash.

"About 1955, the Russians got very serious about decoying our air traffic out of the three corridors to Berlin. They also stepped up decoy navigation signals on the border and coast. The aim was to draw our planes over their territory, where they could legally be forced down. Or shot down.

"This gave them access to a lot of classified information in the aircraft, especially when that aircraft was a late-model fighter or bomber. The B-66 you see here was lured across the border near Wolfsburg in 1960 during an exercise. It was carrying a full set of NATO deployment plans, which, luckily, were destroyed when it crashed. On the other hand"—he changed slides again, this time to show a fully intact F-100 that had made a belly landing in a meadow—"there were too many of these. This airplane was captured almost undamaged, complete with signal codes and full avionics. Its loss forced us to make a lot of expensive changes within a very short time.

"To cut down on the risk of exposure of very important data and equipment, only one route was—and is—available. We had to use our liaison group's ability to travel freely through East Germany to rescue the crew and sensitive matter from airplanes forced down. In 1956 this effort was fully organized, and it began drawing people from everywhere in the European theater—Army, Navy, Marine Corps, Air Force. Because of the small staff allowance at the mission, each man had to be more than just a good driver—he had to be a kind of open agent. At first we tried using a group of officers, but when the Soviets saw our personnel lists, they objected, thinking—correctly—that the officers were more than just window dressing for the mission. They managed to force an amendment to the original agreement, and now we are limited to five officers and fifteen enlisted men." He flashed a new slide, showing twenty uniformed men standing in the sun in front of the mansion.

"Fortunately, the Soviets applied their own standards to our men, thinking that our enlisted people would be as poorly educated and trained and unresourceful as theirs." Brown chuckled in the darkness. "As you know, they were mistaken. Among the group you see there are men with doctorates and master's degrees. And in addition, every one of them is of racing-driver caliber. This skill has given us a whole new role for the mission, one in which it's been highly successful. We call it Recovery." Brown flashed to a slide with a graph depicting successful rescues charted against total known force-downs and shoot-downs.

"As you can see, in its twenty-five years of full operation, the United States Military Liaison Group's Recovery efforts have been increasingly successful. In 1958 they managed to recover about half of the downed crewmen and equipment. In 1968 the figure was up to sixty percent. And today we get almost two out of three Americans forced down. To date, the score is over two hundred and fifty successful recoveries."

He switched off the projector and turned on the lights. Max sat back in his chair, stunned.

Brown sat down across from him.

"Any questions so far, Moss?"

Max was amazed. "If I understand this correctly, Captain, what all this adds up to is a grown-up version of capture the flag. But there are too many holes.

"East Germany is a small country—right? If I remember my geography correctly, it's only about the size of New York State. Given the impressive pieces of real estate closed to our guys, how can they evade the Germans—or, for that matter, the Russians?"

Brown nodded. "It is small. But it's also far behind Western Europe in development. The roads are badly surfaced, unusually narrow, and poorly marked. Aside from a few major four-lanes, there are only five autobahns in the whole country. And the Volkspolizei, the state police, are terrible drivers, who use old cars with little power. After

58

all, for most of their jobs they don't even need cars, since so few people in East Germany have the permit to own one of their own. And the Russians, who maintain a special unit for chasing the downed aircraft and Recovery teams, aren't too much better. I'll show you." He stood up and turned on the projector.

The slide that appeared could have come from a gangster movie. The photographer had taken his picture from the front seat of an American car, looking through the back window. Visible in the rear seat were two very scared and very wet American airmen who were holding on for dear life. And behind them was a white BMW tilted crazily up on its outside two wheels as it tried to negotiate the turn the American car had obviously just completed. A flashing blue light was attached to the top of the car and inside, two men with white peaked caps were covering their faces as their car began its roll.

"This was shot in 1971. You may recognize the American car as a Ford Torino, and I'm sure you'll know that the BMW was a 1964 Sixteen Hundred. The picture is rare, not because the Germans don't usually crash but because they just happened to be near the pickup point for the recovery. Usually our drivers have no trouble outrunning and outwitting them."

"Why don't they just set up road blocks? No, wait a minute—why don't they just *shoot* the Americans?"

"They don't try road blocks very often because, quite simply, there are too many little roads in East Germany, and the average chase takes only a few hours at most. Besides, it wasn't until last year that the Germans had any kind of reliable radio network for coordinating their efforts. And the Russians use the Germans like serfs; although there is supposed to be great cooperation between them, the Russians would much rather simply ignore the Germans. And vice versa. As to shooting, well, there's a specific provision in the agreement that forbids the use of firearms except when someone is fired upon or refuses to stop at a restricted-area entrance."

Moss took the information in, and Brown said nothing, letting him absorb it.

Max was getting confused. For over three decades Americans had been running cops-and-robbers chases in East Germany and he'd never heard a word about it.

"Let me get all this straight, Captain Brown. What you're saying is that these Recovery guys drive hot cars all around East Germany, just waiting to pick up grounded pilots. Okay. But where do they take them? And how do they know where to pick them up?"

Brown flipped through two slides. The third showed a small pile of rocks near an intersection of two dirt roads.

"To answer the last one first, this is the way they know where to stop. Naturally, the cars have constant radio contact with Potsdam so that if they're on patrol they can be sent to the approximate area of a crash. But even if they're not notified, there are special signs that aircrew who are on missions near the border are taught to use to show the Recovery teams where they are. This is an old one; this picture was shot in 1963. We change them all the time, of course, so that our opponents don't get there first.

"The people and equipment are then taken to the Potsdam mission. Since it enjoys immunity from search and seizure, it is, in effect, a little piece of America stuck in East Germany. Once inside, the aircrew are considered safe, even by the Soviets, and can be taken into West Berlin by the mission's regular daily supply run."

Moss sat mute. Unaccountably, he was shaking slightly, and his palms were wet.

The captain went on.

"Not only is the mission sanctuary and intelligence headquarters, it also functions as a garage, too." He showed a slide of a long row of stables that had been converted to modern garages. Some of the steel double doors were open, and Max could see brightly lit working bays inside with the latest equipment. "Since the agreement allows us to house an indefinite number of nonmilitary, nonpolitical 'guests,' we have a staff of civilian mechanics who do all the work on the cars. Each man is carefully chosen, and each one is a top-flight racing technician. They work on the two types of vehicles the Recovery teams now drive—the new Fords you saw at the beginning and the highly modified Jeep Cherokees." He flashed a slide on the screen of a four-wheel-drive Cherokee. It, too, was painted dark blue, and had all the latest off-road racing gear. Brown chuckled. "These four-wheelers go far beyond anything the Soviets or Germans have. They're built to Baja One Thousand racing specs and modified even further in Potsdam. The one you see here is powered by an aluminum four-twenty-seven–cubic-inch Chevy motor that somehow found its way out of the Chevy racing-parts warehouse."

Brown flicked off the projector and turned to Max, who was leaning back in his chair. He ran a hand through his hair and looked at the officer.

"So we know what they do. What's the deal there? Housing, assignments, that kind of thing."

Brown leaned against the wall.

"Naturally, something like this has its drawbacks. Unless you're married, for instance, you can't live anywhere but in the drivers' new quarters near the mission. And the work hours are long. You're a junior partner in a two-man team for the first two years of your assignment, then you become the senior man. Work days are flexible, so you can't always tell from week to week what your schedule will be like.

"On the other hand, you get an automatic bump in grade on assignment and another when you leave. There's hazardous-duty pay and special bonuses for successful recoveries. In addition, of course"—Brown smiled at Max—"the black market still seems to favor Americans there. I'm told a pack of cigarettes is like a pound of gold."

Brown stopped. He switched on the lights.

"That a good enough picture?"

Max shook his head.

"What about the chain of command? Who runs it?"

"Right now, a Marine bird colonel, Jack Martin. He's got a Navy second-in-command and, after that, well, just a bunch of guys who do everything. Radio intelligence, legal aid, and so on. Not much in the way of complicated organizations."

Max shook his head again.

"You didn't understand my question, Captain. I'll put it another way."

He looked steadily at Brown.

"Captain, I've never been known as a good soldier. Spit and polish frankly turn me off. It sounds to me like these guys could be a bunch of crazy dudes having a great time burning up German roads and American gas. Or they could just as well be a lot of brainwashed zombies who drive fast, salute sharp, and smile when the colonel farts. Now, while I wouldn't mind driving a fast car, I'll be damned if I'm going to submit to any more yessir-nosir bullshit after my time is up here. And while it's all very nice to save some American boys from having to talk to the Russians, well, I'm afraid I wouldn't break any bones doing it. So let's cut through the patriotic stuff and get to the truth: What kind of setup is this?"

Brown's face was expressionless. He reached into his pocket and drew out a pack of cigarettes, lit one, and offered the pack to Moss. Max shook his head.

Brown blew out a long stream of smoke. His briefing-master formality was gone. "Moss, given the conditions you've just seen, what kind of setup do you *think* it is? You really believe that the mission needs dumb sons of bitches who can salute nice and whose only goal in life is to make it to twenty to draw their retirement? If you do, you're a bigger fool than your record says you are." He dragged long and hard on his cigarette. "Look. Most of these guys are as screwed up as you are. For Christ's sake, what kind of people do you think fit this set of requirements? West Point ring-knockers? Gung-ho retards? No way. In order to do this job, a guy has to have a lot of education, a lot of guts, and a lot of skill. Not to mention such a damn-your-eyes attitude that he'd have rejected the commission that those things should have automatically given him when he signed up." He jabbed his cigarette toward Max. "And besides that, he's got to be such a goddamn glutton for weird experiences that he signs away four more years of his life just to play with the most expensive race-car toys in the longest cat-and-mouse game ever invented by man. Does that sound like a bunch of *soldiers* to you?"

They stared at each other for ten seconds. Max could feel his heart thumping irregularly. His fingers were cold. He felt the way he did at the beginning of a race, just before the flag came down. His mouth was dry. But his mind was clearing.

"What happens if the outfit is dismantled? The last thing I want is to be part of the real Air Force again."

Brown stubbed out his half-smoked cigarette.

"There's a guarantee clause in the reenlistment contract that lets you out automatically if anything changes to close down the unit." He looked at Moss. His eyes were hard.

"Well?"

Max could feel his heartbeat speed up.

"I need some time to think."

Brown looked at his watch.

"Fine. You've got ten seconds."

Max looked back at him. Off the racetrack, this was precisely the kind of decision he hated. Only two choices. *Do it or don't.* No chance for a slick sideslip. No time for fancy footwork. No way to get out of it. *Do it or don't.* Fish or cut bait. Shit or get off the pot. The wheat from the chaff. The men from the . . .

He grinned at Brown. His heart had settled into its first-lap beat. Strong, calm, sure.

"When do I leave?"

Brown grinned back.

"Tomorrow," he said.

5

THE RAIN HAD STOPPED. MAX STEPPED OUT OF
the Intelligence building and absently put on his hat. The
old wooden door swung silently closed and latched itself
with a heavy *thunk.*

Max looked up and down the flight-line road. It was
as if he'd never seen it before. His eyes burned from the
four hours of briefing and paperwork at Intelligence. It
was night now at RAF Mildenhall. The massive hangars
stood silent on the line, rising into the sky like block-long
skyscrapers. Along the narrow streets of the old Royal Air
Force station, no traffic moved. The pavement glistened in
the reflected light from the bright street lamps. Far away,
across the huge airfield, a jet engine whined like a moan
from another world.

It smelled clean, Max thought. Torrential rains always
brought that peculiar, invigorating smell to Suffolk. The
air was cold, but he enjoyed it now. The hours of sitting in
overheated rooms inside the Intelligence building made
him want to inhale deeply the fragrances of the English
night.

He walked slowly to his little Lotus Europa, now
drenched in a sheen of water. Its chrome-yellow paint
gleamed in the orange light from the sulfur lamps overhead. Max thought he had never seen it look so beautiful.
His footsteps scraped on the asphalt. The sound echoed

off the quiet buildings around him. The ancient brick buildings he'd never paid any attention to in the three years he'd lived and worked here.

He slipped his key into the lock of the door, and then, like a slap in the face, it struck him. He had changed his life. He paused, seeing the silent base with new eyes. It had been comfortable here. A simple job, an easy life. No questions, no agonizing problems. And he had just put his signature on a pile of papers that would thrust him into a completely unknown way of life. By tomorrow night at this time he'd be on the Third Air Force courier aircraft to Berlin.

He was gripped by an overwhelming remorse. This life hadn't been much. He'd treated it with contempt every day he'd lived it. But it had been . . . soothing. And now it was gone.

He corrected himself. No, it would stay. He would be gone. And no one here would know the difference. It was the price he'd paid for his independence.

He slumped into the Lotus' driver's seat. No one? Surely there would be somebody. Lou, maybe. And . . . who else? The people he worked with thought of him as a weirdo. They laughed at his biting jokes and slapped their knees at his impersonations of unpopular bosses, but . . . no. They belonged to a different world. They knew it and he knew it.

A sense of despair crept over him. Listlessly, he cranked the engine over and it rasped to life. Nobody here was close enough to care. For the first time this fact meant something. There was only one person in England who might give a damn about him.

Christie.

He thought of her as they'd parted last month. Another pointless, bitter argument. He couldn't even remember the cause. They'd started the evening well enough, with a curry dinner at Kim's in Cambridge. Then, over drinks at her tiny apartment, things had simply started to happen until her door had crashed closed and he was chirping the Lotus' tires on Jesus Lane on his way back to Barton Mills.

The engine slowly warmed behind him. The note of the exhaust echoed off the buildings and the condensation in the pipe poured out in a little cloud. He rubbed his hands over the worn leather of the steering wheel, thinking about Christie.

Could he really leave without at least seeing her again? Did two years together mean so little? Last night, while he was wallowing in Double Diamond, he thought so. He thought he could just go away. Then it had been back to America. Now it was to . . .

What?

And that made the difference. He needed her. He checked the time. It was still early. She would be home. Alone, he hoped.

Max pushed the choke knob back and snicked the gearshift into reverse. He backed out and drove through the deserted base. Once past the gate, he sped up. In twenty minutes he would be in Cambridge.

It took half an hour. He pulled up in front of the old house Christie lived in, switched off the motor, and looked up at her flat. She rented a little three-room piece of the third floor.

Her light was on.

He got out, opened the foyer door, and pushed her intercom button.

After a moment the speaker popped.

"Hello?" Her lilting English tones came through even the ancient speaker.

"It's me, Christie. Max."

The speaker popped again, but the door didn't buzz open.

"What do you want, Max?" Her voice had turned cold.

"I . . . well, I just wanted to . . ."

"Not this time, Max. It's all over."

He jabbed the button again.

"Listen, Christie, can't we talk about this face to face? I mean, it seems like two years ought to count for something."

66

A motorbike buzzed past on Mill Road, drowning her reply.

"—doesn't it, Max?"

"Look, Christie, for Christ's sake, let me come up and talk to you."

There was a long pause. Then the door buzzed.

He pushed it open and climbed the three flights of stairs. The wood creaked and his footsteps rang in the hallway.

Her door stood open. He walked slowly in.

She sat on the divan, legs tucked under. She was nursing a drink. She had changed her hair, he saw. The fine golden strands were tightly curled. The curls framed her face well, accenting her firm jawline, delicately pointed chin, and high cheekbones. She wore no makeup, but her expressive brown eyes didn't need any. A silk caftan covered her from neck to toe.

"Well?" She said the word like a sentry's challenge.

Max closed the door. Without taking off his overcoat, he went over and sat down across from her.

She stared moodily at him, waiting for him to speak.

"I'm sorry about last month, Christie. Really sorry. I don't even remember what started it."

She tossed down her drink and reached for a cigarette.

"Maybe you don't, but I do, Max." She stuck a Benson & Hedges between her lips and lit it. Her long fingers were shaking. She inhaled deeply, then exhaled hard.

"If you'll remember, it had to do with us. Or rather, you, more specifically."

Max frowned. "No, I don't."

She rubbed the cigarette into an ashtray and jumped up. She stalked to her little window and folded her arms.

"Oh, Max. You remember and you know it." Her slender back was tense. "Damn, Max. Do you really expect me to believe that you don't remember what we were talking about—after?" She turned back to face him. She was angry, her face flushed.

Then he remembered. After. After he got out. That

was it. She'd asked for the hundredth time what he was going to do. And he'd said, also for the hundredth time, that he didn't know. And then she'd gotten angrier and angrier.

She watched him while he recalled, her eyes smoky. He looked up and said, "Yeah, I remember now. I couldn't tell you what was going to happen because I didn't know."

She twisted her pretty lips into a grimace.

"How can you not know? Max, you're only a month away from getting out. You can do anything you want, go anywhere you want. Have you no ambitions?"

He held up his hands and shook his head. "Listen, Christie, that was last month. Things are different now."

She softened.

"You mean we—"

"No. That's what's different, I guess. Before, I could imagine staying here with you. Waiting until you got your divorce from John. Maybe working here, even. But now . . . now it's all changed."

Her eyes were big. She sat down.

"Why didn't you ever tell me you might stay with me?"

"It was just a faint possibility, Chris. Jesus, you knew I was confused. I couldn't face working for my father, and . . . well, it seemed that if things worked out between us, maybe we could . . . you know."

She shook her head.

"I don't know, Max. That's the trouble. I've never known with you. In two years I've learned very little about you. If I had . . . maybe we needn't have fought so."

Max went to the sideboard and poured himself a glass of wine. He cradled it in his hands for a moment, then turned to face her again.

"Maybe you're right, Chris. God knows I've wanted to tell you all the crazy things that happen in my head, but every time . . . well, every time I've ever done that I've lost someone." He downed the wine. "I guess I figured the less you knew about me, the less you'd have to dislike." He sat down again.

She considered him for a moment.

"You're a very smart man, Max. But you don't know much about people if you think that's why you lose friends. Or," she added, "lovers."

They looked at each other awhile. The electric heater tinkled in the silence. The traffic noise from Mill Road drifted up through the windowpanes.

Max's mind was blank. It wasn't going right at all. Finally he said, "Listen, let's try again. First, I'm sorry for last month. Second . . . well, second, something happened tonight that changes everything."

She sat back, eyes wary.

"I've reenlisted to do a special job. In East Germany."

It took a second for the meaning to sink in. Then she blinked and bit her lip.

"The rest is supposed to be classified. But you deserve to know. I'll be driving cars. Fast cars, all over the country. With a group stationed in Potsdam, near Berlin."

Christie reached for another cigarette. Her voice was distant when she spoke.

"When do you start?"

Max hesitated.

"Tomorrow. I have to leave tomorrow."

The cigarette lighter snapped closed and fell to the carpet. Hand shaking, she put the cigarette in the ashtray. Her eyes wouldn't meet his.

"Oh . . . that's nice, Max. I'm glad." S e cleared her throat with difficulty and lifted her face to his. "I'm glad you've found something to do."

The air was heavy with unspoken words.

Max gathered her hands in his. Hers were ice cold.

"Maybe this isn't the right thing to do, Chris. I don't know. If I were sure about us, I never would have done it. I'd have waited. For your divorce, even for your damned doctorate to be finished. But I wasn't . . . and I'm still not."

She was smiling wanly.

"You must have been serious if you'd even considered waiting to go back to the States for another year. You know that's how long it will take me to finish up here."

He nodded.

"I would have done it. If I were certain. But . . ."

She finished for him.

"But you weren't. I know, Max." Her brows knitted together.

"This job——it's dangerous?"

"Well, only a little bit."

She was still frowning.

"Don't patronize me, Max. I work with some East German chemists. The stories they tell aren't funny."

"You're right. It's not a funny job. But it could be fun. As much fun as it is dangerous. I just don't know. It . . . it just attracted me. That's all."

She smiled bitterly.

"Evidently more than I could."

She saw his face work as he struggled with his inner demons. Suddenly she leaned forward and put a finger to his mouth.

"Never mind, Max. We have one last night together. Let's make the most of it." She stood up and drew him to her. Surprised, Max met her kiss. He felt tears on her cheek. Her arms went around him and she held him tight. Then she pulled back slightly and said mockingly, "Max Moss, soldier boy, goes off to the wars." She laughed in her low, husky way.

Max swept her off the floor and held her in his arms. He scowled mightily and growled, "You've been asking for this for a long time, Scarlett. And now you're going to get it."

She frowned and went stiff in his grasp.

"What's the matter, Chris? Gable not good enough for you?"

Christie shook her head.

"I just wish you wouldn't try to make everything a joke, Max. Because sometimes it isn't."

He kissed her, brushing her long eyelashes with his lips.

"I know," he whispered.

Then he carried her into the little bedroom.

The rain returned at two in the morning. Max lay

wide awake and listened to it sprinkle tentatively, then stream down in earnest. Beside him, Christie stirred in her sleep. She turned and lay on her side, away from him.

He ran a finger down her soft skin, then lightly kissed her neck.

Carefully, he slipped out from under the covers. The light from the street lamp nearby provided a dim twilight for him to navigate through her cramped bedroom. He collected his clothes, then stood at the doorway. The soft orange light threw a warm glow across her naked body. He gazed at her for a moment, then shut the door.

He dressed quickly, then took a sheet of paper from Christie's typewriter stand and began writing. He gave Christie power of attorney and, on another sheet of paper, assigned to her all rights to his Lotus. Then he signed and dated the logbook to reassure the skeptical bookkeepers at the Ministry of Transport office downtown.

He thought for a moment, then scribbled a long note to her. By the time he was done it was nearly three o'clock.

He pulled out the keys to his Lotus and dropped them on the notes. He unlatched the door and stepped into the cold stairwell, pausing to take a long look around the apartment. Then he took a deep breath and locked the door behind him.

A few moments later, the cabby was incredulous.

"Are you sure, mate? All the way to bleedin' Milden-hall? That'll cost you over ten quid."

Max shut the door of the big Austin taxi.

"Sure am. Let's go."

The cabby shrugged and switched on his ENGAGED light. The diesel clatter rattled up and down the narrow little street of darkened houses.

Max looked up as the cabby pulled out. He thought he saw a pale face at the curtain in her window. The cab was gone before he could be sure. But he smiled anyway. He asked the cabby if he'd ever been to Germany.

6

"THE WAY I SEE IT, ONLY A GRUNT COULD LOVE A Warthog."

The voice came from behind him. As usual.

He ignored it.

The voice continued.

"Fact is, the way I hear it, they're going to give Warthog guys commissions in the artillery. That way, they'll save on pilot training." Chuckles followed.

He sighed. Nothing ever changed. He turned around and saw the three who were chuckling. Typical. Two first lieutenants and a young captain, all scrubbed shiny clean, with yellow silk ascots tucked into their brand-new flight suits. Each guy seemed to be wearing at least five different patches, each with some brave message. There were malicious gleams in their eyes, sneering grins on their faces.

Fighter jocks. Always the same.

They were from Lakenheath, he saw. Even worse. F-15 fighter jocks. They thought of themselves as the elite. MiG hunters. Roamers of the sky. Knights riding silver needles miles above the earth. He cleared his throat. Their grins grew forced.

Solemnly, he sat up straight. They tensed.

"Oink, oink," he said, and turned back to the front of the briefing room.

Their startled responses were lost in the noisy bustle as the crews began filing in.

Buzz McCulloch wasn't particularly bothered by their sniping. In a way it was easy to see their point. The Warthog *was* ugly, because it was a single-purpose airplane. Made to fly and fight low and slow, right in the weeds at a battlefront. A tank buster, bridge destroyer, troop killer. Flying artillery. And that's why the ground troops loved it. It was the one Air Force airplane that had proved that it probably would not kill them instead of the enemy.

McCulloch looked around the room for the other twenty-nine A-10 pilots. Most were already sitting down. That was another thing. For some reason A-10 guys—who never referred to their airplane as the Thunderbolt II, the way God, the Air Force, and Fairchild Republic wanted them to—always seemed to take their job more seriously. Maybe it was because they flew so low. When you spend your flying day down with the grunts, you care about the same things the grunts do: weather, enemy positions, and troop movements. Which was why you listened well in briefings if you were an A-10 pilot.

Today, thought McCulloch, today is serious. Today we find out if the last three years of endless training have been worth a damn.

There were those who would say that Captain Sawyer F. McCulloch was a man who took his work *too* seriously. But the Air Force hadn't thought so. When the ultrasecret biocybernetics project began that resulted in the A-10F he would fly today, the Air Force hadn't hesitated in picking McCulloch as one of its test pilots. Physically fit, he had combat experience in the Middle East, a loving family, and a calm disposition. But more importantly, he had the eyesight of a bedouin and the reactions of a Muhammad Ali.

His wandering eye picked out the other three A-10F pilots. Each one flew an airplane so secret that their own crews and maintenance equipment had followed them over from the States on a special C-5.

A colonel on the raised platform rapped for silence. The room grew quiet. The colonel looked back to the door behind the assembly and waited. When the door opened, he said, "Gentlemen, the wing commander," and everyone sprang to his feet. A brigadier general stalked up the aisle. On the dais, he said, "At ease, gentlemen," and the crewmen sat down.

"In a few hours," began the general, "we will begin the joint NATO exercise Mickey Mouse. As you know, it will be a fairly large-scale operation, involving elements of five NATO countries. However, some of you may not know that the three squadrons of A-10s based here will have a special mission. They will participate in a separate exercise. This one is called Tom and Jerry. Colonel Byrd will now brief the A-10 people on that exercise."

Byrd rose, switched on a huge projection of their exercise area, and began to speak.

"The three A-10 squadrons will leave here for the intermediate at Leipheim at oh-eight-forty-five today. After a refuel and final check, they will then proceed to the forward operating location at Edemissen—here." He pointed to a spot on the map. "At this FOL, laser designators will be fitted, weapons will be armed, and you will receive external stores. Your forward air controller will be there to finalize your Army coordination, but you will fly your missions with no actual FAC on hand." This last point was met with some murmuring.

"Tom and Jerry is a test of your ability to join Army Cobra helicopters and ground units in killing Warsaw Pact tanks. It is a three-day field test. For the occasion special West German Leopard units will act as the Soviets. They will have the most sophisticated SAMs, antiaircraft, and antitank hardware. This operation will take place in the heavily wooded area near the border, and it will take place regardless of weather. Each of you will receive detailed instructions on quarters, targets, units, and umpire ID at your FOL. This includes the four special aircraft flying today with the three Bentwaters squadrons."

The colonel sat down, and the general took over again, explaining the larger exercise in greater detail. McCulloch's pencil was busy, one part of his mind noting the vital points, another already back in the cockpit of his "special aircraft."

74

His fascination with the airplane always puzzled his friends. Which was because to them the F model was almost identical with the previous versions of the A-10. Twenty-two extra inches added to the twin tails was the only visible change. Otherwise, the A-10F was still the ungainly Warthog. Mottled gray-black paint covering a fuselage about fifty-four feet long and wings about fifty-eight feet from tip to curled tip. Two big GE high-bypass-ratio turbofan engines sat behind the wings, Caravelle style, in huge cowls. They had to be huge to mask the infrared signature of the engines on enemy tracking screens. The main landing gear never fully retracted; it folded up into nacelles in each wing, leaving some rubber protruding so that even without landing gear extended, the airplane could land safely. An enormous seven-barrel 30-mm Gatling gun stuck out of the rounded snout. It could fire at the rate of forty-two hundred rounds per minute—and each depleted-uranium round could knock a huge hole in any tank's armor. And it could carry eight tons of weapons on its wings, twice as much as the capacity of a World War II Flying Fortress.

This was the standard Warthog. But his airplane was even deadlier. Although equipped with a large array of navigation equipment and radio gear, the old Warthog couldn't fight in bad weather or at night. Because of the superb visibility from the pilot's seat, effective flying could take place in remarkably bad conditions, but really nasty weather found the A-10 home on the ground. The F had no such problem. It could find a target in a pitch-dark storm and put the weapon right on it. Thanks to its use of the latest avionics, it was a genuine all-weather aircraft.

But this wasn't what made it so secret that it had to have special guards everywhere McCulloch parked it. No, it was because of the Jesus Box.

McCulloch smiled as he thought of it. He touched his helmet bag with his boot as he continued to take notes. With the Jesus Box, warplanes had leaped ahead into the twenty-first century.

The engineers at Edwards hadn't called it that, of course. Just as they hadn't called the F the Wonder Warthog. They detested that kind of irreverence. Only pilots would call something like the Biocybernetic Control Unit a Jesus Box.

McCulloch recalled the first time he'd seen the thing, three years ago. It had been a lot bigger then—a black box taking up half the right side of the cockpit—and the helmet had been painful. But the principle had been the same. When he slipped on the helmet, brainwave amplifiers had picked up the proper emissions and turned them into signals the computer could use to control the functions of the airplane's armament. That had been staggering enough—they told him it wasn't actually reading his mind, just responding to strong electrical commands—but when they'd got it fine-tuned a year later, the results were even more astounding. They'd managed to reverse the whole effect as well, so that not only could he arm, target, and fire a missile just by concentrating on doing it but now they had worked out a way for the airplane to tell *him* things—without his asking. They had been plugged into each other, he and the airplane.

McCulloch shook his head. No matter how many times he used the Jesus Box, he couldn't get over it. When he was in the cockpit, it seemed so natural to delegate a part of his brain to "listening" to the airplane—the radar, the navigation systems, the flight alarms. They had given each system a kind of sensory identification, so that when the radar picked up a bogey, he could "taste" it immediately. Just as he could "hear" infrared scanning. The time gap between the airplane's "learning" of a potential threat and his reaction was thereby cut enormously.

And so, he thought grimly, it had to be. The modern battlefield had become a maze of electronic-warfare systems, each trying to jam and destroy the other. No wonder the Air Force—which was in grave danger of failing to convince even itself of the survivability of so slow and clumsy an element as a man—had spent billions on perfecting the biocybernetic system. And no wonder it had been so secret. He had even agreed to receiving hypnotic suggestions to ensure that he did not inadvertently disclose his work. And as far as he knew, he'd kept his mouth absolutely shut—as had the other three Wonder Warthog pilots in the room. Besides them, a colonel in the C-5, and a general in the airborne command post, nobody in Europe knew the real story behind the F model. Everyone else thought it was simply an all-weather version of the old Warthog.

He came out of his reflections automatically when the briefing wound down. He looked down at his pad. He had taken three pages of small, neatly written notes. A useful trick, one that had stood him in good stead throughout college. He stood to attention while the general strode out.

He looked at the clock as the crowd of aircrewmen began to break up into noisy groups. It was 0730. Takeoff in an hour and fifteen minutes. He picked up his helmet bag and put on his flight jacket. On the back was painted a color portrait of Philbert Desenex, secret identity of the Wonder Warthog comic-book character created by Gilbert Shelton.

Behind him, someone laughed and yelled, "Oink, oink."

He smiled and thought again about the Jesus Box. About how the A-10 had been chosen over all other aircraft to test its potential. And smiled wider as he remembered how absurdly easy the box made it to dodge even the newest surface-to-air missiles.

He waved at the smirking F-15 pilot.

Outside, ground crews were preparing their airplanes for the flight. As he left the auditorium he saw that it was another gray, rainy dawn. Just as the weather people had predicted.

On the flight line, a jet engine screamed into life, followed by another.

He headed for Operations to get his maps and a cup of coffee.

November 1 was going to be a long day.

7

KOSHKA WAS DOING HIS FIFTIETH SIT-UP JUST AS
the telephone rang. He sprang off the rug and had the receiver off the hook before it could ring again. He looked
through the open door to the bedroom. She was still
asleep. He pulled it shut and spoke into the receiver.

"Yes."

"Comrade Colonel, Kolyachin here. Forgive my intru-
sion, but we have received an important signal from
Groundhog."

Koshka smiled. Not only did Kolyachin know where
he was, he also knew that Koshka would want to know
what their agent in England had to report. A good man,
Kolyachin. He had chosen his aide well.

"What did Groundhog report?"

" 'Mishka left on time.' "

Koshka's smile widened. The KGB, with whom they
shared Groundhog, had also chosen well. He looked at his
watch.

"Excellent, Kolyachin. Please call the director in Berlin and tell him to implement his part of the plan. And also
inform Colonel General Malakov. I believe today he will
be at group headquarters."

"Yes, Comrade Colonel. I have already checked. He is
there now. Is there more?"

Koshka absently fingered a scar on his naked thigh, thinking.

"No. I will be at the field in an hour."

"By then, Colonel, I will have the flight at Stendal. I will personally check each aircraft."

"Good, Kolyachin. Have Vanya prepare the gunship for me."

Kolyachin was surprised.

"You will command from the air, Comrade Colonel?"

"Only if necessary, Kolyachin. I'm sure the comrade director will be up to the job. But one can't be too careful."

"Of course, sir. If there is nothing—"

"No," said Koshka, and hung up.

He walked over to the window. Outside, East Berlin was working through another dreary morning. Little traffic moved through the streets. Silent crowds shuffled to work. The old apartment shook as a streetcar passed below and clattered by. He dropped the blinds and went back to his exercises.

He was on his fortieth push-up when her voice came through the door.

"Yuri? Are you still there?"

He grinned as he strained through another push-up. His face was flushed, the cords standing out on his neck. He wasn't as young as he once was. Forty push-ups used to be nothing.

She opened the door. He looked up. She was naked. Her long brown hair flowed in disarray down to her shoulders. She rubbed her eyes—her huge violet eyes—and smiled at him, yawning.

"What are you doing?"

Koshka jumped up, breathing hard. A thin film of sweat covered his wiry body.

"Exercises, *lyubovnitsa.*" He looked her up and down slowly. "You should try it sometime."

She smiled coyly.

"I don't need to with strong Russian bears like you, Yuri."

His smile froze and she turned pale. He saw the look

79

of fear on her face. Even with whores, he thought bitterly, even with them there is no trust.

He made his smile broaden.

"This bear hasn't got his money's worth yet, *Liebchen*." He strode over and slapped her naked buttock.

She squealed and ran back into the bedroom.

Koshka checked his watch. A little more time left. He jumped into bed, squeezing her breasts. She giggled prettily, but he didn't notice. He was already thinking about Mishka.

8

BARON KARLFRIED HASSO LUDWIG VON LUSTOW would never have understood Nubs Pierce. Or why he wanted to tear out the beautifully carved ceilings of the baron's stables. The baron had been a man of unremitting conservatism, who would have treated Nubs Pierce with the same cold contempt as that he had meted out to Otto von Bismarck. The baron had been appalled by Bismarck's influence on the German Confederacy and had demonstrated his displeasure by exiling himself from Berlin. He built himself what he called a country villa on the banks of the Havel River in Potsdam, where the river widens and turns sluggish enough to be considered a tiny lake. His country house was the model of German Neo-Classicism, with six floors (two belowground and four above), grand Corinthian columns, an elaborate coat of arms over the windows of the great central hall, and, of course, an enormous stable. The care lavished on the mansion itself was matched by the architecture of the stable. For if the baron loved anything as much as the little lake in the Havel, it was his horses.

The first thing Nubs Pierce had thought of when he saw the lake had been how you could hold a hell of a hydro race on its calm waters. The baron, having died in his country house half a century before Nubs was born in Lubbock, Texas, wouldn't have understood that, either. Luckily for the United States Army, the baron's point of view no longer mattered. Just as the opinions of his last descendant, Baron Willi von Lustow, didn't matter. Willi had been a squadron leader in the infamous Luftwaffe mystery group, KG 200. One night in 1943 he'd taken off from a snowy airfield near Stalingrad and never returned. So when the United States Army decided in 1947 that it needed a military-liaison mission on the other side of the Berlin boundary, the Von Lustow country house was chosen. It was vacant, it was secluded, it was fairly near the Berlin checkpoints, and, best of all, it would probably infuriate the Red Army's General Malinin that the U.S. Army had gotten it before he could.

Nubs didn't know anything about the baron. He'd heard about Willi, and Malinin was a name that he vaguely recalled from some mimeographed orientation papers. All he knew about the baron's country house was that it was the most impressive pile of rocks he'd ever lived around. And that the baron's second floor over the stables had to come out so that he could install the new power hoist he needed.

In fact, he thought glumly as he stared up at the intricately carved walnut ceiling, it might be damn well necessary to rearrange the whole place. The thought of what Colonel Martin would say to that made him grin. And that made him spit out some of his chaw. He lowered the left side of his face and, with practiced ease, shot a brownish spurt of Red Man at the ground, his eyes still estimating the work to be done on the ceiling that fifteen Bavarian artisans had labored over for three years.

Max Moss stopped dead. The little bald guy had just spit sideways on his shoes.

Moss reached out and tapped the smaller man on the shoulder.

"Say, fella, that wasn't too nice."

The small man lowered his hands from his hips and turned around slowly to face Max. He was about five five, completely bald, thin as a bunch of sticks, and had a face as wrinkled as a prune. Glacier-blue eyes looked out from under bushy white eyebrows, and a pointed nose, which had been broken too many times to reset in its original place, overhung a wide slash of a mouth. He was dressed in a dirty white jump suit with a Firestone patch over one breast pocket and the word "Nubs" embroidered over the other. A bulge in his left cheek shifted to his right as he considered Max.

"Wanna run that one by again, sonny?"

Max cleared his throat and pointed to his shoes. The brownish ooze was running off onto the ground, staining the concrete.

"I said, it isn't nice to spit on a guy's boots."

Nubs glanced down.

"You oughta be a tad more careful, boy." He looked Max up and down. "You a new driver?" he asked, without concealing his feelings about all drivers—old, new, and unborn.

Because he had been here only three days, and because the old man was so fragile-looking, Max swallowed his retort.

"Yeah, I'm a new driver, all right. Who the hell are you?"

The rain drummed on the tile roof far over their heads as Nubs stared at Max. In another service bay a mechanic was whistling erratically to a tune on the radio. An air wrench whined.

"How long you been here, boy?" he said finally.

"Three days," Max said.

Nubs nodded. "Figures. This your first visit to the garage?"

"Except for a look a couple of days ago," Max said, "it sure is. But who—"

"Name's Nubs, boy."

The older man stuck out a greasy hand.

Max looked at the hand. It was huge, completely out of proportion to the rest of Nubs's body. Max shrugged and shook it.

"Max Moss, Nubs. Now, how about this stuff on my shoes?"

Nibs flicked a look.

"You're right," he said, pronouncing the words *yer raiht.* "Better get that stuff cleaned off. Eats through shoe leather real nice." He tossed Max a rag from his back pocket.

While Max was wiping his shoes Nubs said, "You come over to get acquainted with the shop and the iron?"

Max straightened up.

"Yeah. I've spent the last three days over in the mansion there, getting briefed all day and all night long. Aside from a couple of jogs by the shore, this is the first time I've had a chance to get over here. The colonel said I was to check with a Mr. Pierce. You work for him?"

Nubs didn't smile. "Hell, boy, I *am* Mr. Pierce. Only if you want your iron to get you through that gate over there, you'd best never call me that." He pointed to the name on his jump suit. "Nubs. Just Nubs. Got it?"

Max shook his head. A beat-up old Texan running the garages. Why not? Nothing else in this place made much sense.

"Sure, Nubs."

Pierce nodded. "Good. Now, you might as well get to know this place, because if you're anything like the rest of them, you'll be seeing a lot of it. Nubs's Number One Unbreakable Rule, I call it. You bend a car, you work on it with the boys. You sure as hell won't find no decent mechanic out there"—he jerked a thumb toward the gate—"so you'd best know how to fix 'em."

They'd been standing in the old main entrance to the stables. Big wooden double doors installed by the baron's workmen had been replaced by a roll-up steel door. A small office—once the special domain of the baron's livery master—stood next to the door. Nubs pointed to it as they walked deeper into the building.

"That's my office. I don't keep track of you boys, I don't keep track of your damn crashes, I don't keep track of parts. You want to know any of that stuff, you talk to

Carl, Jake, or Sam back there. You got another problem, see me there." They walked on.

"Up above is where me and the boys live. Lousy steam heat, but otherwise pretty fair for a good ol' boy from Lubbock."

They turned a corner and the main garage area lay exposed, its central aisle at right angles to the entrance. Bright fluorescent lights hung from a plain acoustical ceiling. Stainless-steel benches lined every wall, and sparkling tools hung on endless pegboard racks. A recently poured concrete floor supported three hydraulic jacks and a hoist. The room was almost a hundred feet long. No trace of the original stables was visible. A single Jeep Cherokee, badly mangled in a recent accident, was being readied for the attentions of three men and a Port-A-Power sheet-metal straightener.

Max was impressed and said so.

Nubs grinned. "Yeah, we got a fair little shop here. With the parts shack in back, the engine room over there, and the stuff we got in here"—he tapped his forehead— "me and the boys can keep just about anything running any way you'd like."

One of the men working on the smashed Jeep looked up just then and saw them.

"Hey, Nubs, we need some—" He stopped and stared at Max. "Marty? Marty Morrison. Is that you?"

Max turned red. He'd recognized Carl Haskell the moment he'd seen him.

Carl jumped down from the Jeep and walked over, rubbing his hands on a rag. The other two mechanics were staring with curiosity. He looked just the same, Max noted; dirty-blond hair, cheerful, rawboned face, huge body.

"Damn, Marty. Never figured to see you after Daytona. What brings you out here?" He stared at Max's unmarked flight suit.

Nubs spit on a piece of cardboard. "Mind telling me what's going on, boys?"

Before Max could speak, Carl had turned to Nubs and said, "Shit, Nubs, this here boy had the fastest Chevy at

Daytona. Why, the sucker nearly won the Sportsman in—"

"It's like this, Nubs," Moss said, cutting him off. "I raced under a pseudonym. Maxwell Taylor Moss, aka Marty Morrison, out of Ohio. Ran a '77 Malibu."

Nubs looked at Moss again. "Reckon I remember a Morrison did some winning down home. You that boy?"

Carl broke in. "Sure is, Nubs. Hell, he was a real terror. I mean he could put just about any old boy into the wall." He turned to Moss. "But what're you doing *here?*"

Max's face closed up. "Well, Carl, I had some trouble. Joined up. Air Force. That's how I'm here."

Nubs spit again. "If you boys don't mind, let's get on with it, okay? Carl, get back there and make that Jeep pretty again while I take Mr. Moss *and* Mr. Morrison around the rest of the tour."

Carl smiled his easy smile and bounded back to the Jeep. "Stop by upstairs sometime, Marty. We'll pop a few and talk some."

Max said nothing. Even in the middle of an East German stable he couldn't escape his past.

Pierce was talking.

"I don't know, and I don't want to know, Moss. You wouldn't be here if somebody didn't think you could cut it—I mean besides Carl over there—so I don't care. Got it?" He punctuated his last word with a liquid shot at an old coffee can under a bench.

Max nodded.

"Good. Over here, we got the maintenance board. You can tell how your car is doing by when we—"

A shout interrupted him.

"Moss. Sergeant Moss. Are you in here?"

They turned back to the main door. There, dripping from the steady downpour, stood a man in a Navy officer's raincoat.

Moss recognized him. Lieutenant Commander Aldrich. Second in command at the mission. Max raised his voice. "Over here, Commander."

Aldrich waved him over. Max nodded at Nubs and walked toward the Navy man.

Aldrich wasted no time. "Moss, the colonel's decided

to accelerate your schedule even more. Apparently Shipley and Carmichael aren't doing too well in Berlin." He inclined his head toward the Jeep. They had turned it over on a remote mountain in the south the day after he'd arrived. "That means we're running tight right now, so he's asked Sergeant Wilson to partner you until they're out of the hospital. Then your schedule can be set back to normal." Aldrich saw the look of dismay on Moss's face and smiled. "Don't worry, Moss. Wilson's an old hand, and you won't really be on a patrol—it'll just look like it to our friends across the wire."

Moss said nothing, and they turned to cross the circular courtyard to the mansion.

Aldrich looked at his watch. "It's nine now. After your next briefing you can take off after lunch. Okay?" Max nodded.

They ran from the garage entrance. They had a fifty-yard sprint through the rain to get back to the mansion, across the circular driveway and the central grass, where the flagpole stood. The flag whipped in the wind. The rain had gotten heavier, and the lights from the mansion's windows glimmered weakly in the gloom. Max knew that it would be cold in the old building, the steam registers beneath the windows in every room unable to cope with the chill. The five fireplaces would also be going furiously, and on the top two floors, where the electronics and radio rooms were, the technicians would have their space heaters blazing away. The main floor, with its two huge dining rooms, formal foyer, and drawing room—which was used as a briefing room—would be coldest of all. Even the basement code rooms and computer cells would be warmer.

Max and Aldrich stooped and threw open the doors, stamping their feet on the mat. Moss unzipped his old flight suit and hung it on the coat rack in the rear of the foyer. Aldrich did the same with his overcoat. He noticed Max's chevrons and said, "Well, I see you got your new stripes on."

Max looked down at his technical-sergeant chevrons. The colonel had told him to sew them on immediately. He'd never expected to be a five-striper. You couldn't do it in one term, and by the second term—well, he still wasn't used to thinking of spending another four years in the Air Force. Even in these circumstances.

Aldrich had seen enough men come into the mansion from all branches of the service to recognize the distracted melancholy in Max. Although the recruiting techniques varied according to the individual, almost without exception the men selected were first-term enlistees who had been about to leave the military. And no matter how interesting the mission seemed at first, sooner or later, most of them wondered if they'd made a big mistake by signing on a second time.

"Buyer's remorse?" he asked, grinning at Max as they walked up the short flight of stairs into the magnificent hall.

Max forced a wan smile. "Not really, Commander. Just can't get used to it. That's all."

They walked past a suit of armor covered with condensation. It *was* cold.

Aldrich nodded. "I know the feeling. I was going to get out myself until they offered me this job. I think I'd rather have yours, though. Always wanted to drive race cars."

Before Max could answer, they were in the briefing room. An arched doorway connected it to the smaller of the dining rooms, and huge windows overlooked the river beyond the manicured lawn. Both steam heaters were hissing, but the temperature was still in the low sixties. A crystal chandelier hung from a high, sculpted-plaster ceiling, and expensive Turkish rugs were spread over the parquet floor. The fireplace crackled as a thickset man fed it wet wood. He stood up when they approached.

Aldrich introduced them.

"Max, meet Ike Wilson, the only man to ride a motorcycle through the colonel's flowers and live to tell the tale."

Wilson said nothing, simply sticking out his hand for Max to shake. He had a grip like iron. Even though he was at least two inches shorter than Max, he had the stance and bearing of a man with phenomenal strength. Max guessed him to be about forty. He wore old-style flying sunglasses and had a neat mustache and close-cropped hair blacker than Max's. His face was expressionless. He looked like a man who always stood on the balls of his feet. Waiting.

Aldrich motioned them to the chairs arranged around a briefing easel.

"Max, I understand that you've already been brought up-to-date on our goals here and on some of our history. Ike can probably fill you in a lot better than any of the briefings, though, since he's been here almost seven years." Max looked over at the silent master sergeant, who, like Max, wore an Air Force uniform. He hadn't known it was possible to take a second tour.

Aldrich continued, flipping up the cover on the map board. "What I want to do before you take off after lunch is give you an idea how we arrange our patrols and what kind of surveillance you can expect from the Vopos and the Russians." He frowned for a moment. "Moss, didn't you once live in Germany?"

Max said, "Yes. When I was a kid, my father had an assignment in Berlin. Around '63. We were here for about a year."

Aldrich nodded. "Good, that means you have at least some idea about what to expect. Things have changed in Berlin considerably, but you probably saw that when you landed on Monday." In fact, however, when he'd stepped off the courier airplane, Max had been rushed through the Berlin Command's paperwork so quickly and driven down the Avus autobahn so fast that, in the confusion and darkness, he had actually seen almost nothing of Berlin. Except for the checkpoint on the Königstrasse, of course. And even there, their special license plates had allowed them through with only a pause for the East German military policeman to check the numbers against his master book. And the ten minutes from there to the mansion had been through a Potsdam that was virtually deserted. Since then Max had been staying in the new, hotellike barracks for the drivers and working in the mansion every day. He had seen nothing of the countryside at all.

Aldrich hadn't noticed his reverie. He was pointing to a large map of East Germany, which was divided into five colored zones.

". . . the operating radius of the cars, we've sliced up Germany into these areas of patrol. The center of the slices is here at Potsdam, and, although the actual amount of ground in each area is different, each can be covered in the same amount of time. You leave here in the morning, drive for a day, a night and a day, and return the next evening. You have complete freedom of travel, of course, so you stay overnight in a *Gasthaus* or even a hotel, depending on how close to a major city you are. And, of course, your route is always as different as you can make it so that the Vopos and Russians don't get an MO on you. As Ike can tell you, shaking the tail car they stick on you right outside the gate isn't too hard, but if you establish a pattern they can follow too easily, it makes it damned hard to make a successful pickup. Questions?"

"As a matter of fact, yes, sir. First, aren't we under constant surveillance out there? Surely something like one of our Fairmonts or Cherokees can't go unrecognized by the Germans. So how is it possible to be free of them?"

Aldrich sat down. "You have to remember that these people are used to a system of government that doesn't reward initiative. Everyone who sees your car will probably know you're American—but so what? The only time they'll call in the cops is when they're told to. We've had cases of farmers leaning on their shovels watching while we've made successful pickups right in their fields. It's not so much that they hate their leaders, just that they've learned not to get involved. So the only guys who really try to find you are the special Volkspolizei teams and the military cops. Even regular Vopos pounding a beat in the boonies will usually just watch you without reporting. After all, we've been doing this for over twenty-five years now, and our blue cars are as much a part of the scene as the white BMWs of the Vopos or the gray army trucks of the Soviets."

Max thought for a second, then said, "Okay, so we can roam all over—except for the permanent restricted zones—take pictures, make notes, pick up pilots and equipment, and come home without interference. What about the tails?"

Aldrich pointed upstairs. "We've got complete files on the guys the Germans assign to tail our cars, including the secret-service people. You should memorize the faces, cars, and habits of every one of them so you'll know what to expect. Ike knows them all."

Wilson smiled a thin smile. He had still not said anything. Moss noticed a tiny blue tattoo on the back of his left hand. It was a heart with "Margarete" written across it.

Max turned back to Aldrich. "Once we've made a pickup, I assume the Russians and the Vopos pull out all the stops to block us off?"

Aldrich nodded. "Right. That's why we've got the latest radio and navigation gear in each car. They're scattered almost as thin on the ground as we are, so you've got some advantage on them. But they always know where you're heading."

Moss broke in. "Which brings up another thing—why don't they just put a roadblock out on the gate road? Seems a lot easier than chasing all over the countryside."

Aldrich grinned widely. "They tried that, back in '58, I believe. And they got the people in the Recovery car, too. Even managed to break a few bones in the driver and his partner—purely by accident, of course—before they were done. We didn't say anything, but the next day, the Soviets' mission near Frankfurt—I'm sure the colonel briefed you on how theirs is set up—found itself mysteriously surrounded by construction equipment. They protested—all the missions are guaranteed secure access by the agreement—but the local commander just said the road needed repairs. And the next week, when a Soviet car was going like hell through the construction area, a grader just happened to back up into the road. A general and colonel got it in that one, I believe. Since then nobody's tried roadblocks on the entry road."

Aldrich stood up and walked to the fireplace. "You

have to realize, Max, that this whole thing is like a house of cards. The French shut down their mission long ago, and the British use theirs purely for a bit of spying and trading secrets with the Germans. We're the only mission that does recovery anymore. So we and the Soviets have to be very careful anytime we or they want to take things even an inch further than the agreement specifies. For instance, there have been some desperate attempts to stop our cars from escaping. But outside of a restricted zone, nobody's ever been shot at. Not once. The reason is that the Soviets know that if they opened up, the whole game would collapse. And they want their mission even more badly than we want ours."

He held his hands out to the fire. "Even something like building the new barracks you're staying in caused headaches. They were sure we were trying to build some kind of secret weapon system, or at the least a new radar. It took months to convince them that the cutbacks in our budget in '81 made it impossible to keep ferrying the mission drivers back and forth from the Berlin barracks. So they finally agreed, but a full colonel in Soviet Technical Intelligence was posted on the site during construction."

Aldrich walked back to the maps. "Anyway, all this means that it's unlikely you'll have to deal with anything other than the surveillance you've already been told about. Helicopters, cars, aircraft—yes. But don't worry about a tank suddenly appearing on an open road and blowing you away. It won't happen."

With that, Aldrich settled into a long discussion of the precise patrol zones, the duty-roster scheduling, and the maintenance requirements of the Recovery teams. By the time he was finished with the last page of the flip chart it was lunchtime.

Aldrich glanced at his watch and winced. "Jesus. I've got to get up to EuCom headquarters. Ike, are you ready to take an orientation cruise with Max today?"

Wilson, who had said nothing during the briefing, nodded. His voice was a deep rumble. "No problem, Bob."

Max was startled. He'd been told that most of the mission people called each other by their first names, ignoring rank when no outsiders were around. But this was the first time he'd heard it. He looked quickly at Aldrich. The Navy man hadn't noticed. He was absorbed in gathering up his gear.

"Okay, then. Max, I'll see you tomorrow after breakfast. Come on up to my office and we'll go over special rescue procedure." With that, Aldrich hurried out of the room.

Max turned to Wilson. Ike was looking intently out the window.

"Damn rain isn't going to stop. We might as well catch a sandwich and get going." He glanced at Max. "How about it, Moss?"

It was the first thing Wilson had said directly to him. Max was a little annoyed.

"Sure, Ike. Whatever you say." If Wilson caught the slight edge of sarcasm, he ignored it. He got up and was almost out the door before Max was out of his chair.

Lunch was spent in near silence. Every time Max would try to start a conversation Wilson would grunt a monosyllabic reply and quash it. After an hour Max still had no idea what kind of man Wilson was. Except quiet, thought Max sourly as he finished off his roast beef.

Wilson looked at his watch and stood up, catching Max in mid-swallow. "Time to go," he said. Max gulped down his coffee and hurried to catch up. The staff dining room was only a little less elegant than the two official dining rooms. A huge chandelier hung from the ceiling and the five dining tables were covered with blindingly white Irish linen. The kitchen and serving staff were superb, each one a German civilian whose credentials in cuisine and ability to keep his mouth shut were impeccable. As everywhere else in the mission, there were no divisions between ranks. The five officers ate where the enlisted men ate; the only difference was that the three married officers lived in Berlin and commuted.

By the time Moss caught Wilson he was nearly at the

front door. Max had had enough. He grabbed Wilson's arm and said, "Listen, Wilson, I don't know what your problem is, but I sure hope we can solve it. Because if I understand the deal, you and I will be partners for some time."

Wilson stood stone-still. Without facing Moss, he said quietly, "Moss, let go of my arm."

Max let his hand drop. Wilson turned around to face him. Somehow he seemed not as short as he had.

"You're right, Moss. We will be partners. And you'd better learn something right now. As of this moment, I'm your only insurance against a bunch of Vopos with no objections to broken bones. *Your* broken bones. If I were you, I'd stop worrying about stupid chatter and start worrying about that." During his speech his voice had never been raised, had never betrayed a hint of anger.

Max was shaken. An aura of deadliness surrounded the man like a thick robe.

Without waiting for Max to answer, he stepped into the rain.

Ten minutes later, they met in the garage. Max had gotten his gear from the barracks room. Although it stood to reason that Wilson lived there, too, he had not seen Wilson, who was standing next to Nubs Pierce when Max ran through the open main door to the old stables. Neither man looked up as Max approached.

Max drew closer and heard Nubs speaking.

". . . turbo's set on ten pounds, Ike, so don't screw around with it. Last time you took it up to fifteen we had to replace every damn gasket in the motor. Aside from that, she's just the way you drove her last."

Wilson nodded, looking into the open engine bay of the almost-new Ford Fairmont four-door sedan. Max joined them. The engine almost made him gasp. In all his years as a racer he'd never seen such a lovingly crafted engine. The 302-cubic-inch Ford V-8 had been carefully worked over by the Recovery technicians; it was balanced, lightened, ported and polished. A new camshaft, a new ignition system, and the AiResearch turbocharger made it an all-new power plant, capable of spinning out five hundred horsepower at maximum turboboost.

Nubs turned to Moss. "Carl says you was a good runner. Ever drive a turbo?"

Moss nodded. "Yeah, but not in a racer. Had an old Mustang that I breathed on a little."

Wilson cut in. "This automobile will outperform everything you've ever driven, Moss. Including your NASCAR stocker." Moss's eyebrows rose. So Wilson knew about his racing.

Nubs said to Max, "Come on, Moss. You need a little prerace check of this ol' hoss." He then took Max all around the car, pointing out its modifications one by one. As he did so Max detected the pride in the broad Texas drawl.

As a connoisseur of cars, Max knew the pride was deserved. Even to one used to the fire-breathing race cars of the superspeedways, the Ford was impressive. It rode on a completely new suspension, built entirely in Germany by the Ford of Europe competition department and further tweaked by the mission's wizards. Double gas shock absorbers controlled each wheel, damping them enough to permit a rock-steady ride. Drilled racing disc brakes hung on each axle. Fat Goodyear endurance racing-style tires bulged out of the fenders, their thin sidewalls specially reinforced for the job by Goodyear. Inside, the standard Ford interior had been gutted and replaced with special seating and instrumentation. A Litton inertial navigation system was installed between the two front racing seats, its map readout centered on the dash between the driver and passenger. "Navigator" would be a better term, thought Max as he puzzled over the complex digital displays and dials in front of the passenger seat. A full-spectrum radio filled up the space in the dash not taken up by the shifter and the navigation system. The driver had gauges for speed, engine rpm, oil temperature and pressure, turboboost, fuel-cell pressure and level, battery condition, and a host of minor idiot-light monitors.

The steering wheel was small and thickly padded with

leather. Max saw that it had triggers built into the rim and that a microphone was installed flush with the horn button. Nubs saw his look of amazement and said, "Like our little touch, eh? That's so you can call for help when you got your hands full of steering wheel."

Wilson slammed the hood down and slipped the hood pins through their links. "Let's go, Moss. I'll fill you in on the car as we go. It'll be dark by five."

Max unzipped his bag, took out a notebook and microcassette recorder, and put the bag in the trunk. He noticed the oversized batteries, large tool box, emergency supplies, and M-16 rifles. A shiver ran down his spine. He climbed into the passenger seat, slammed the door, and pulled on his six-point harness. The interior smelled of leather and fiberglass. Racing smells.

Wilson gave Pierce a filled-out form. Max recognized it as a patrol sheet.

"We'll be taking a quick run through Area One, Nubs. Out the E-eight, up to Salzwedel on the seventy-one, then back on the little roads through Osterburg, Genthin, and Brandenburg. Should be back by five or so, unless the Reds have the one-oh-seven road closed down again between PRZ fifteen and sixteen."

Pierce spit a wad of brown stuff at a crawling spider.

"Just watch the boost, Wilson. And don't try to cross any more damn streams with this thing. You wanna do that shit, use a Jeep."

Wilson said nothing. He walked around the car, stooping once to check the ground clearance, then got in. He adjusted his harness, switched on the radio and the inertial nav system, and said to Moss, "Make a note in the log." Max took the small blue book from his door compartment, opened it to November 1. "Training patrol: Wilson, Isaac, master sergeant, and Moss, Maxwell Taylor, tech sergeant. Area One. Terminus: Salzwedel. Estimated time of patrol, five hours. Time of departure"—he looked at the digital clock set in the dash—"twelve-oh-five." He pointed at the radio. "See if the guard channel is working—squawk the identifier."

Max pushed the small red button that sent out their

Mayday signal to the men on the fourth floor of the mansion. A small beep came from the radio. In a second a yellow light appeared below the switch. Wilson grunted. "Signal operating instructions for the day are alpha-alpha-nine." He selected the appropriate frequencies on the radio, switching the alpha-numeric indicators to A-A-9. He squeezed the triggers on his steering wheel and said, "Peter Rabbit, this is Brer Wolf. How do you read?"

Instantly, from the central speaker, a voice said, "Brer Wolf, this is Peter Rabbit. We have you five-by. Out."

Wilson sat still for a moment. He removed his sunglasses and took out a small chamois rag tucked into a corner of the cockpit. As he cleaned them the only sound in the car was the breathing of the two men. Finally Wilson turned to Max, and Max saw that his eyes were almost clear, a strange color of gray. Wilson regarded him impassively a moment before he slipped his dark glasses back on. He flipped up a toggle switch. Max heard the rapid clicking of a mechanical fuel pump from the engine compartment.

Wilson slipped the five-speed gear selector into neutral and turned the key. Instantly the dashboard lit up, the needles swinging off their dead pins.

He twisted the key another notch and the engine exploded into life, filling the garage with thunder.

Wilson looked at Moss.

"Let's go," he said.

9

BY THE TIME THEY WERE TEN KILOMETERS
south of Salzwedel, Max knew a little about Ike Wilson and
a lot about East Germany. Or rather, he thought, I've
found out a few things about Wilson and remembered a
lot more about Germany. Things that had been fuzzy images impressed in a nine-year-old boy's consciousness as
he stared out the rear window of his father's staff car had
become scenes that seemed naggingly familiar when he
noticed them through the window of the speeding Ford.
Then they would suddenly snap into focus as they mated
with the visions from twenty years ago. A farm cart with its
dun-colored and unrecognizable burden piled high in
back, being pulled by a dispirited dun-colored horse and a
stolid citizen of the German Democratic Republic sitting
in front. The endless gray-green forests. The narrow, un-
posted roads, covered only with gravel, asphalt, concrete—whatever came to hand. And the little farm towns
spread out along the deserted roads, their rebuilt habita-
tions barrackslike and drab. From the moment they'd left
the relative bustle of Potsdam—once the favorite suburb
of the German entertainment community—things had
grown more and more familiar. And more and more depressing.

Wilson hadn't noticed, thought Max. The second he'd
dropped the clutch outside the garage at the mission and

spun the tires on the concrete driveway, he'd been a changed man. His deadpan expression had been rolled up like a shutter to reveal a thin, wolfish grin that had stayed fixed for the last two hours of driving.

Coldly precise with his movements at the steering wheel and shifter, Wilson drove the Ford as if he were riding a wild horse, forcing it to do his will. It was as though he were trying to kill the car. Small beads of sweat stood out on his forehead. But the strange grin never varied.

Max had to admit to himself—grudgingly—that Wilson was, for all his lack of sympathy for the car, a splendid driver. The wide Goodyear tires started to rise off the surface of the road on a thin film of water at any speed over seventy miles an hour, but Wilson took them up to ninety anyway, savagely booting the car sideways around corners on the smaller roads. On the Helmstedt–Berlin autobahn—the main ground artery linking Berlin with the West—Wilson had discovered that the better road surface would allow even higher cruising speeds. So, despite the heavy, slow traffic and the intermittent sheets of rain, he nailed the throttle and held the car at over ninety for long periods of time.

Max was busy trying to learn everything, his head swiveling like a nervous fighter pilot's. But Wilson never seemed to take his eyes off the road ahead. Because of that, he'd taken Max completely by surprise when he'd suddenly started quizzing him about features of the road, the terrain, the surrounding cars, and the route.

Wilson's deep voice hardly paused for the hundred miles to Salzwedel, always pushing Max to notice this culvert, that insignia of a Soviet armored division, another small dirt road that led to a stream that fed into a river inside a permanent restricted zone. It was as though the act of driving released the gates of his mind, allowing him opportunities and reasons for speech he never indulged in once the car was stopped.

It was when he'd sensed the pattern to Wilson's loquacity that Max managed to get him to talk about himself. It rankled Moss that everyone around him seemed to know everything about him, whereas he knew nothing of them.

So it was a small triumph when Wilson began a burst of his typical clipped sentences about his own life. They were on a featureless stretch of autobahn, ten minutes from their turnoff exit onto the northbound road to Salzwedel, when Ike finally responded to Max's question about how he'd learned the two languages necessary for Recovery work.

Eyes still fixed dead ahead, Wilson replied, "Easy. My mother was German. Been speaking it since I was a little kid. And I learned Russian when I was stationed in Turkey. Wasn't much else to do. Especially since they didn't have a decent racetrack in the whole damn country." And then he'd been silent until they came to their turnoff.

Max made a note of the time as they rolled to a stop on the exit road. A striped bar hung across the road. Four Vopos and a paramilitary guard stood inside a shelter looking bored. One of them peered at their license plate and shouted something. Wilson rolled down his window and told the guard in German that they were from the mission. He shrugged and pushed the button that lifted the barrier. Wilson slipped the car into first and shot through the gate, spraying loose gravel backward from the spinning tires. Muffled shouts and curses came from the guardhouse. Wilson's smile broadened.

"Little ritual we always go through. Guy named Steiner runs the post. Happen to notice the guns they had?"

Max was startled. "Uh—guns?"

"Kalashnikov-nineteens. New, the latest automatics from Moscow. Wonder what those guys are doing with them. Log it."

Max wrote the information in the little blue book, and he recognized the uneasy feeling in his stomach. It was, as always, the fear of failure. He knew he could drive as well as any of the other men at the mission, but how could he ever develop observational skills like Wilson's? A chill settled on him as he felt the stirring of despair. He had to wrench his mind away from the depression into which it so easily sank. Wilson's tattoo caught his eye.

"Hey, who's Margarete?" he blurted out.

Wilson's mouth tightened, making the grin a grimace.

100

"Nobody, Moss. Keep your goddamn eyes out the window, not on me." He downshifted for a corner in the little road. The car immediately slued wildly sideways, the rear wheels slipping over the edge of the asphalt onto loose dirt and gravel. Wilson swore violently and kept the throttle all the way open, steering into the slide. The car steadied as the speed increased, and just as a large pine tree seemed about to cave in Max's door, Wilson upshifted and the car shot back onto the road. The near-accident had taken less than two seconds. Max was petrified. He didn't mind driving like this, but he hated riding helplessly. He shuddered and gasped.

Wilson looked at him for the first time. His grin was gone.

"Sorry, Moss. It's just . . . well, I don't much like to talk about her." He was silent for a while. The road unwound in front of the car like a glistening gray ribbon. There was no traffic. No towns. Just dense forest that grew right to the edge of the road. The high-speed wipers swished across the windshield in a blur. The engine sounded strong, the V-8 loafing along in fifth gear. Max realized with a start that the red line painted on the tachometer indicated that the Fairmont was theoretically capable of doing 170.

Wilson spoke again.

"It was during my first tour in Berlin. Met her at a dance. Got close, y'know? Real close. Then one night she kind of broke down. Finally got her to tell me about it, and it turned out she was supposed to pump me about the mission. But she couldn't do it. Wasn't a spy, see? Just a girl . . . until *they* found out about her across the wire. Figured they could get her to do a little work, right? She still had family on the other side. You know the story. Well, she wouldn't do it." They were doing over 120 now. Wilson sat like a robot, hands automatically making minute steering corrections as they shot down the country road.

"One night she didn't show. I got worried. Called in some buddies, and we went looking. Found her in an alley near Checkpoint Charlie. She'd fought hard, it looked like. But they'd got her anyway. Cut her good." His jaw muscles were jumping. Sweat was pouring down his face.

"So I talked 'em into another term. Because one day"—he squeezed the leather wheel until his knuckles stood out—"one day the pigs that did it will be on the road somewhere. And I'll be there, too."

Max tore his eyes away from Wilson's face as the car crested a hill. The Ford rushed over the top, pitching slightly as it settled back on its suspension. Max saw a farm truck directly ahead of them. He braced himself against the grab rail and yelled a warning to Wilson.

"Look out, Ike."

Wilson took a half second longer to react than he should have. He blinked swiftly and instead of jamming on the brakes, which would have eliminated what little traction they already had on the slippery road, he whipped the speeding Ford to the left.

The farmer slammed his open door closed just as the Ford *whoosh*ed by in a shower of spray. Max glanced at him as they hurtled past and then looked ahead again.

"Ike. A car."

But Wilson had already seen it. Coming straight at them was a gray sedan. Max knew there wasn't enough time for them to slip back into the right lane. He watched in horror as they closed with the oncoming car. He could see its terrified driver frozen at the wheel.

Wilson suddenly jerked the steering wheel to the left. The Fairmont immediately turned off the road, fishtailing wildly. He did not ease up on the gas.

The Ford slithered along the wet grass next to the road. Wilson desperately worked at the wheel to keep it straight.

Suddenly they were washed in the spray of the gray sedan as it whipped past them. Max felt the car rock from the backwash and prayed that Ike could keep it on all four wheels. He darted a glance at the trees barely three feet from the car.

Wilson began to ease the Ford back up onto the road. The right front wheel juddered as it encountered the edge of the pavement. Max began to feel easier, then was startled by Wilson's curse.

"*Shit.* Hold on, Moss." Max saw a huge stone marker ahead in their path. He closed his eyes and waited for the impact.

It never came. Wilson jammed the gear lever into fourth and spun the wheel all the way to the right. The Ford lurched up onto the road, missing the stone by inches. Then it began to slide. Wilson steered into the slide, gently keeping the power on. They were still shooting down the wet road at over a hundred. It seemed for a second as though the Ford would settle and come back under control. But the road was too wet.

The car continued its slow slide, then went past the point of forward control. Max opened his eyes just in time to see the beginning of their spin.

Wilson gritted his teeth. He released the steering wheel, then centered it. They stopped their spin. But they were sliding backward. Wilson grinned wolfishly and jerked up on the hand-brake lever. As if by remote control, the Ford swapped ends instantly. And suddenly they were in their own lane again, still alive.

The tires hissed on the asphalt and the car rocked gently as Wilson fed it power. He looked over at Moss. For the first time his smile was wide and unaffected.

"Hope you don't mind bootleg spins. Brakes would've put us right into that old guy's load of shit."

Max let go of the grab bar. His heart was thumping wildly. He just couldn't get used to not driving.

"Sure, Ike . . . anytime. Next time, though, holler or something, okay?"

Wilson chuckled, and as easily as that, the barrier was down. The older man began interspersing his questions about what Moss observed with questions about Moss himself.

Max was wary at first, leery of Wilson's lightning-quick change of mood. But gradually he began to answer Wilson's queries with more candor. All but the last one Wilson had asked before they entered the turnaround in Salzwedel. The one about why he was in Recovery.

Without thinking, Max had said, "Hell, it seemed like the right thing to do at the time," and said no more. Wilson shot a glance at him, but Max was withdrawn. Why *was* he here? The last few days of intense learning had left no time for introspection. When he'd finally fallen into his bed after a day of relentless cramming, he hadn't even wanted to talk to the three or four other Recovery guys who drifted in and out of their barracks. The missionary motel, they called it, and few stayed there long. With the rotating shifts, a crew would arrive, debrief, fall asleep, and then either take a day or two off in Berlin or go right back on the road. There was little socializing. They were hardly a jolly crew of merry men, thought Max.

So why do it? Why not be back there in beautiful Santa Barbara, lying in the sand a hundred feet from Castagnola's Seafood Emporium? Or with Christie in Cambridge?

Wilson interrupted his brooding.

"Check out the tower on the left, Max."

Moss looked out the left-hand window. Wilson had slowed the Ford to less than thirty miles an hour, bringing angry honking from the truck behind them. A large black latticework tower stood in the forest about a half mile away to the west, well inside the border restricted zone. Approaching Salzwedel on this main road, they were less than ten miles from the three rows of barbed wire and booby traps that marked the border between East and West Germany. Max noticed that the tower was topped by a rapidly oscillating dish.

Wilson accelerated. "Make a note, Max. New Soviet Apple-type multiple-use tower set up one kilometer south of Salzwedel, one kilometer west in forest. Time: fourteen-fifteen hours."

Max finished writing and said, "Is that unusual?"

Wilson slowed again as they entered the outskirts of Salzwedel.

"Yeah. Unless they're up to something across the way there." He inclined his head to the west. "But that's damned unlikely right at this spot at this time. See, there's a NATO exercise scheduled for today down by Wolfsburg, and the Russians usually avoid stirring things up with decoys or jamming when our troops are just across the bor-

104

der." He frowned as they passed a long line of Soviet Army trucks and armored personnel carriers parked in Salzwedel's town square. "Better note this, too, Max. Looks like a whole motorized company of radio troops from—let's see—yeah, from Sixteenth Frontal Aviation Army HQ in Finow."

Max looked up. "Finow? That's northeast of Berlin, isn't it?"

Wilson nodded. He turned onto the southbound road off the square, followed by curious stares from several Soviet soldiers in a corner café.

"Sure is. And radio troops have only two functions in life: eavesdropping on us and jamming us." He paused, thinking. "Listen, get on the horn and—" He broke off, looking in the rearview mirror. "Oops."

Max flipped down his visor, to which a mirror was attached. He saw a dirty white BMW behind them. Inside were two men. One was holding a microphone.

"Vopos," said Wilson. "After we lost Fritz outside Potsdam, I thought they'd leave us alone. Maybe they don't like us being so near these radio guys." They rumbled through the southern suburbs of Salzwedel, followed about a hundred feet back by the BMW.

Wilson nodded at the radio.

"Don't broadcast now, Max. Let's see how dedicated those guys behind us are." They picked up speed as they exited the built-up area. The rain had stopped, Max noted. If Ike was going to do any fancy stuff, it was just as well.

Wilson looked quickly at the map display in the inertial navigation system. It showed them heading southeast on Route 71. The digital distance-to-base readout stood at 82/131, indicating that they were that many direct air miles/kilometers from the mission in Potsdam. "Look here," Ike said, pointing to a junction a few kilometers farther down. "This is the Winterfeld crossroads. We'll turn east toward Osterburg there. That way we'll have some small hills, a lot of farm roads, and at least ten intersections to lose these birds with. What do you think?"

Max looked up, surprised at Wilson's asking for his opinion. However perfunctory, it made him feel better.

"Sure," he said.

Wilson grinned and pressed his foot to the floor. The Ford leaped forward, and as 4,500 RPM came up on the tachometer, the turbocharger, whose turbine blades were spun by the recycled exhaust gases, made its presence felt. A new scream came into the exhaust note and they burst ahead, the tires spinning despite the speed of eighty miles an hour. Wilson's grin widened as the BMW shrank in the distance.

"Nice," he said, "but that was Müller, I think. We won't lose him that easy."

And they didn't. It took all of Wilson's concentration to gain enough ground in the open country to drop the white car a mile behind. Once they had lost the Germans from direct view Wilson kept the throttle down, sliding wildly around the muddy little farm roads, scattering chickens and geese in one village, villagers themselves in another. After half an hour they were only a few kilometers from Osterburg. Just before a level crossing Wilson locked up the brakes and slid the car to a stop. Max's body hurt from being thrown against the seat harness.

Wilson looked past Max to the right. There was a firebreak in the dense forest. He engaged first gear and pulled off the road into the break. It was barely wide enough to allow the car through. Underbrush scraped the sides as they crept along. Finally the trail—it was hardly a road—opened abruptly into a meadow large enough for the car to turn around in. Wilson spun the car on the wet grass until they were facing the way they'd come. Visible far down the long tunnel of the trail through the trees was the farm road. Wilson nodded, satisfied. He shut off the engine.

"How about a cup of coffee, Max? No harm in letting old Müller work a little harder, eh?" He released his harness and reached back over the seat for the thermos bottle.

"How did you know about this firebreak?" Max hadn't even seen it.

Wilson propped his sunglasses up on his forehead while he poured two steaming cups of coffee. "Used it once before. About a year ago, I think. Doesn't look like anybody's been here since, either."

Max drank the hot coffee in silence.

Wilson glanced at the clock. "Almost a quarter to three. In ten minutes we'll head on through Osterburg to Route one-oh-seven, then on south to Genthin. By then Müller will be on the carpet for losing us." He laughed at the prospect.

Max rolled down his window. Rainwater was dripping noisily off the trees into the brush. Far away, Max heard the hissing of tires on pavement. He looked down the fire-break just in time to see a flash of white go by.

Wilson laughed again, and Max determined to listen very carefully next time Ike Wilson spoke. He swallowed his scalding-hot drink and asked Ike to explain the fine points of the inertial navigation system. He took careful notes as Ike obliged.

At precisely the same moment, eleven miles southeast of where they sat, Ivan Kolyachin was strapping himself into the cockpit of the lead MiG-25 of Koshka's Felix flight. Waiting.

10

MCCULLOCH TASTED THE RADAR JUST IN TIME. He pulled the Wonder Warthog up over the trees for another shot at the Gepard antiaircraft tank, and simultaneously felt the Jesus Box telling him about the SAM radar a thousand meters south. He reacted instantly. While he ordered a Maverick radar-homing missile to launch at the SAM installation with one part of his brain, he jerked the stick hard left and stood the A-10F on its wingtip. He pushed the throttles all the way forward and held on. It had taken 320 milliseconds. The SAM radar needed 350 milliseconds to lock on to him.

He clipped the branches of the dripping pine trees with his left wing and his on-board computer told him through the Box that he could still make a good run at the Gepard. Making his decision, he did a rollout to the right. He kept the power on as he dived to the ground again, relying on the terrain-following radar and his Jesus Box–enhanced instincts to keep him out of the trees and rocks, which were briefly visible through the fog. At five hundred meters, he loosed a one-second burst at the Gepard, whose crew had just switched on their twin radars. They were too late. The 30-mm depleted-uranium slugs tore through the 25-mm armor and exploded inside, detonating the tank's ammunition. Less than a second after they had seen the A-10, they were dead.

Still flying through the trees, he throttled back to two hundred knots. His infrared scanners told him through the Box that a heat-seeking missile had been launched at him from the ground. He asked the computer for help and, 290 milliseconds later, pulled back sharply on the stick. The Warthog groaned, but he fed it full power; seconds later, the General Electric turbines wound up again, helping him gain altitude. Two thousand feet above the ground, he was still in zero-zero cloud and rain, but the missile had tracked him. He felt its probing infrared and stood the plane on its right wing, almost stalling. He allowed the A-10 to fall over backward and dove straight toward the ground. After a loss of four hundred meters he applied dive brakes and picked up the IR scanner on the ground with his forward-looking sensors. He switched on the infrared gunsight and the little light source on the instrument panel again shot a minute beam into his eye. As he focused on the target indicator set into his head-up display on the windscreen, the computer calculated the angle of fire from the position of the pupil of his eye, as determined by the reflected infrared beam in his eyeball. While the missile was staggering around trying to find him, he fired an IR missile of his own at the ground source. One and two-tenths seconds later, it disappeared in a ball of high-explosive fire.

He had destroyed a complete surface-to-air missile launcher, a Gepard AA tank, and a missile source of unknown size in less than two minutes. His sensors were quiet momentarily, reporting no further threats, and he took stock of the battlefield situation.

Since 1430 hours, when the ceiling had dropped below standard A-10 minimums, he and the other three F models had been the only aircraft flying in the battle zone. And since then, if his recollection was correct—and his computer told him it was—the four of them had destroyed fifteen main battle tanks, twelve AA tanks, nine SAM launchers, twenty trucks of various sizes, and six bridges. Also, an unknown number of ground troops had been eliminated. Not bad for a half hour's work, he thought. Especially in weather like this.

He checked his fuel. He'd been over the target for nearly two hours. According to the plan, he was to break off at 1500 and orbit a small hill to reform with the other three Wonder Warthogs. There was no fire from the ground now. He asked the Box for a scan of the radio, starting with the "enemy" frequency.

". . . *Verdammt*. How did he get in so fast? One moment we had him; the next, the deadlight says he's killed us all. How—"

"Don't know, Captain. All I saw was a flash on the infrared scanner and then nothing. Fritz says that he got the Gepard, too."

McCulloch smiled and switched to the "umpire" frequency.

". . . No, Major, there's nothing you can do, I'm afraid. Captain McCulloch destroyed your company fair and square, according to our sensors, and that's the way it'll have to read."

Not bad, McCulloch thought again. He looked down at the Jesus Box, tucked into the space the caution-light module had occupied before conversion. It was a small black plug-in box about seven inches wide, five high, and eleven deep. It slipped neatly into the right-hand dash panel, with four simple switches on it and a single multipin connector. His flexible helmet lead snapped into that. It was the umbilical that tied him to the airplane. And survival.

He looked at the time, projected in digits on the head-up display on his windscreen: 1458. Time to break off. He and the others had proved today what a Wonder Warthog could do, he thought. And we still have two more days. Not to mention nights.

He gently brought the stick back and climbed to two thousand feet again. He knew that the Airborne Warning and Control aircraft radar was good enough to pick him up at that height, and after the confusion in the valley they'd probably like to have a nice, clean blip on their screens up there at forty-five thousand feet.

Since his orbit point was only ten miles from the valley, it took him just a little over two minutes to get to it. The whole area was socked in, just as it was ten miles to the east, but his terrain radar and infrared scanning allowed him to spot the little eighty-meter hill. It stood in a kind of marsh, he saw as he lost altitude gradually in a gentle spiral. He switched over to the A-10 radio frequency.

"Hello, Warthog flight, this is Warthog One."

"Wart One, this is Wart Four. Am at angels one and closing to rendezvous. Do you see me?"

McCulloch found him on the long-range scanner against the clutter of the background.

"Roger, Wart Four." He was still about thirty miles north.

"Wart One, this is Warthog Three. Wart Two is on my wing. Will arrive in fifteen." They were even farther north. He allowed his A-10 to whistle quietly downward while he awaited the others. At one thousand feet he leveled out and relaxed. In half an hour they'd be debriefing at Edemissen, then a long shower and a beer would top off a fine day.

Below Buzz McCulloch's circling A-10F, a man stared up at the drizzle and mist, listening. As McCulloch's plane whined overhead, unseen, he picked up a portable radio transmitter, setting it on the roof of a brown Volkswagen Rabbit. He carefully aligned the compass dial, then aimed a small tight-focus dish antenna according to a preset mark on the dial. He flipped the ON switch and repeated one word three times into the microphone.

The man then jerked the radio off the roof and threw it inside the car. He jumped in and sped away toward the little town of Wahrenholz, where, to the townspeople, he was a respectable postal clerk.

Twenty-three miles northeast, the radio troops in the base of the mobile tower that Wilson and Moss had seen south of Salzwedel received the three-word message. The senior sergeant, who took the message, scribbled it on a piece of paper and handed it across the cramped compartment to a captain. The captain then picked up a receiver, turned to his keyboard, and punched a telephone number into it. Two seconds later, Colonel Yuri Andreyevich Koshka answered his phone.

The captain did not identify himself. He simply said, "Felix, Felix, Felix," and hung up.

Comrade Colonel Koshka smiled and then had his radio operator make two more calls.

And Captain Sawyer F. McCulloch circled the Könns-chiers-Berg again, waiting for Warthog Four to rendezvous.

11

KOLYACHIN'S EARPHONES CRACKLED INTO LIFE.
He sat strapped into the cold cockpit of the huge MiG-25
at Stendal airfield, exactly fifty-two air miles from Mishka's
orbit point. His engines—and the engines of the four other members of Koshka's special Felix flight—were running
as they sat on the runway, cockpit canopies closed, ready
for the word. Then the tower operator relayed Koshka's
message: *Go.*

Kolyachin reacted instantly. He slammed the dual
throttles forward and the enormous Tumansky turbojets
coughed and then began to spin up to war-emergency
power for a short-field takeoff. In two seconds they were
at maximum rpm. Kolyachin held the brakes against the
shuddering fury of the seventy thousand pounds of thrust
that was trying to hurl the big black airplane into the air.
He spoke once into the radiomicrophone to the other
men. He said simply, "Let's go," and released the brakes.
It was exactly 1500 hours.

He was slammed back against the headrest almost immediately. Full-power takeoffs in Foxbats were punishing
to both man and machine. But Kolyachin's Foxbat, like the
others, had been specially prepared by the Mikoyan-Gure-

vich experts for their unique role. In seconds he was traveling at 190 miles an hour. He pulled the stick back and the sleek fighter leaped into the rainy afternoon. He did not check behind him. He knew the others would be there.

He pulled up, barely clearing the trees, and switched on his complex radars. Terrain-following control was not an American exclusive. He had already calculated that it would take Felix flight a little over three minutes at full power to cross the fifty-two miles between the airfield and their quarry. The entire operation could not consume more than seven minutes at the outside. After that their presence over West Germany would be known, and the jamming of the massed radio troops along the border would be considered dangerous by the NATO allies. The risk of retaliation then was too great. But all they needed was a few precious moments.

The darkening countryside hurtled underneath the needlelike nose of his bobbing aircraft. Just over the border restricted zone, they broke the sound barrier. Not even Kolyachin had done that before while relying on his terrain radar. The aircraft was steady as the airspeed kept climbing. At eighty thousand feet, the newest Foxbats could fly at almost four times the speed of sound—more than thirty-five hundred miles an hour. This close to the ground, he held their speed to just over Mach 1. It would be sufficient for their surprise and would allow just enough time to slow down and trap the A-10.

His predetermined braking-point alarm went off. Savagely, he jerked the throttles back and the MiG's swept wings shook with the load. He took control from the terrain-following computer. He already had the A-10 on his screens. He took the flight in a wide circle around the American and one by one they peeled off and formed a kind of cup to the west of him. He applied full power again, armed his missiles, and shot in on the American's tail. He still couldn't pick him up visually, but the infrared and radar signatures were unmistakable, despite the intense jamming. As he prepared for the closing, Kolyachin glanced at the time: 1504. Three minutes to herd the American the twelve miles back over the border.

McCulloch had been distracted by the jamming, so when he felt Kolyachin's radar and IR scanners right on his tail, he reacted sluggishly. For a few critical seconds he did nothing, watching the five blips form up behind him. Then he realized that something was amiss. The weather was still zero-zero. No NATO aircraft would engage in such dangerous flying. And the jamming . . .

He applied full power, and the turbofans began to wind up to maximum. But agonizingly slowly. The lead blip was only two miles from his tail. He quickly considered what was happening. It could only be a desperate attempt to capture either him or his aircraft. For a moment he marveled at the chance the Soviets were taking. This chase amounted to an act of war. And then the lead blip was right behind him. He jinked the A-10 around, trying to head south. But another blip—by now he recognized the telltale radar signature of a big MiG-25—was already there. He was being corralled. Only one way to go.

The plane behind him had slowed to his airspeed, now at around three hundred knots, and his engines—which had no afterburners—slowly began to accelerate. He consulted his computer. The only possibility this close to the border was to dive across, then break due north, heading for the parrot's beak of Wentland, West Germany, which stuck like a peninsula into East Germany. He checked the time, estimating how long it would be before the AWACS controllers realized what was happening in their big E-3A at forty-five thousand feet: 1505. By 1510, he figured, it would all be over.

One way or another.

He dove to the ground, keeping his power on. Behind him, the tailing blip did the same, still staying about a thousand meters back. McCulloch grinned. So they had terrain-following capability. Let's see how good it is, he thought.

The paratroopers of the 505th Airborne Infantry's First Battalion, who had been involved in the maneuvers, were digging in for the night. They hadn't expected any more aircraft because of the miserable conditions. So when the A-10 screamed through their bivouac, barely

115

clearing the stumpy trees, followed by a massive black airplane that shook the ground with its passage, they could only look at one another. A captain thought it was suspicious; they were, after all, across a small canal that marked the border with East Germany. He picked up the command phone and made a call.

McCulloch looked down. They were over the border. He was sweating now. Adrenaline pumped through his body. He had to break north in a few seconds. The A-10's engines screamed. He switched off the laser simulator used in scoring hits in practice. His only luck today had been that they insisted on his carrying real weapons in the exercise. He had four Sparrow air-to-air radar-homing missiles and 1,350 rounds of deadly 30-mm ammunition. He knew the value of the Jesus Box, and was not going to allow it to fall into Russian hands.

Behind him in the fog and rain, Ensign Kolyachin smiled. So far their plan had worked. They'd expected the American to run for the ground. Fine. They were as comfortable flying ten meters off the deck as he was. And now they were over home territory.

McCulloch saw the steeple of a church on his forward-looking radar. Perfect. At the last moment he split to the right of the steeple, then applied full dive brakes and stood the A-10 on its left wingtip in a hard left turn. He knew the MiG would try to follow, and he also knew it couldn't. Nothing except a Harrier or helicopter could turn with a Warthog. Especially a Wonder Warthog. He caught a glimpse of the bell tower as he began his maneuver. The airplane hammered and shook, the stick jumping in his hands. He was buffeted around the cockpit, but he held on, hoping the g-suit would keep him alive through the seven-g maneuver.

Kolyachin was taken by surprise, but recovered almost instantly. The American was trying to make a break north. He hauled the big Russian fighter around, but McCulloch had gained two thousand meters on him in the seconds Kolyachin had delayed his turn. He cursed and flipped on the radio.

"Samarov, he's turned north. Do you have him?"

Samarov's reply was instantaneous.

"Yes. Shall I fire on him?"

Kolyachin did not hesitate.

"If he tries to go through, yes." He jammed the MiG's throttles forward, kicked in afterburning, and closed the gap to the now-northbound A-10.

McCulloch found a small road cut through the dark forest below. The computer told him the distance between the edges of the wood was sixty feet. Just enough. He dove down to less than twenty feet off the deck. Radar had shown no cars or traffic on the road. He throttled back to 280 knots and flew along the road, wingtips brushing the trees.

Samarov's MiG overflew him on an interception course, as McCulloch had guessed it would. Confused, Samarov watched the American's radar blip pass *under* his and jerked the black fighter around in a wide turn. He was desperate. If he let the American escape, his career was finished. Before he'd completed his turn, he fired an AA-13 air-to-air missile at the American. It left the underside of his MiG in a burst of flame.

The Jesus Box told McCulloch immediately. It would take the Soviet missile 2.5 seconds to close with and destroy the A-10. One hundred milliseconds after it left the MiG, McCulloch responded with a Sparrow missile. He also deployed drones from his underwing stores as a countermeasure to confuse the enemy's radar. On the screens of the pursuing MiGs, it suddenly looked as though there were ten identical A-10s, each flying in a different direction. One second after he saw that, Samarov's AA-13 was intercepted by McCulloch's Sparrow. There was a ball of flame as the missiles collided. Samarov gritted his teeth and kicked in his afterburners. He *knew* McCulloch would be down there—and then Samarov knew no more, for the second Sparrow that McCulloch had launched two hundred milliseconds after the first flew right into the Russian's gaping jet intakes and exploded.

Kolyachin saw it happen. He felt fear. They had been

told this American aircraft was only a ground-attack fighter. How could it hold off five MiG-25s? He knew now their only hope was to down the American. In three minutes he would be back over West Germany.

Kolyachin kept his MiG at full power, then dove from his three-thousand-meter height back into the rain. He was now flying directly at McCulloch. The American could not avoid a missile launched from straight ahead. The A-10's blip steadied as the advanced Soviet radars found the real airplane and disregarded the decoys. Kolyachin, now also flying along the road, launched an AA-13. And pulled up.

McCulloch's Sparrow was fired almost simultaneously. The fireball of the converging missiles lit up the area for miles. Kolyachin rocketed right over the A-10.

McCulloch knew that his single remaining Sparrow wouldn't help him much. There were still four Foxbats. He regretfully abandoned his northward flight and pulled up above the trees again, now heading northeast.

Kolyachin watched him on his scanner while he was turning back, inverted in a full-power loop. He grinned. His loop would bring him back in front of the American for another head-on attack. This time he would wait until the last possible second. And fire *two* AA-13s.

McCulloch watched Kolyachin's maneuver, his mind racing. He knew what the Russian was trying to do. But the Soviets had no idea of the usefulness of the A-10's 30-mm Gatling gun. The other Russians were standing off, also watching. McCulloch smiled. No initiative, those boys. Good pilots, but followers. And then Kolyachin was back at his level.

The two aircraft hurtled toward each other with a combined closure speed of over nine hundred miles an hour. Their lives were measured in fractions of seconds. Kolyachin was the best pilot Koshka could find, flying the most advanced interceptor the Soviet Union could build.

But he didn't have the Jesus Box.

McCulloch did. And in the milliseconds that counted as they shot toward each other in the fog over the East

German pines, he used it. He linked his combat experience with the Box's sensors and computer—and launched his last Sparrow just as Kolyachin pushed the button on his missile launcher. Before he could push it a second time to fire another one, McCulloch had also triggered a hundred slugs of deadly 30-mm depleted uranium at the Foxbat.

Kolyachin didn't even have time to be surprised. His missile was destroyed one hundred meters from its launch bay, and the 30-mm fire immediately smashed his titanium aircraft to shrapnel. All that was left after his MiG exploded were minute bits of foillike metal expanding in a boiling cloud of destruction.

McCulloch flew right through it. Some of the tiny metal bits *ping*ed off his windscreen.

The men in the three remaining MiGs knew their lives depended on getting McCulloch. As one, they abandoned their dispersed positions and swung their radar sights on him. They flew in a wide V formation, just far enough apart so that if one exploded, it wouldn't damage the others.

McCulloch saw them behind him and knew he had run out of options. They could fire too many missiles, and he had no missile defenses left. In low-level, one-on-one dogfights he stood a decent chance. But this way . . .

He searched the ground. Broken forest, some farmland, a few roads. If he could get the Warthog down, he could destroy it on the ground with the built-in destruct mechanism. And the Recovery people might even be able to get him out. The MiGs closed in behind him, and he made his decision.

He applied full dive brakes, throttled back, and aimed for an elongated meadow just across a small creek. He fell more than flew over the tall trees and pulled back on the stick slightly, trying to get the nose up for a belly landing. Just before he hit, he shut off all the power with a mental command through the Jesus Box. At the last second, he finally saw the ground. He was still doing almost one hundred miles an hour.

The MiGs screamed over just as he hit. He'd misjudged the size of the stream, and his tail assembly just touched the bank. It jerked the A-10 down immediately. The tail section, although tough, wasn't built to take such landings, and everything aft of the main wing spar broke off. The automatic sealers went to work, but too late. The aft fuselage exploded in a huge sheet of white flame. The forward section bounced once, then flipped sideways. Both wings ripped off, spewing fuel on the stubble-covered field. The cockpit section spun, then bounded forward another hundred feet and stopped, leaving a long furrow in the rain-soaked earth.

McCulloch, protected by a titanium bathtub of armor, had survived all but the last flip, when the canopy had been torn off and he had struck the earth with his head before the fore section had rolled upright. After a few seconds he regained consciousness, but could not move. His head lay against the side of the cockpit coaming on jagged Plexiglas, the remains of the canopy. The double twenty-four-volt batteries had not torn loose, he realized through a red haze of pain, because he still felt the pulsing of the Jesus Box. Just before he slipped again into unconsciousness, he ordered it to broadcast a continuous Mayday signal on the guard frequency of 243.0 kHz. Then his eyes closed.

The MiG pilots were confused. Their look-down radars had shown the A-10 losing altitude—and then they'd lost the blip just as they were preparing to launch their missiles. They turned back just in time to see a strong infrared signal on the ground. They passed over the area, flying with flaps and gear down to make a slow radar search, but no aircraft-sized blip appeared on their screens. After another flyover the acting leader called off the futile search.

If the A-10 were still in one piece, Koshka would have to find it himself.

On the ground.

12

SEVEN MILES ABOVE THE EAST GERMAN MUD, AN
American Air Force master sergeant frowned at his radar
screen. As one of the ten radar monitors on board the Airborne Warning and Control Boeing 747, he had the specific responsibility for keeping track of activities over the
border area where McCulloch had crossed and then
crashed.

He watched the confusing blips for a moment, first
losing and then finding them again against the background.

"Major? Could you check this, sir?"

The watch commander came down the aisle between
the banks of screens.

"What, Sergeant?"

"Looks kind of like an engagement right here, sir."

The major studied the screen intently. The blips had
disappeared again.

"Did you have your tape on?"

"Yes, sir."

"Then back it up and we'll watch it on the monitor."

The radar technician rewound a high-quality video
tape that constantly recorded the images on his main
screen. Then he played it back on a small TV monitor
built into his console. The images appeared along with a
small time check in the upper left corner.

Together they watched the puzzling encounter. The observable action had started at 1504 and lasted four minutes.

"What do you think, Major?"

The major plugged his interphone jack into the technician's console.

"Station Nine to commander."

"Go, Nine. This is Number Two."

The major hesitated.

"Sorry, General, but isn't General Phillips available?" He was talking to the second in command, a Marine brigadier general. The AWACS plane carried flag-grade officers from all services.

"Negative. Indisposed at this moment. What's the problem?"

"Well, sir, here at Nine we have on tape what looks like an incident. Over the border at map reference AG-seven."

"Put it on the monitor here, Major."

The master sergeant pushed the buttons to transfer the recorded radar image to the command center on the big airplane. After a moment the general came back on the air.

"I see what you mean, Major. Comments?"

"Could have been a screw-up from the Tom-and-Jerry pilots, sir. They were in that area."

"I see. You don't suspect Soviet activity?"

The major hesitated again.

"No, sir. But I think we should check—"

"With the NATO commander. Affirmative. I'll do it."

"Yes, sir. Station Nine out."

The general dialed the ground commander at Wolfsburg.

"Jake? Bob here, upstairs. Listen, have you had any unusual air activity in the last fifteen minutes?"

The general commanding the maneuvers shook his head.

"Negative, Bob. But I'll check with Air. Hold one." He covered the field phone and called to a nearby Air Force colonel.

"Frank, any odd things going on upstairs in the last quarter hour?"

"No, sir."

The ground commander took his hand off the phone. "As before, Bob. Nothing."

"Thanks, Jake. Out."

Just then General Phillips, the Air Force commander in the AWACS aircraft, came back from the head.

"Anything happening, Bob?"

The Marine nodded to a television terminal. "Just something a little odd over AG-seven. Have a look." He played the tape back.

General Phillips studied the confusing traces carefully. It was easier for him to piece together the events than for the Marine; he had been a combat fighter pilot for twenty years. Suddenly he turned pale. He grabbed a phone and squeezed the transmit button.

"Get me Tom-and-Jerry liaison, pronto."

The Marine general frowned. "But, Phil, I already checked with the ground commander—"

"They don't know anything about the A-10Fs we've got in there," Phillips said, covering the mouthpiece. "I just hope—"

He broke off and spoke into the mouthpiece again.

"Yes, this is General Phillips, AWACS. Colonel, do you have a missing A-10?"

The colonel at Edemissen looked at his deputy.

"Not that I know of, General."

"What about the F models?"

The colonel looked out the tent flap at the fog.

"They're the only ones still up in this soup. I'm told they're on their way back right now. Would—"

"Put me through to the flight leader, Colonel." Phillips was sweating.

There was a long pause while the radiotelephone was patched into the command net. Then a crackling hiss came from the general's earpiece.

"This is Mother Goose. Warthog One, do you read?"

The static continued. The general tried again.

"Warthog One from Mother Goose, do you read—"

123

"Mother Goose, this is Warthog Three. Sir, we have lost contact with Warthog One. We assumed he was already down at the FOL."

"Negative, Warthog Three. When did you have last contact with Warthog One?"

"Ah, Mother Goose, that would be around fifteen hundred."

The general looked at the radar monitor. It was stopped at the beginning of the tape, flashing the time of first radar reading of the incident: 1504.

"Roger, Warthog Three, take your flight in. Mother Goose out."

General Phillips swiveled to face the surprised Marine general.

"Bob, somehow we've lost a very important airplane. I think the Soviets have forced him down in the East zone. Get on to the radio-intercept boys downstairs and see if they've got anything to help us. And get a flash precedence message out to Third Air Force, SHAPE, EuCom, and the Pentagon." He swiveled back to the console before the Marine could reply.

Phillips sat frozen for a few seconds, not seeing the flashing lights on the board in front of him. The big airplane banked gently as the pilot made his orbit turn high above the earth. Through a window in his tiny airborne command center, he could see the sun blazing above the cloud and fog.

Phillips picked up the red phone and spoke to the operator.

"This is command. Get me Colonel Jack Martin at the Potsdam mission. Priority one."

He was connected at 1522.

Three minutes before, Colonel Yuri Koshka had ordered Karl Stachel's ground units into the search area.

13

YURI KOSHKA PLACED THE TELEPHONE RECEIV-
er carefully in its cradle. He ignored the three officers
standing uncomfortably in front of his desk. He stood up
and walked to the window overlooking the airfield at
Finow.

So. Stachel's men were in their cars and on their way
to the crash area. The Vopos were alerted, and military
and paramilitary search teams were being readied. For
now he could do no more.

He stared at the darkening fog and silently cursed.
Damn Kolyachin. He had been the best. Still, it had not
been expected that the American would fight so well. It
simply made the capture of his aircraft and the pilot himself all the more important.

One of the officers cleared his throat noisily.

Koshka turned his cold stare at the man. A lieutenant
colonel in Technical Intelligence. Like himself, a party
member. But younger. Much younger. One who had ambitions, thought Koshka.

The lieutenant colonel waved at the map.

"If the comrade colonel wishes, we can prepare a helicopter search effort using—"

"The comrade colonel does *not* wish it, Khreshkov.
Until the fog is driven away by the northeast winds—which
Captain Ulyanov here assures me will take place within

125

three hours—we cannot risk helicopters. Or any other aircraft."

The lieutenant colonel nodded and remained silent.

Koshka considered him for a moment.

"However, Comrade Khreshkov, there is something your people can do. Have the radio troops stop dismantling their installations along the border. Have them turn their antennas back into East Germany. Have them monitor all transmissions on all frequencies. We must augment the normal electronic intelligence of the Germans with every possible effort."

The other man clicked his heels together.

"As the comrade colonel wishes. What kind of transfer network would the colonel like?"

Koshka sat down again. He pointed to his telephone.

"You will arrange it so that all relevant messages come directly to me. I want minimal delay in transmission of potentially useful intelligence. Understood?"

Khreshkov nodded. His expression betrayed nothing. What Koshka wanted would require huge expenditures of manpower and energy. But it was said in the GRU that Koshka got what Koshka wanted.

Further conversation was cut short by a single ring of the red telephone on Koshka's desk. It was the direct line to the Kremlin. Before he answered it, he waved the others out.

When they had closed the doors, he picked up the receiver and said, "Koshka."

There was a pause. The line was filled with static and eerie whistlings. It was a direct laser link, untappable.

A voice said, "Koshka, this is Boris. In a moment Comrade Tchaitov will come on the line. I just wanted to tell you that he is very upset."

Koshka smiled grimly. The Kremlin had known almost as quickly as he had. Perhaps more quickly.

"Yes, Boris. Thank you. I will not forget."

There was a repeated clicking, then another voice spoke. It was Tchaitov.

Without preamble he said, "Well, Comrade, I expect

you have an explanation?" It was more a statement than a question.

"Yes, Comrade Director. The American aircraft was more capable than we expected." He spoke without inflection, but his palms were clammy.

"Correction, Koshka. More capable than *you* had expected. There were, you'll recall, those here in the GRU who did not agree with your plan. Who said—correctly, as it turns out—that the risks were great and the chance of success small. No doubt you have some comments on that?" Tchaitov's voice was icy.

Koshka spoke without hesitation.

"Yes, Comrade Tchaitov. First, we had no alternative. The Central Committee itself demanded that we capture this aircraft, and this was our best chance. We will have others. Second, it is not over. My pilots simply reported that their ground-search radars did not find any objects the size of this aircraft. All that means is that it has broken up. Quite possibly, the pilot is dead. But there is still a strong likelihood of success in the primary goal."

There was silence on the line for a moment. Then another voice spoke. It was, Koshka realized, a GRU staff conference call. He must be wary.

"Comrade, this is General Bortsoi. What measures have you taken to ensure this strong probability of success?"

Koshka quickly outlined his arrangements for ground search. But his mind was racing past this conversation. It was clear that he had more enemies in the GRU than he'd realized. This conference was unprecedented. Even when he had captured the PanAvia Tornado fighter from the West Germans in 1980, his only contact with the directorate had been a congratulatory message and a bottle of vodka.

It was certain that he would have to do much better than that before Director Tchaitov sent him any more vodka.

Tchaitov came on the line after Koshka had finished explaining his strategy.

127

"Yuri Andreyevich, we know you are under great strain. So are we all. But this operation has the highest political consequences. There is evidence that the United States will not react the same way to this operation as it has in previous times. Even now, they have placed many groups on standby alert. This alone makes it imperative that you succeed. The situation is very tense. The Premier himself is involved now. Do you understand?"

The line howled with static. Of course he understood. He was to be sacrificed in case anything backfired. But he had always known the stakes. The game was still worth it.

"Do not worry, Comrade Director. In twenty-four hours I will have the aircraft—or what remains of it—in transit to Plesetsk for your technicians. Good-bye." He hung up. His abrupt ending of the call would infuriate Tchaitov, but there was nothing he could do. With the rest of the directorate on the conference line, he would not dare recriminations against one who—so far—had not failed.

Koshka looked down at his hands. Palms down on the desk, they were trembling. For the first time.

14

THE RADIO SNAPPED ON JUST AFTER THEY'D passed through Osterburg going south. Max leaned over and adjusted the gain as the mission's identifying code came through on frequency A-A-9.

"Brer Wolf, this is Peter Rabbit. Stand by for a double play."

Wilson said nothing, but slowed the car. His eyebrows arched slightly. Max knew that in today's signal code, "double play" meant a first-priority message. The radio operator didn't wait for them to answer.

Max scribbled furiously as the message came over the speaker in the dashboard.

"Brer Wolf, we have a cancan dancer at Uncle Joe's farm. Repeat, we have a cancan dancer at Uncle Joe's farm. You're the RLH. Repeat, you're the RLH. Out."

Max checked the code. After a few moments he read back the message.

"There's an aircraft down somewhere in section zero-oh. Exact location unknown. We're supposed to make the recovery." He looked out the windshield. They were on the main road from Osterburg to Genthin, normally a fast two-lane highway full of military traffic from the Soviet base at Stendal. This afternoon, though, the fog had slowed everything to a crawl. The map reference quoted in the signal was north of Osterburg. Max looked at Wilson, who was checking the fuel levels and engine condition.

"We'll have to turn around and get north. All we can hope for in this soup is that the guy's beacon is working. Otherwise, we won't even be able to see a road marker." He peeled off his dark glasses and glanced in the mirrors. Not too far behind them, the misty glow of a truck's headlights shone in the fog. There was no northbound traffic.

"Okay, Max. Looks like you'll get to find out about more than just the countryside today."

Moss nodded, silent. Well, he was just along for the ride. Wilson would handle the whole thing.

Without warning, Wilson jerked the wheel to the left and downshifted a gear. He floored the accelerator and the Ford did a perfect 180-degree turn into the other lane. Tires spinning, the car stopped for only a fraction of a second, then fishtailed back toward Osterburg. Max had expected this maneuver, so he was braced and holding on. Wilson strained to see through the mist as they rocketed past the creeping traffic going the other way. Visibility was down to less than a hundred feet.

Without a word, Max turned on the bank of fog lights set in the grille. Wilson nodded and kept staring intently into the gloom, peering just ahead of the irregular zone of illuminated fog and highway.

They went through Osterburg without much slackening of speed. The town was shut down anyway. Only one old man had to jump clear of the speeding Ford. Wilson smiled as they saw him leap for his life. Max swallowed.

On the other side of Osterburg, Max switched on the radio direction finder and set it to the guard frequency. He turned up the gain, but all they heard was an occasional burst of static and background hissing. On the north side of Osterburg, the road was completely deserted. Wilson slowed to twenty as they strained to find signs of the aircraft they were seeking.

Thirteen kilometers north, Max thought he heard a faint beep from the radio. He held a hand up to Wilson, staring intently at the speaker.

"Hold it, Ike. I think I've got something."

Wilson switched off the fog lights and shut off the engine. He coasted to a stop on the side of the road. A blanket of silence enveloped them. The engine tinkled softly as it cooled.

The beep came again, faintly, through the static. Max slowly swiveled the loop antenna on the roof. When it was standing perpendicular to their line of travel, the beep suddenly became stronger. Max switched on the electronic link between the inertial navigation system, the car's small computer, and the direction-finding apparatus. In a second a glowing line was traced due east from their position on the main road. The computer estimated that the signal strength indicated a distance from the transmitter of less than five miles. Max looked up, surprised.

"Is that possible? How could a guy have gone down so close to a town and not have been captured right away?"

Wilson looked out the window.

"In this stuff anything's possible. Besides, this area isn't all that heavily populated. Out there"—he pointed to the right—"out there is a big chunk of real estate with almost nothing on it. A few miserable villages, dirt roads. That's it. So our boy could've lucked out."

Wilson studied the map for a moment. He switched on the engine and, while the loping idle of the big V-8 evened out, said to Max, "Keep the computer link going. I think we're going to have a hell of a time getting to him. I know the roads out there pretty well, but when you can't see your damn hand in front of your face—well, you get the idea."

After a few moments Wilson spotted a tiny gravel road leading to their right. He turned off and the line on the electronic map almost paralleled the road. He grunted and idled down the ten-foot-wide track. He rolled down the window on his side and Max did the same on his. The gravel crunched under the fat tires. According to the map, they were within five hundred yards of the signal source.

Wilson shut off the engine again. The only sound in the still fog was the tiny beep coming from the radio. He got out and motioned to Max to do the same. They stared into the mist, straining eyes and ears. Nothing.

Wilson waved Max back in. They went up the road another hundred yards and repeated the process. Again, nothing. Neither man spoke.

The third time, Max went a little farther from the car. He walked into the fog and something caught his toe. He bent down and picked it up. A dense, fused piece of metal. He called to Ike.

Wilson nodded when he'd hefted the metal.

"Yeah, it's from an airplane, all right. Must have blown. Let's go up another hundred." They got back in the car and inched forward. Max noticed another, larger piece of metal in the ditch next to the road.

His throat dry as they got out, Max stared at the metal fixed in the glare of the headlights. And so he missed the trench that tripped him. He fell headlong into the ditch, which was actually, it turned out, a small creek. He staggered to his feet and stared at the rupture in the earth. It was like a furrow. Something big had suffered an enormous impact here.

All at once Max saw that the gouge extended across the lip of the ditch and into a fog-shrouded field. He clambered back up to the road, where Wilson was turning over the large, flat piece of aluminum.

Wilson looked up as he approached.

"What happened to you? Little early for mud—"

"Never mind the cracks," Max said. "Over there is a very big, very deep gash in Mother Earth. Seems like we ought to find out where it goes."

Wilson's eyes narrowed. He dropped the aluminum. "Show me."

Wilson stood on the far side of the ditch, looking at the irregular trench. He said nothing, then bounded back to the car.

"Come on, Max. I think there's an access road to that field back there." They jumped into the car and Wilson slowly backed up. A hundred feet away, he found the road. The shiny black mud showed no tracks.

Wilson eased the big Ford along the road, peering out into the field, which was now on their left. After he had gone a hundred yards, he stopped and listened. Nothing. He shrugged and looked at Max.

"Feel like a little off-road excursion?"

Before Max could answer, he had the Ford jouncing over the stubbled furrows. The lights bounced crazily up and down, making weird patterns in the still-heavy fog. It was getting darker. In an hour, thought Max, it'll be pitch-black.

Then they saw it. The blackened, blasted skeleton of an A-10 tail assembly, wrenched and twisted from its impact with the ground. Their headlights pierced the gloom, bringing out the stark details. Wilson didn't get out. He studied the wreckage for a moment, then looked to Max's right. Another, smaller furrow led off into the murk. He swung the car around and they started alongside it.

They passed a broken-off wing, but Wilson gave it no attention. The pattern was clear to him now; from his long experience, he was able to reconstruct the crash.

"If anyone's alive, he'll be at the end of this trench," he said.

Max switched off the radio direction finder. The beeps were stronger now, annoying him. He knew they were close.

And then it was pinned in their headlights. The fore section of an A-10 lay nose-up and leaning to the right, still sitting in the hole it had dug as it had hurtled across the East German earth. From behind it, they could see that the canopy was gone.

Wilson eased the car out alongside the shattered fuselage and turned so the lights were bearing full on it. He left the engine running and climbed out. Max followed.

Wilson saw the pilot first. He sat upright in the cockpit, his head leaning against the fragments of canopy left

133

wedged in the sealing edge. He was too far up to reach. Wilson called to him, but he didn't respond.

Ike went back around to the lit-up side of the nose. He found the emergency-hatch trigger for the boarding ladder, which was built into the side of the airplane. He pulled the flap away and activated the ladder. Moss held his breath as the ladder slowly emerged. Wilson called back to Max.

"Get the med kit. We may be able to do something. Looks like he hit the dirt with his head." As Max went back to the trunk of the car Wilson climbed up the ladder.

When he was halfway up, the fuselage groaned and shifted slightly. Wilson froze. It was balanced precariously on a mound of earth. After a moment the groaning stopped and he continued slowly up the ladder.

He reached the top and peered inside. The main power was off, but a light on a small panel on the right side of the dash glowed feebly. The pilot's helmet—a grotesque affair like no Air Force helmet Wilson had ever seen—was plugged into the glowing panel. Wilson reached carefully across the cockpit and felt the pilot's bloody face. It was still warm. Balancing himself, Wilson felt for the jugular vein. It pulsed erratically. The man was still alive. But the odd angle of the silver helmet and head alarmed him. If his neck wasn't broken, it was close to it.

Max arrived at the foot of the tilted ladder with the med kit.

"*Ike.* Is he alive?"

Wilson looked down. "Yeah. Barely. Looks like his neck is broken, though. Give me the kit."

Max balanced the awkwardly shaped plastic med kit in his right hand and stretched full length. Wilson gingerly leaned backward and stretched for it. He swore. Too far.

"Stay there, Max. I'll come down."

He carefully moved one leg down a rung, then the other. Wrapping his right arm around a rung, he leaned back down again.

"Okay, Max, give it to—"

There was a sudden metallic crack and one ladder stanchion pulled away from the fuselage. The ladder

134

swung out wildly, and Wilson looked up just in time to see the other stanchion break off. He flung his arms up to grasp the cockpit coaming, but the momentum hurled him away from the fuselage and slammed him into the earth. He had time for a half-choked cry as he fell. And then he lay still.

Max stood rooted to the spot. He stared down at the twisted body of Ike Wilson, garishly lit by the seven high-power fog lights from the idling Ford. He was unable to take his eyes off him. The older man lay facedown, one arm outflung but rotated in a way that meant it had to be broken in at least one place. The other arm lay twisted on his back. Palm down. And from a deep gash blood pumped from his forehead. He didn't move.

Max didn't know how long he stood frozen. The only sounds were the quiet, distant rumble of the Ford and his hoarse breathing. Slowly, painfully, his mind began to move again. The cold pierced his clothes. He began to shiver. As the blood continued to ooze from Wilson's head wound an absurd thought repeated itself over and over in Max's stunned mind.

This wasn't a fantasy. He wasn't a spectator. It was real. It was happening. To him.

Then Wilson groaned. A convulsive shudder shook Moss.

It was real. *Real.*

Wilson moaned again.

And Max Moss willed his shaking hand to reach down to him.

15

STACHEL CURSED. FIRST IN GERMAN, THEN IN
Russian, finally in English. He cursed the Americans, the
Russians, the West Germans, and the Mercedes in which
he was creeping slowly northward through the fog. He
cursed volubly, expertly, and loudly. But the fog didn't
lift. And the Mercedes still crept forward at less than thirty
kilometers an hour.

The driver ignored him. He was already traveling as
fast as safety permitted. Indeed, since a twilight condition
was the most dangerous, he was already going too fast.

It maddened Stachel that the road from his headquarters in Magdeburg to Osterburg was uncrowded but
fogged in. His five ground-search cars were scattered all
over the map, unable to converge on the target area quickly because of the damnable fog. And that fool Müller had
let one of the Potsdamers slip through his grasp less than
two hours ago. He was surrounded by idiots.

He picked up the radiotelephone in the back of the
powerful black Mercedes 450 SEL and called his directorate headquarters in Berlin. "When will the fog lift?" he
asked. The answer was the same as it had been for the last
hour. "By six o'clock, *Herr Direktor*."

At least the Americans had to deal with the same fog.
He had to assume that the Potsdam car had been in the

crash area and was even now trying to find the airplane. The thought gave him little comfort.

Then he smiled. But if I'm uncomfortable, he thought, how must Comrade Koshka be feeling right now? Stachel well knew the enemies Koshka had in Moscow. He'd worked hard enough to get to know them. If Koshka came up empty-handed on this one—especially after ruffling the Yankee feathers so badly—there was little question that the whole system would be revamped. A new organization put in place of the one Koshka commanded. And there was also little question as to who would run the new organization.

He, Karl Stachel, would turn it into a German operation. The GRU would be happy to oblige, since its own people had failed so consistently. And once it was an all-German system . . .

From long practice, Stachel stopped short. He knew the pitfalls of grandiose dreaming. But this particular fiasco was his biggest break in years. If they lost the American, Koshka would be discredited and recalled to Moscow. If they found him, the chances were excellent that Koshka's fighters would have bungled and ruined the precious equipment the Russians were after. Whatever it was. Whenever there was a bad-weather force-down, the aircraft was usually written off, along with the pilot. And Koshka could survive that situation no better than an outright failure. So his only chance was to capture both the hardware and pilot intact.

Looking out at the murk, Stachel stroked his goatee and grinned as he thought of how slim Koshka's chances were. Then the grin faded, and he realized again the desperate need for *his* people to get to the plane before anyone else. Müller and the rest had been handpicked for this mission. They knew that Stachel wanted neither plane nor pilot to be in any condition that could benefit Koshka. So if they arrived first, they were to arrange things. Just enough to allay suspicions.

But they had to get there before Koshka.

He began cursing again. And still the fog didn't lift.

16

MAX HAD FINALLY STOPPED THE BLEEDING AND
had the inflatable splints in place when Wilson regained
consciousness. There was a dark bruise over his left eye.
The swelling kept the eye shut.

The right eye opened slowly as Max nervously read
the instructions for the anesthetic hypodermic. Max didn't
see Wilson looking up at him.

When he spoke, Max jumped.

"Max ... what's happening?" Wilson's voice was
weak.

Moss sat back on his haunches.

"Jesus, Ike. I thought you were dead. No—don't
move. You broke both arms, bad. I'm just going to give
you a painkiller."

Wilson shook his head groggily.

"No. Listen, you've got to get that guy up there in
shape to travel. The Vopos will be here soon." Wilson began struggling to get up.

Max held him down.

"No way, pal. Don't move." He injected the clear fluid
into Wilson's lower back and rolled him over gently. Wilson's arms were held immobile, crossed over each other
on his chest.

He closed his good eye. "Okay, Max. But get that guy out. We have to get out of here, and fast."

Max looked up at the A-10. He'd forgotten about the pilot while he was trying to patch up Wilson.

With the boarding ladder ripped out of the fuselage, the only way up was with the collapsible ladder they had in the trunk of the car. Max eyed the distance to the canopy and estimated that their ladder would bring him only to the edge. He'd have to scramble up over the coaming to get to the pilot. Thinking about the unsteady fuselage did not make him relish the prospect.

He shook himself out of immobility. There was nothing for it. This time it was up to him.

Max bent and gently picked up Wilson's limp body. He knew Wilson couldn't walk, so he'd brought the car closer. He half carried, half dragged the semiconscious man to the rear door, which stood open. He carefully rested Ike against the doorsill and slipped inside, then he pulled him into the car and laid him on the seat. He propped up Ike's head with a rucksack, covered him with a blanket, and strapped him in. Ike was still drifting in and out of consciousness, mumbling.

Max got out and took a deep breath. He dragged the folding ladder out of the trunk and extended it to full length. It seemed hardly strong enough to hold itself up, let alone a man.

He laid it against the skin of the fuselage, planting the feet of the ladder carefully. It seemed steady. He began climbing. The ladder bowed under his weight but didn't give way. Gaining confidence, he inched his way to the top. On the final rung he was closer to the canopy than he'd calculated. He would be able to lift himself up and straddle the cockpit, reaching in to the pilot.

Despite the chill and the slight breeze that had sprung up, Max was sweating heavily. His mouth was dry. He couldn't swallow.

The pilot was sitting as Wilson had described him. His eyes were closed, his face covered in still-wet blood. His hands lay limply in his lap. Max noticed the weird helmet and its connector to the panel. He reached in and felt

139

for a pulse in the throat. It was there, barely. He hoisted himself carefully over the edge and sat down, legs astride the cockpit, facing the pilot.

Before Max could reach in again, the pilot's eyelids fluttered. He coughed and a trickle of blood ran out of his mouth. Slowly he opened his eyes. He saw Max and did not react for a second. Then he tried to speak.

Max couldn't hear him. The man's lips were moving, but even the soft rumble of the Ford's exhaust covered the words. He leaned forward. The fuselage suddenly shifted and the man's eyes closed as his head moved a fraction of an inch. His face tightened. Max knew then that he must have a broken neck or back. The realization sent a shiver down his spine.

The pilot opened his eyes again. This time they were slightly clearer, the lids higher. The pain of the movement had shocked him more awake.

His words were slurred and agonizingly slow, but distinguishable.

"Can't let . . . them . . . get . . . Jesus . . . Box. Take . . . helmet and"—there was a long pause while he struggled to speak through his pain—" . . . box. Set . . . destruct. Under . . . under . . . seat." His eyes closed again.

Max looked at the helmet. So it *was* special. He followed the coiled connection line to the panel, which was still lit by a feeble yellow bulb. It was a quick-insert black box. You didn't even need a screwdriver to get it out. If the four flanged Dzus fasteners at the corners were twisted, it would slide out.

But if he took the helmet, he'd have to move the pilot's head. And the man clearly needed expert medical aid.

The seconds clicked by relentlessly. Max couldn't make up his mind. As usual, he thought bitterly. Come on, Moss. Show us how smart you are now. The helmet or the man? You get to decide, Maxwell Taylor Moss. You get to play God.

Max wiped the sweat off his face. To hell with the helmet. This guy was going to die if he didn't get some help. He leaned forward to feel the pilot's throat again. He shifted his position slightly to reach better, and the fuse-

140

lage groaned. And then groaned again. Max froze in mid-reach, and suddenly the whole nose section rolled to the left.

Max barely hung on. His butt slid across the open cockpit. He grabbed the coaming and gritted his teeth as the Plexiglas splinters dug into his flesh. The wreck wobbled back and forth for a moment, then slid backward into the furrow about three feet. It halted with a dull *thwack*.

Max let out his breath raggedly. He looked at the pilot again and gasped. The man's eyes were wide open, the mouth formed in a soundless scream of pain. The last movement of the aircraft had killed him.

Max managed to stop the vomit just behind his teeth. He'd seen death before, but always in the hot-blooded atmosphere of a racetrack. Not like this. Not some guy he didn't even know. Some American forced to crash in hostile country. He fought back the bitter bile and gulped in huge lungfuls of cold air.

He didn't even know the man's name.

Slowly, carefully, Max took his hands off the sides of the cockpit. The fuselage felt much steadier. Experimentally, he rocked back and forth, ready to grab the cockpit rails again. Nothing. It was as if the plane were anchored in bedrock.

He set to work. First he unplugged the helmet connector, then unsnapped the straps of the helmet itself. He closed the man's eyes before he took off the helmet, which was much lighter than it looked. Inside were dozens of fitted foil-covered foam pads.

He had to sit on the opposite side of the cockpit to get at the panel the man had called the Jesus Box. The strangeness of the name hit Max as he worked at the Dzus fasteners. The panel itself gave no clues. The only legend it bore was BCU. And that could mean anything. In seconds the box itself was out. He rested it next to the helmet on the floor of the cockpit. Then he punched the pilot's seat-harness release button and the parachute release.

He may not have been able to do much for the guy, but he was sure as hell going to take him home.

Miraculously, the ladder was still in place. It tilted

backward precariously, but Max edged down gingerly and reset it. He got a length of nylon line from the Ford's tool kit, checking on Wilson while he was at the car. Ike was still mumbling incoherently, eyes closed.

It took almost ten minutes to lever the pilot's body out of the cockpit and lower him to the ground. Max was covered in a greasy film of sweat before he was done. And when the body slipped onto the ground at the foot of the ladder, Max slumped back into the pilot's seat. He rested there for a moment, looking at the instruments. He had no idea what was secret on this aircraft. He looked for the pilot's log. It was gone. The man must still have it in his flight suit. There was nothing else in the cockpit; everything loose must have been thrown out when the plane crashed.

Getting the pilot into a body bag wasn't easy, but urgency gave Max strength. The big Ford trunk wasn't quite big enough for the dead pilot and the emergency equipment, too, so Max unhesitatingly threw out the toolbox, spare tire, and the M-16 rifles. They would do him little good tonight. And he had to find a way back to Potsdam tonight or not at all.

The thought stopped him in his tracks. He was, for all practical purposes, lost. The nav system could tell him how far from the mission he was, but it couldn't help him evade what he had to assume was a massive manhunt. Or keep him clear of PRZs. And according to his briefings, there was little hesitation on the Soviets' part to shoot first in those zones and ask questions later. If there was a later.

The Ford coughed once before it regained its smooth idle. He'd been here too long. He finished fitting the pilot's body into the deep trunk, threw in the helmet and Jesus Box, and slammed the lid. Now for the destruct switch on the airplane.

He found it easily enough under the seat. A simple timer; once it was turned on, it was armed, and only a hidden reset button would allow it to be turned off. He cranked it as far as it would go. Max had worked only on transport aircraft, but he suspected that this bomb had a short fuse—even on its maximum setting. He slid back down the ladder, kicked it away from the plane, and ran to the car. Jerking open the door, he fell into the deeply bucketed racing seat and checked the car's instruments. All okay; engine hot from idling so long, but nothing serious. He looked back over the seat to Wilson, who was still semiconscious. Max buckled his own harness and, as gently as he could, eased the blue Fairmont out of the depressions the tires had made. The fog seemed to be lifting; the little breeze was becoming stronger.

Good for them, bad for him.

He tried to collect his thoughts. First get to the road before the plane blows. Then find a route back. Don't think past that. *Don't.*

It took longer to jounce across the rutted field than he'd remembered. Then he gunned the car onto the slick dirt road and found their tire tracks. He followed them back to the small gravel road.

At the intersection he stopped and put the shifter in neutral. Behind him, Wilson was breathing hoarsely. Max poured some coffee into a cup and wet Ike's lips. He drank the rest, his hands shaking.

Now what? Left or right? He switched on the nav system's cathode-ray tube. The CRT warmed slowly and finally painted a picture of his location. The distance-to-base readout stood at ninety-five kilometers, and the map display showed they were a few klicks east of a tiny village called Dobbrun. He thought for a moment, then punched the keys that asked the computer to list the names of all the towns within a ten-mile radius. He read them anxiously as it printed them on the screen.

Königsmark. Rengerslage. Osterburg. Krevese. Düsedau. Seehausen. Falkenberg.

Falkenberg. The name resonated in his head the moment he saw it. It wasn't just another name. It meant something. Something about—something about another mansion, a big mansion . . .

Not a mansion, a castle. Schloss Falkenberg.

Suddenly memories came flooding back. The rides to the country from Berlin with his father in '63. The long, long rides. And at the end the fairy-tale castle where he

143

and the little German girl could play all day long and not disturb them.

Them. His father and . . . *her*. Gisela Koch.

Max smiled. He had a destination.

He checked the way to Falkenberg, dropped the gearshift into first gear, and drove up onto the gravel road, heading north.

It wasn't much of a chance. But it was better than none.

17

MÜLLER LOST THE HELP OF THE SOVIET RADIO troops and their powerful equipment just before the fog began to lift. They had been guiding him to the location of the American aircraft by triangulating the plane's Mayday signals. Although the signals were weak, the Soviets were able to get a reasonable fix.

But suddenly the signals stopped, and Müller had only a vague notion of where to go. He knew the plane was down somewhere between Seehausen on the north, Osterburg to the south, and Havelberg to the east, but that was all. There hadn't been enough for more accuracy; the signals had been too weak and erratic.

He cursed and slowed the white BMW, pulling off the road and stopping. Grabbing the map from his assistant, who said little and thought less, Müller glowered at the 125 square kilometers of his search triangle. His was still the closest car to the scene. The director was stuck in the fog at least twenty minutes away, and the others were widely dispersed. Say half an hour for them, with the fog.

He lit one of his precious Marlboros—a gift from the director—and pondered the problem. It was fairly open country. Fields, farms, some forest. Not much else. First thing, then, was to drive around every field that had a usable perimeter road. Legwork. He sighed heavily as the Marlboro smoke filled the car. The life of a policeman.

By the time he was rolling slowly along the road to Dobbrun, windows down and eyes red from staring into the gloom, the fog was beginning to disperse. The little two-liter engine of the old BMW didn't like crawling at such a slow pace, so he occasionally had to rev the engine. He had just done so on the gravel road when his assistant, who was looking east, said something that was covered by the whine of the motor. Irritably, Müller idled the engine and looked over. The man was pointing to the field on their right. Müller stared hard out the window. And then saw it.

A large, indistinct mass about a hundred meters into the field. It lay at the end of a deep trench, recently gouged out of the earth. It had to be the American plane. Quickly, Müller drove north along the ditch while the other man aimed a portable spotlight out into the field. At such a distance it only dimly illuminated the wreckage, but Müller was able to see a twisted tail assembly. He found the farmer's northern access road—there were no tracks on it—and drove down the edge of the field parallel to the wreck. Opposite it, he spun the plastic wheel of the BMW and drove over the furrows. The little car bounced and jerked heavily.

At the tail section, Müller stopped. Playing the bright spotlight over it, he saw that another piece had broken off and continued across the field during the crash. He followed the rent in the earth and saw the nose section. Jumping back into the car excitedly, he called the director.

Stachel had been wandering around the A-10 site for ten minutes before the fifth car finally slid to a halt in the field. There were now four white BMWs and one black Mercedes all standing around the battered A-10 nose section, lights aimed at it.

Stachel was in a murderous mood. He kicked the spare tire found near the plane, picked up an M-16, and shouted at the silent group of men who stood in a ragged semicircle around him.

"*Idiots.* They have already been here. The pilot is gone, something is missing from the aircraft, and all you can do is tell me about the damned fog. *Idiots.*" He hurled the M-16 at the ground and the men flinched.

Stachel whirled to face Müller.

"And *you.* If we had known that they were already gone, we could have saved valuable time. Why did you not tell me about this"—he waved his hand at the debris from Moss's car—"and the American tire tracks?" His face was turning red, the blotches a deep purple. His calf-length Prussian-style greatcoat swirled as he stalked back and forth.

Müller gulped.

"*Herr Direktor,* I came in from the other road." He pointed back across the field. Stachel silenced him.

"Never mind. Excuses are of no use now." He paused, breathing hard. His back hurt and he was hungry. He stared blankly at the A-10. He had to move fast. His plan could still work. Of course, the easiest thing to do was simply to bungle the capture of the American, but that would not shed much favorable light on him. No doubt it would discredit Koshka as well, but it had to seem—had to *be*—clear that his people had worked smoothly and efficiently. He again faced the men.

"So. We will fan out and allocate one major road to each car. Maintain a low radio presence; the Americans can listen to us as easily as we to them. Do not alert Soviet troops, and do not enlist the aid of civilian policemen. We do not need their help. Yet." He began pacing. "The Americans have at least an hour's lead on us. But we know they must go to Potsdam, and as the roads converge we will be waiting. Only Müller and I will canvas the local area; the rest of you take your roads and patrol them toward Potsdam. I will inform the Soviets." They still stood, waiting uneasily.

"Well? What are you waiting for, fools? *Go.*" They scrambled to their cars and one by one jounced across the stubble-covered field. Stachel turned to Müller.

"It seems our American friends did not successfully detonate their destruct charge. Or—does it, Müller? Perhaps it only has a long fuse, eh?" He turned and glared balefully at Müller.

"What? Oh ... yes, *Herr Direktor.*" He shuffled his feet. What was Stachel trying to tell him? The man was so damnably unpredictable.

There was an extended silence. Stachel maintained his icy glare. Müller became more and more uncomfortable.

Finally he blurted out, "*Herr Direktor*—is the *Herr Direktor* suggesting that we explo—"

"The *Herr Direktor* is suggesting nothing, Müller." Stachel almost snarled. "The *Herr Direktor* is telling a certain underling that if he expects to have any future in the German Democratic Republic's Volkspolizei, he'd better make certain the Americans *did* detonate their device. Does the underling understand *that?*"

Müller fell back. Stachel was like a madman when he was angry. He became a human tank, steamrolling over all opposition. He nodded vigorously.

"Yes, yes, *Herr Direktor*. The Americans blew up their plane successfully, using a long timer. It appears that it went off after we left." Sweat rolled down his face.

Stachel's anger was snuffed out as if by a switch.

"Excellent. Unfortunate, of course. But excellent." He began buttoning his greatcoat. "Now, you will see to it and we will begin our search. I will head south and you will go north. It will probably be the same automobile you let escape earlier today. I trust you will recognize it."

Müller flushed. He tried to answer but could only stammer.

Stachel waved a hand.

"Do not worry, Müller. If you can capture these Americans, no one will ever know that you are the one responsible for allowing them to recover their equipment and pilot. Now, get to work." Stachel yanked open the rear door of his Mercedes and worked his bulk inside. His driver stared straight ahead. A good man, thought Stachel. Sees nothing, hears nothing, knows nothing. Stachel tapped his shoulder.

"Let's go, Hans. South, toward Osterburg."

As the car jiggled over the bumpy field Stachel picked up the radiotelephone but didn't switch it on. What to tell Koshka?

There was no doubt that Müller would see to the total destruction of the plane. The little man was petrified of failure. And Koshka need never know the details. But even in the ashes it would be clear that no human had been aboard. And the Russians were far too clever in rebuilding wrecked NATO aircraft; they could even notice the missing piece of cockpit hardware. At least, he had to assume that they would notice. No, Koshka would have to be told something like the truth. He punched the buttons that gave him direct access to Colonel Yuri Andreyevich Koshka.

Koshka picked up his phone before it had stopped ringing.

"Yes?" His brown eyes were circled by tight lines, his mouth drawn into a livid slash.

"Comrade Colonel, it is Comrade Stachel. I have news."

Koshka smiled thinly. Stachel always called himself "comrade" when the news was bad.

"And so, *Herr Direktor*?"

Stachel cleared his throat. Koshka winced. He hated people who made guttural noises into a telephone.

"Bad news, I'm afraid, Comrade Colonel. The Americans—"

"—have already been to the crash site. Yes, *Herr Direktor*, when so much time elapsed before your call, I suspected as much. What are you doing?"

Stachel did not hesitate. In his most efficient voice he said, "Naturally, we have a maximum effort under way. All civilian policemen, all DDR paramilitary personnel, and, of course, all my own people are on the road already. We will certainly apprehend the Americans before they get near Potsdam."

149

Koshka's smile faded. His face was grim.

"Let us make one thing clear, *Herr Direktor*. There is no possibility of failure. None. I know the niceties of the agreement made by the Stalinists years ago, and it must, for appearances' sake, always seem that those agreements are scrupulously adhered to. But those Americans will *not* return to Potsdam. Do I make myself clear?"

Stachel was astounded. Koshka was telling him to kill the Americans if necessary. He was even more desperate than Stachel imagined. A slow, sly smile spread across Stachel's face.

"Of course, Comrade Colonel. I will ensure it."

Koshka's reply was a jab to the gut.

"No, Stachel, *I* will see to it. In twenty minutes I will be leaving to take command of the operation. I will do so from the air. The wind is reported to be clearing away the fog, as predicted, and this operation is too important to us all to have anything less than maximum effort. *To us all,* Stachel. Do you understand?"

Karl Stachel chewed his lip. He understood, all right. Koshka had somehow found out. He did not trust him. Somehow Stachel had walked too clumsily along the razor's edge. He would have to move fast—but carefully.

"Yes, Comrade Koshka. I understand. Where will you actually be?"

Koshka consulted a large map on his desk.

"You are now heading south on Route one-eighty-nine. I will rendezvous with you at the airfield at Stendal. Where my MiGs are stationed. If I am not there when you arrive, you will wait, Stachel."

How had Koshka known where he was? Suddenly Stachel felt frightened. Really frightened, for the first time. He was playing with plots against a man—and a nation—that were both utterly ruthless. And they held most of the cards.

Then he remembered the swaggering of the illiterate Soviet troops, the rape and plunder after the war. True, there had been Nazis who needed to be purged. But thousands of Germans had died needlessly under Russian boots. He gritted his teeth.

In his most unctuous manner he said, "Of course, Comrade Colonel. I will be there. Any further instructions?"

Koshka was puzzled by Stachel's reply. He had been able to detect not a hint of the resentment and fear that Stachel must be feeling. As he had reminded himself many times before, Stachel was a man to be wary of. A good Marxist, undoubtedly. But almost certainly a renegade nationalist, too.

"No, Comrade Director. Carry on." He replaced the telephone receiver without waiting for Stachel's reply.

His new aide knocked on the door and Koshka called him in, still pondering Stachel.

The young ensign—as expressionless and almost as tough and well trained as Kolyachin had been—clicked his heels politely.

"Comrade Colonel, Vanya reports that your helicopter is ready on the field."

Koshka looked up and nodded. The ensign clicked his heels again and marched out.

Koshka stood and absently began gathering his gear. Nine-mm pistol. Ammunition. Field glasses. Infrared scope. He ticked off the items as he packed them into his rucksack. But his mind was wrestling with the snowballing effects of this operation.

It had become a far more deadly affair than a simple capture. His informers hadn't been able to tell him all of Stachel's plans—the man was too skilled at hiding things he didn't want exposed—but he had enough to know the goals. And the damnable thing was that Stachel was being far cleverer than Koshka had ever expected. The man had left no trail of guilt, no evidence. And, worst of all, there was now no doubt that his enemies in the Intelligence Directorate were somehow allied with Stachel, at least temporarily. No one was moving in Moscow to hinder this operation—they really did fear the new A-10 too much for that—but the all-out assistance he had expected was lacking.

As he walked out the door to his big office he cast a look backward.

Strange. In all the years he'd occupied it, he had not

left a personal mark anywhere. It was cold, sterile. The official portraits of Lenin and the Premier looked stonily down on what might as well be an empty office.

It was as though he'd never been there.

He slammed the door and left to board his helicopter.

18

THE VILLAGE OF FALKENBERG WAS DESERTED. IT consisted of no more than twenty houses, a few drab shops, a single service station, a weary-looking church, and a small *Gasthaus*. Either all the occupants were gone, thought Max, or they were sitting behind tightly closed blackout curtains. The effect was the same. Nothing moved as he drove into town.

At the crossroads he turned east. He had never seen the village in all the times his father had brought him to the nearby castle. So it seemed likely the castle was to the east or south of town. And since he'd come up the south road, that left the east.

He drove slowly, but his mind was in turmoil. Wilson sounded worse. In the drive to Falkenberg, Max had kept their speed down, both because of the fog—which finally seemed about to dissipate—and because Wilson had begun to tear at the straps holding him to the back seat. Max had to stop once to cinch them down.

He kept his mind off the body wedged in the trunk. If he let himself contemplate all this too deeply, he knew that he'd slip into a kind of helpless panic. Movement was the best thing—the only thing that would help.

He handled the big Ford as if he'd been born in the driver's seat, but he gave it no thought. Driving, after all, was something he knew he did well. And this car was a jewel. He had felt the instant response and power through the gas pedal, and it had taken all his concentration to keep from pressing it down hard. The impulse simply to make the car go as fast as it could—to *anywhere*—was enormously difficult to suppress. But Wilson's condition couldn't be overlooked. And the fog . . .

He saw with a start that the fog was completely gone. The last few miles from the village had brought him into a countryside of rolling hills. Heavy forest—not the depressing ranks of pines that had been planted with deliberate, military precision, but the naturally wild and dense forest—covered the hills. The moon wasn't up yet, but all the clouds were gone. The stars cast a faint light over the country. Had he not been gripped by a fist of fear, Max would have thought the scene beautiful.

Suddenly he recognized the fence running along the road on the north side. Tall, arrogant blocks of granite. The castle's outer fence. If he remembered correctly, the gatehouse would be about a mile farther east.

He slowed to a crawl the last mile, switching off the Ford's headlights. There had been no traffic on the road. He hoped his luck would continue. And then he saw it, ahead on the left.

The gatehouse hadn't been changed. His childhood memory had made it larger and more grand, but it was the same. A rambling two-story affair in the style of the area: half stone, half whitewashed clay, with a glazed-tile roof. His mouth went dry as he saw that light shone through the windows of both floors. A wisp of smoke curled out of one of the four ornate chimneys. He looked around the entrance. A dark Mercedes was parked in front. It looked elegant but well used, about six years old. Leaning against one wall was a bicycle and next to it an unidentifiable gray motorcycle.

He remembered that the gatekeeper always seemed to have dogs in the yard. He and the little German girl—Frau Koch's daughter, he suddenly recalled—would often come down the long driveway from the castle to play with them. Big, friendly German shepherds. Tonight, there were none.

154

He looked up the dark drive toward the castle. It was invisible from the road, set back about three quarters of a mile. He could just make out a chain across the entrance to the driveway behind the gatehouse. A small white sign hung from the chain. It was too far away to make out the words, but knowing what it said suddenly became very important to Max. He thought of ways to slip past the gatehouse to read it, then remembered the night-vision field glasses in the glove compartment. He unbuckled his harness and rummaged through the glove box. Finally he found them, a small pair of very heavy binoculars.

The sign came into focus with the ten-power glasses. There were only two words on it: EINTRITT VERBOTEN. Entrance forbidden. Max's heart began to pound faster. So the long chance was no chance. There hadn't been a sign when Gisela Koch lived in the castle. He let the glasses fall into his lap and stared out the window.

Behind him, Wilson suddenly jerked upright, straining against the straps. Max whirled just in time to see him looking feverishly around. His eyes had the glassy look of a man in a deep delirium. A sheen of sweat stood out on his face.

"Where . . . where are we? We'll get—"

"It's okay, Ike, it's okay," Max said, gently forcing Wilson back down again and securing the straps. "We're okay. Take it easy." Wilson looked uncomprehendingly at him. Pulling another hypo from the med kit, Max injected Ike with its contents immediately. Shivering, Wilson didn't even notice. He began to quiet down as the drug took hold.

Max turned to look at the gatehouse again. Now that he was actually here he realized that it was all a hopeless gamble. He stared through the dark at the details of the little gatehouse, remembering.

He thought of the last time he'd seen it, nearly twenty years ago. He'd been standing up in the back seat of his father's staff car, watching it disappear out the rear window while Eric Moss—it had been Colonel Eric Moss then—sat hunched in the driver's seat, shoulders eloquently rigid. He never knew why their visit to Gisela Koch's wonderful castle had been cut so short. He'd been playing in the garden with her daughter—now he remembered her name: it was Hansi, short for Johanna—when his father had come storming out of the castle. Without a word, he'd jerked Max off the ground and half dragged, half marched him to the car. A few moments later and Schloss Falkenberg was only a memory, one that Eric Moss never spoke of and one that Max had all but forgotten about.

Until today. And now it was of pounding importance that he recall everything he could about the blond, gracious woman his father had been involved with. Because she might be his only way out of the Vopo dragnet.

He strained to picture her as she would be today. *Then* she had been barely thirty, newly widowed. Her husband had been in the East German government, and soon after his death she and Eric Moss had met at some state function. The first time Max had seen her was on their first visit to the castle. She'd left her Berlin apartment and returned to her ancestral home. Her maiden name had been Alexandra Gisela Maria von Falkenberg, Max remembered; a name fit for a princess, and so she had seemed to him as a child. She had been tall, even statuesque, with radiant blond hair and sparkling cornflower-blue eyes. When she'd introduced him to her daughter the first time, Max had been disappointed that the girl had none of her mother's traits: she had been dumpy, brown-haired, and giggly.

A flashing red light on the dashboard shook Max from his reverie. He blinked and saw that the water temperature was rising from prolonged idling. He switched on an auxiliary electric cooling fan and the light faded. He took a deep breath and surveyed the gatehouse again. It was time to act. The question was, could there be any point in hoping that the brief encounter between the Mosses and the Kochs two decades ago would help him get back to Potsdam? Even if Gisela were still here, he thought, she'd be over fifty years old. And age in these parts tended to make people wiser. Not to mention more suspicious.

He looked again at the keep-out sign. It wasn't likely she lived behind that sign. The East Germans didn't put up that kind of notice to protect the security of middle-aged women.

His face twisted into the mocking smile his friends knew so well. So. Here he was again, arguing the different sides of the problem, stalling. Always stalling. Only there wasn't any time for that. Now he had to act, and quickly. Parked across from the only lighted house within miles was not the place to avoid detection by the Vopos. Better a running chase back to Potsdam than a sitting-duck capture here.

But he couldn't bring himself to drive away. He looked again at the gatehouse. They wouldn't know anything about him and his precious cargo. And out in this deserted countryside, strangers must always be stopping to ask for directions. Why not . . . why not an American, lost on the way to Berlin?

Even if those in the house were hostile, they could only watch him leave. And if he suspected them of too much curiosity, he could always double back.

He decided the risk was worth it. If they knew Gisela Koch, and if she still lived in the area, she still might be able to help him. But he must be careful not to ask too intently about her; that would lead the Vopos right to him.

He sat for a second more, then engaged first gear and switched on the lights. He drove into the yard and stopped, leaving the lights on and the engine running.

The night air was cold, still carrying the taste of the clammy fog. He hurried across the yard to the door and lifted the huge old brass knocker, bringing it down hard.

After a few moments a light came on above him and a man's voice asked who he was.

"Sergeant Max Moss, U.S. Air Force," he yelled back in German.

There was a long pause. Then the voice asked, "What do you want?"

Max responded with his tale about having lost his way. There was another pause. He was getting really cold.

Then the voice said, "Very well," and the door swung open. Max stepped inside.

He was in a long, old-fashioned reception hall. An-

157

tique furniture stood along both walls, and there were closed doors leading everywhere—upstairs and to both sides.

He turned to face the man who'd let him in. He was heavy, less than six feet tall, with massive, almost Neanderthal features and black eyes that peered suspiciously out from under heavy black eyebrows. He wore a simple brown-tweed suit, old-fashioned and a little worn. He regarded Max silently.

Max cleared his throat. "Uh, thank you. Now, I wonder if you could help me with the way to Berlin?"

Neanderthal Face slowly looked him up and down. Max's blue uniform was dirty and torn at the knees. His shoes were muddy. A trace of blood stained one of his shirt sleeves. He didn't look like an innocent traveler.

Before the hulking German could speak, Max looked down and laughed.

"Ah, look at me. This is what happens when you try to change a punctured tire in the fog. Perhaps I could clean up after we talk about the way to Berlin?"

The man's eyes narrowed. His voice was disconcertingly high for a man with such a huge frame.

"Perhaps, Sergeant. But first, tell me—"

"*Rudi.* Who is that?" He had been interrupted by a female voice from one of the side rooms.

The Neanderthal shook his head like an angry bull. He looked at Moss.

"Excuse me, Sergeant. I will be back in a moment." He stalked down the hall, leaving Moss alone. He didn't invite him to come in or to sit down.

Rudi opened a door on the right and spoke too low for Max to hear. The woman's reply was equally indistinct. Then Rudi carefully closed the door and returned to Moss.

Rudi stopped and looked hard at Max, his face expressionless.

"She says you are to come in. Follow me." He spun on his heel and Max noted that, like many very large men, he was much lighter on his feet than he looked.

He opened the heavy oak door and Max stepped into

the cheery warmth of a drawing room lit by a crackling fire. The room was twenty degrees warmer than the hall. Tall old velvet-covered chairs ringed the fire. He could see silver hair on the woman who sat with her back to him, facing the fire. She had heard them come in and stood up to meet them, her face set in a smile.

They looked at each other and the color drained from Max's face. The smile froze on hers and a spot of intense red appeared on each of her cheekbones. They stared at each other for what seemed a long time. And then Rudi shuffled uneasily behind Max. She jerked her cornflower eyes away from Max and spoke to Rudi.

"Thank you, Rudi. I will help this young man. You may go." There was a slight catch in her voice.

Rudi grunted and shut the door behind him.

Max looked at her again. She stood only about five two. Beneath the bulky white cardigan and long print dress she wore, her figure could have been slender. The graceful, carefully manicured hands spoke of someone who cared enough to ensure that it would be. Although she was clearly well into middle age, her face was still shapely, though laced with a fine network of tiny wrinkles. She wore little makeup, making her large, steady eyes the perfect complement for her silver hair. She wore it in a severe bun on the back of her head. A crucifix hung from her throat. She unconsciously reached up to touch it while she returned his searching gaze.

There was no doubt. She was Gisela Koch.

She broke the silence.

"Please excuse me, Sergeant. But for a moment you ... you reminded me of someone." She spoke in heavily accented English.

Max smiled.

"Please, let us speak German, Frau Koch. It will be easier for us both. You don't recognize me?"

She again fingered the crucifix, her eyes wide.

"You know *me?*"

"Of course, Frau Koch. You are the only woman I met in Germany I have remembered. But it's not surprising you don't recall me. After all, I was only a boy—"

"*Max,*" she cried out. "Max Moss. Can it be so?"

His smile faded. "Yes, I'm afraid it can. I'm sorry to burst in on you like this, Frau Koch. And I wish I had time to be more sociable. But time is short. Very short. And I need your help."

She sat down and waved him to a chair. Her eyes had narrowed. She took in every detail of his uniform.

"I see, Max. After so many years . . . there is trouble?"

"Yes. But before I ask your help, you should know my situation. Then you may not wish to help."

She waited.

"You see, Frau Koch, I am running. From the Vopos, from the Russians. It's a long story, but that's the crux of it. I have a wounded friend outside in a car who must have medical attention soon. And I have to get to a certain place in Potsdam. Before . . . before they catch me."

Gisela didn't move. She sat straight in the velvet chair. The snapping of the fire was the only noise in the room. She regarded him steadily for a long moment. When she spoke again, her voice was calm.

"No, Max. You need not expect anything from me but as much help as I can give. You will tell me of your needs—directions, food, whatever you wish—and I will provide them." She hesitated and glanced at the door. "But softly, Max. *He*"—she pointed to the closed door— "he has excellent hearing. One of the reasons, no doubt, they assigned him to me. Like the others before him, he reports everything." She saw Max's look of surprise and smiled.

"Yes, Max. We have that much in common, whatever else has changed for us. The Vopos are my enemies, too."

Max blinked again in surprise. Then he drew his chair closer to hers and began to relate his story in an urgent whisper.

But Rudi wasn't eavesdropping outside the door. He was far more interested in the idling Ford in the yard. As soon as he had closed the drawing-room door he had slipped to a darkened room and looked out the window.

When he saw the Ford clearly, he smiled. His heavy

160

features became warped in a savage grin as he picked out the telltale signs on the Fairmont.

So. A Potsdamer.

He studied the car carefully, noting each detail. It had obviously been in deep mud, most of which had dried on the splash panels, fenders, and tires. Some was still wet.

Rudi let the heavy curtain fall back over the window and picked up the telephone receiver on the desk. Then he hesitated.

Perhaps there was more to know before he called headquarters.

He replaced the receiver. If he were to gain some valuable advance information for Berlin, he might be able to escape this miserable assignment. And he was sick to death of snooping on the high-and-mighty Koch bitches. In the two years he'd been assigned to the gatehouse women, they had revealed nothing of use to the state. Nor, he thought sourly, had he even been able to get the young one horizontal. That was apparently for officers only.

He would investigate the car further. It might be his ticket out of this godforsaken forest. He eased open the door to the office and listened for a moment. They were whispering in the drawing room. Good. Let them talk.

Rudi switched off the hall light and ducked out the front door. It shut behind him with a solid *click*. Balancing himself on the balls of his feet, he slid his deadly little Makarov pistol out of its holster and carefully began circling around the yard to the Ford.

Gisela cocked her head in the midst of Max's hurried telling of the story. She had heard the faint sound of the front door closing. She held up her hand to silence Max and listened intently. Swiftly she rose and went to the window, where she parted the drapes and scanned the yard. When she turned to face Max, her face was grave.

"Max, Rudi is investigating your car. Can he learn anything from it that may hinder you?"

Max frowned. "No, I don't think so. Only that Ike is injured and unconscious."

She nodded and let the curtain fall back. "Good.

Since Rudi is gone, we can talk more freely. But he will be outside only a few moments, then he will undoubtedly call his superiors to report. We have little time."

She fell silent, frowning and biting her lip while she looked at him with unreadable eyes.

At last she spoke again.

"Max, I can help you get to Potsdam. I could supply you with detailed instructions to evade the police, instructions that would allow you to use roads and farm tracks that even they don't know about. But it would take too long to tell you all that. And even then you could still easily get lost in the countryside."

Max shrugged. "Maybe so. But without—"

"No, Max. There is a better way. One that would help us both. Please wait here for a moment." Max's reply was cut short by her abrupt exit from the room.

He jumped to his feet and strode to the window. Rudi, he saw, was a crouching dark shadow across the muddy yard. He appeared to be studying the Ford. Max closed the drapes and swore. His options were running out even before he could choose any. Rudi would soon have enough to close the Vopo dragnet around him.

The door swung open. Gisela walked in, her face strained. Max started to tell her that he had to leave, and then he realized she wasn't alone.

A girl—a young woman, actually—stood silently beside her. She was almost the same height as Gisela and also wore her hair in a tight bun; in the firelit tableau it took Max only seconds to see that she was a younger version of the elder Koch. Slender, graceful, and poised, with almond-shaped gray eyes, the young woman regarded him steadily in frank appraisal. Her face was highlighted by prominent cheekbones and a firm jawline, but full, generous lips softened any hardness in her features. Like Gisela, she wore a calf-length print dress and simple shoes. Neither the dress nor her severe hairstyle could conceal her obvious beauty.

Gisela said brusquely, "Max, this is my daughter, Johanna. No doubt you will remember her as Hansi?"

"Remember her? Well, yes, Frau Koch. But only as a

162

little girl. Not as a woman." He cleared his throat awkwardly.

Johanna Koch's sudden smile illuminated her face. "And, Max Moss, I seem to recall you as an aggressive little Ami brat who loved to pull my pigtails." She spoke in a warm contralto that carried across the room like musical notes.

Max flushed. "Excuse me, Fräulein Koch. I didn't intend—"

"Enough pleasantries, Max." Gisela's voice was strained and there was an edge of urgency in it. "We haven't the time. I brought Hansi here for a reason, and it wasn't so that the memories of a five-year-old girl could compete with those of a nine-year-old boy." Max flushed again. She was right. Their time *was* too short.

Gisela pulled her sweater tighter about her. "Max, I have a proposition for you. Any moment Rudi will realize that there is more to your story than you told him. Therefore we haven't the time for instructions. You must be on your way immediately. Which means that if you are to have any chance of success, you must take someone with you to show you the way." She paused and looked keenly at Max.

"That someone will be Hansi, Max. My daughter will guide you to Potsdam."

Rudi kept out of the headlights as he approached the blue Ford. Warily, he sought a view of the interior, but the windows were steamed over. He would have to get closer.

Inside the car, Ike Wilson had fallen into a delirium. He seemed to be tied up and in a prison cell. The bastards were trying to get him to talk. They had him strapped down. But he was too smart for them. He wriggled and thrashed and groaned, and suddenly was free. He lay still, listening for the tread of the sentry outside his steel door. Nothing. He looked down at his arms. They were wrapped with some kind of tape. Probably broke 'em while I slept, he thought. The bastards. Well, they didn't hurt much. And when the guard shows up again . . . He thought of the pistol tucked into his boot.

Rudi saw the Ford shake and stopped dead. So there

163

was someone in there. He must be more careful. But the fact that he couldn't see anyone's head above the window-line made him curious. Perhaps, he thought, perhaps they have a captive. One of us. A comrade.

Rudi darted forward, gun ready. He knelt below the windows of the car and worked his way along the metal flank. The only sound was the bass thrumming of the idling engine. The movement inside had stopped. He peered inside the Ford, trying to see through the fogged glass. There was nothing in the front seat. But in back he saw a prostrate form.

He looked back at the house. The American was still inside. He slipped along the side of the car and peered in at the man on the back seat. All he could tell was that the man was bound, his head propped up on some kind of bundle. He wasn't moving, and his arms were crossed.

Rudi stared a long time, but the man's eyes remained tightly shut. The suspicion grew that he was a comrade.

He reached down and eased the door handle out. It was unlocked. He swung the rear door open.

Ike Wilson had been watching the bastard, waiting. Every night they'd come by his cell to taunt him about Margarete. Tonight there'd be a little surprise for them. He watched through slitlike eyes as the guard opened the door. It was time.

Rudi jumped back as the man's eyes flew open. They were the hot eyes of a madman. Transfixed by them, he did not see Ike Wilson painfully raise his right arm. Until it was too late.

Rudi got his Makarov up a fraction of a second after Wilson squeezed the trigger of his little .22-caliber pistol. Rudi's gun went off and blasted a 9-mm hole in the Ford's dashboard. And then he fell into the mud like a bag of wet cement, a neat little hole punched in his forehead and a jagged wound twice as big in back, where Wilson's dum-dum had tumbled out.

A second after the double *crack* rang through the night, Max pounded down the hall, threw open the door, and sprinted to the Ford.

164

Rudi's body lay sprawled in the mud, feet toward the open rear door. Max paused only long enough to make sure that he was dead and then reached in to check Wilson. He was still clutching the pistol. But his eyes were closed and his head lay against the seatback. Max crawled in and looked for wounds. He found none and noted that Wilson's breathing had steadied. He rolled up one eyelid and confirmed that Ike was unconscious. Max took the little gun out of Ike's limp hand and strapped the wounded man back in.

He surveyed the damage to the car. Rudi's bullet had gone through the passenger-side window and smashed into the dash. Max checked the circuits and, one by one, the green lights came on. Only one red light showed. The radio. He fingered the shattered electronics grimly. They were really alone now.

He turned to Rudi's body just as Gisela and Johanna came running out of the house. Hansi bore an ancient shotgun, Gisela a large kitchen knife.

"No need for those. One's dead, the other's unconscious." Both women stood over the dead Vopo and stared down at him, their faces expressionless in the glare of the single bulb over the gatehouse doorway. Suddenly Johanna spit at the corpse and raised the shotgun as if to smash the skull.

Gisela snatched the weapon away from Hansi. "No, *Liebchen,* no. I know how you feel, but we cannot waste time on this pig now." Hansi slowly relaxed and the wildness went out of her eyes.

Gisela faced Max. "This changes nothing, Max. You and Hansi must be off immediately. She can—"

"Hold it, dammit." Max slammed his hand against the Ford. "Just a damned minute. This is all going too fast." He drew a long breath.

"I know, Max. It must seem hard to understand why—"

"Hard to understand? Jesus, that's the understatement of the year. Ten minutes after I show up, you're trying to send your own daughter off with someone you haven't seen in twenty years, a guy I never saw before is dead, and you figure it seems hard to understand? Well, it sure as hell is, and before another thing happens you're going to start explaining. *Now.*"

Gisela put a hand on his arm. "Yes, Max, I see. And I shall explain. But it will have to be done quickly, you understand? So you will have to take many things I say on faith alone." She paused, waiting for Max to reply. He said nothing, so she continued, eyes focusing beyond Max, on the past. Hansi shivered in the cold.

"You may not remember it, but Eric—your father—left me because he was convinced that I had tried to spy on him. My first husband, Wolf, was a loyal Communist, high in the counterintelligence service. Your father knew that, but he loved me—I never doubted it, not for a moment. But his people—your people—told him that they had proof the Vopos were using me as an agent to spy on him. He demanded to know if it were true, and I told him the truth. That they *had* ordered me to spy on him but that I couldn't do it." She hesitated, biting her lip.

"He wouldn't believe me. He cursed me and left. The Vopos were enraged. *They* believed I had been planning to defect by marrying Eric. They had always suspected me of trying to use Wolf's connections to protect my 'aristocratic' standing anyway. So, after my affair with Eric, they took the castle away from me and Hansi, and assigned us to the gatehouse. Ever since, we have been the chatelaines of the *Schloss*. No more. Just caretakers in our own house—when they aren't using it for Party functions." Anger stole into her voice, chiseling away the carefully controlled tone.

"For twenty years we have lived like this—spied upon by Vopo pigs who follow us everywhere. Pigs like this one." She kicked the body in the cold mud. "We are prisoners here as surely as if we were in a steel cage."

Max shifted impatiently against the side of the Ford. "So why didn't you defect?"

Hansi answered. "We tried, many times. But even though we have many friends among the local people, there was no one strong enough to help us. And the one time we contacted the Americans, we were rebuffed. They thought we were too risky. That we weren't worth the effort."

Max ran a hand through his hair. "So now, Fräulein Koch, you figure the way west is with me. Well, I'm sorry, but I have specific orders that no one—*no one*—other than American nationals is to be transported in a Recovery car. It's part of the original agreement. In fact, they made damned sure I knew that it's the most vital part of the agreement."

The strain of trying to convince Max was beginning to tell on Gisela. Her lips trembled and she tried again, desperately.

"Max, I'm not begging a favor. I know about the rules. But they're bound to be here any minute. You can't hope to penetrate their cordons without guidance, and whatever lead you may have had, you've already lost. But you can still make it. I can gain you some time by misleading them enough for you and Hansi to slip through."

The wind gusted, bringing the chill of the recent rain into Max's bones. He realized suddenly that this proud woman was offering her life in return for her daughter's escape. Because no matter what their fate on the road to Potsdam, he knew that Gisela would be doomed. And she knew it, too.

Max's head ached. Colonel Martin had made it crystal clear that the consequences of taking Germans in a Recovery car were enormous. But he stood no chance of getting back to Potsdam without help.

Twisting in on itself, his mind cried out for a time to unravel everything. He caught sight of Rudi's body again.

"What about him? How will you explain him to the Vopos?"

Gisela smiled wanly. "He will be in the Mercedes. And the Mercedes will be out of sight. I will say that you cut the telephone wires and that he left to report from a public telephone in the village."

"And Johanna? How will you explain her absence?"

Her smile disappeared. "I will say you kidnapped her at gunpoint. As a hostage."

Max jerked. "Gisela . . . they'll never believe all that."

She seemed to shrink within her sweater. "Perhaps. But even so, you will gain time."

Max glanced at Johanna. She stood a foot from her mother, tears running down her face.

"You know what will happen to you?"

"Yes, Max Moss. I know what it means to stay here. But I have had enough. This is no life; it's mere existence at the whim of pigs. I have no future except Hansi. And Hansi can still live." She clutched Max's arms in desperate, nervous hands. "Max, you cannot refuse me. You must take her with you. You *must.*"

"Johanna, what about you? Do you think this plan will work?"

She slowly shifted her gaze to Max. Her gray eyes were luminous in the dark. They held him while she answered.

"I know this. I know that we cannot all go. And that we cannot all escape. Someone must remain to misdirect the police, and there . . . there is logic in my mother's plan. But it would be better if you took my mother. She knows the area better than I. And I may be able to gain more time for you than she."

Gisela whirled to face Hansi.

"*No.* Have I schemed and bled to raise you these twenty-four years only to have you throw your life away for me? *Never,* Johanna. You are the future and I the past— through you I will escape, and *they* will have failed." She reached out and held her daughter's head in both hands. "I know it is not easy, child, but you must go, not I. Remember how we planned for this moment all these years? How we would savor the freedom? Then don't fail me now. Be strong, and *go.*"

Johanna stared wordlessly at her a moment longer. Then she embraced her mother.

For ten long heartbeats Max watched as they held each other tightly. He felt the stirrings of panic as the decision loomed over him. Take one and leave the other to die in a Vopo torture cell? Take both? Take neither and play the game correctly into certain capture? It was exactly the kind of multifaceted no-win argument he'd loved in college. They'd all loved them, he and those naive kids. They'd stay up all night long, arguing one side, then the other. Only now he didn't have all night. He didn't even have another minute.

He suddenly slapped the Ford. "*Fuck* the agreement. And fuck the goddamn game. We're going." Startled, Gisela and Hansi separated and looked at him without understanding. He had spoken in English.

He forced a grin. "Sorry, ladies. But if Hansi and I are going to stay ahead of them, we'll have to leave right now."

They stared a moment longer as his words sank in. Then Gisela stood on tiptoe and kissed him on the cheek. He felt the hot tears on her face.

"Thank you, Max. I—"

"Don't thank me, Frau Koch." He had cut her off savagely. "I'm leaving you to face the Vopos and there's no guarantee my government will allow Hansi to defect even if we make it. She might be sent right back."

She smiled broadly, eyes shining. "They may, young Max. They may." She took Hansi's hand and looked back at him. "And then again, they may not. But it is an even chance, no?"

A lump in his throat suddenly choked him and stopped his reply. Max gazed at the desperate hope in Gisela's face and the despair in Johanna's. Then he wrenched his eyes down to the body at his feet. He stooped to grab one arm, and, wordlessly, the chatelaines of Schloss Falkenberg joined him. Together, they dragged the sodden corpse to the Mercedes.

19

MÜLLER ALMOST MISSED THE TIRE TRACKS. The lights of his little BMW caught the drying mud streaks that emerged from the Schloss Falkenberg gate, froze them for a moment in their yellow-white beams, and then he was rushing across them. It took another second for their meaning to register. When it did, he slammed the BMW to a stop, then whipped it around and drove back to the gate, eyeing the tracks as he approached.

A car had entered and left within the past hour. He stopped the car and peered into the gatehouse yard. No cars stood parked there. Only a bicycle and a motorcycle. He set his jaw and drove in, the slick mud squishing under his tires.

In the middle of the yard he shut off the engine and surveyed the scene. His assistant sat silently, waiting for orders. The mud was churned up near the gatehouse door. Tracks led clearly to the porch. A second set of tracks indicated where another car had obviously been recently parked.

It was definitely suspicious. A light showed on the lower floor of the gatehouse. Smoke drifted from a chimney, light against the dark sky. The Koch Mercedes was gone. At another time, under other circumstances, Müller might have ignored this fact. But not tonight. Not on this road. And not with an Ami in the area.

"Stay put. I'm checking the gatehouse." His assistant nodded silently. Müller grabbed a flashlight and jumped out of the BMW. A few seconds later, he knocked on the oak door, hand on gun.

The door flew open and Gisela Koch's distraught features greeted him.

"Thank God. I thought it might be—"

"Yes, Frau Koch? Thought it might be who?"

Her hand went to her mouth. She shrank back from him.

"Oh—you aren't Volkspolizei? I thought Rudi had called."

Müller nodded. "Yes. We are the police. But no one called us. Frau Koch, an American car is in the area. Have you seen it?"

Before she could answer, Müller's eyes narrowed and looked past her to the hall. "Say, where is Rudi Glaser? He's supposed to be here."

"Yes, I know, Officer. But when the Ami took my little Hansi and cut the telephone wires, Herr Glaser decided to chase them and call you from the next village. That's why—"

"Stop, Frau Koch. No more, please. I must report." Müller scowled. "You say the telephone does not work?"

Gisela shook her head, eyes wide. "No, no. The Ami—"

"Never mind. You will please stay here while I send word with the radio in my car." He turned and slipped through the mud to the white BMW. He didn't see the tiny smile on Gisela Koch's face.

Stachel's Mercedes slued to a halt in the muddy yard a quarter hour later, followed within minutes by Koshka's helicopter. Stachel was speaking with Müller when the big Mi-24 gunship settled heavily onto the middle of the road. The Germans straightened as the Soviet colonel strode through the mud, heedless of its effect on his highly polished boots.

"Well, Herr Stachel? Do you know where the American is yet?"

Stachel shook his head. "No, Comrade Colonel. But we know for sure where he has been."

Koshka's narrow face darkened dangerously. "We all know where he has *been, Herr Direktor*. He has been to the field near Dobbrun. We know that much by the mysteriously delayed explosion of the A-10. What we need to know now is where he *will* be."

Stachel stepped back a pace under Koshka's verbal blast. He swallowed a retort and spoke unctuously.

"And that is what I wished to tell you, Comrade Colonel. Müller and I have spoken with the woman who lives here. She claims that an American sergeant kidnapped her daughter and drove west, and that Unteroffizier Glaser left to tell us of the fact."

"Glaser? One of your men?"

"Yes, Comrade Colonel. He is assigned to the Koch women—to report anything, ah, unusual."

"And why didn't he report the American?"

Stachel grimaced. "The Koch woman says that he couldn't—the American cut the wires."

Koshka grunted. "So. Do you believe this?"

"No, Comrade Colonel, I do not. I have known this woman a long time and am familiar with her file. She has tried to defect many times. I believe she is lying."

Koshka was growing impatient. He slapped his thigh absently and said, "Stachel, I am less interested in your case histories of unreliable women than I am in the location of the Americans. Stop telling me what you *believe;* try instead to concentrate on the problem at hand. If the woman is lying, then by all means liquidate her, but first find out where the Yankees are."

Stachel clenched his fists in silence, then bowed. "As the Comrade Colonel wishes," he said icily. He turned on his heel and stalked across the yard to the gatehouse door. He slammed it behind him. The bang echoed out over the chill night.

Koshka ignored him, lost in thought. Standing uneasily half at attention a few feet away, Müller coughed. Koshka swiveled to face him.

"So, Herr Müller, what do you think?"

Müller colored and stammered, "Uh . . . well, Comrade Colonel, I'm sure the director knows better than I."

"Don't hesitate to disagree with your superior, Müller, when called upon to do so by higher authority. It marks a man as someone to watch."

"Yes, sir. At first I thought Frau Koch was telling the truth. But then I saw that one set of tire tracks goes east out the gate, and the other west. If Unteroffizier Glaser *had* decided to chase them, why did he not follow them? And why did he not call by now? It's very puzzling."

Koshka pointed down the eastward tracks. "Where does the road go that way?"

"Wendemark, Comrade Colonel. And then on to the Elbe ferry near Havelberg."

Koshka pondered for a moment, then slapped his thigh in decision. "Obviously they have gone east, or one of our men would have seen them. So they must be even now nearing the ferry. Müller, you will collect the director, and both of you will head toward Wendemark and the ferry. I will go by air to ensure that our quarry doesn't escape by a side road. And before we leave, call the ferry. Is there a police unit there?"

"Yes, sir. Three men. One on each side of the river and one on the ferryboat."

"Good. Radio the commander that if he sees the Americans, he must detain them at all costs. He is to shoot if necessary. Understand?"

Müller nodded eagerly. "Yes, Comrade Colonel. At once." He ducked and ran off toward the gatehouse. Yuri Koshka started back to the helicopter. Halfway there, he called to the running man, "Müller! Tell Herr Stachel to hurry—I want to speak with him before we leave." Müller waved acknowledgment and ran into the house.

Gisela Koch sat erect in her fireside chair. She was pale and the whiteness of her knuckles stood out as she

173

clasped her hands. Karl Stachel studied her silently through hooded eyes from his position on the sofa.

"Frau Koch," he said at length, "we both know your story to be a complete fabrication. Americans running from us, whatever else they may do, do not kidnap German girls. And whatever sins Glaser may have been guilty of in his police service, he was not rash enough to simply chase off after a suspicious Ami car without first calling his superior." He stood heavily and spread his hands before the dying fire. He spoke while staring into the red embers.

"Furthermore, we both know you have been trying to leave the Democratic Republic for years. It does not take much imagination to put tonight's events together in their proper order." He fixed his unblinking gaze full upon her. "We know all about your fondness for Americans. And you must know that this Ami was trying to get to Potsdam. The conclusion is obvious. You and he overpowered Glaser, disposed of his body, and he left with your daughter. The difference in this case being that she left willingly."

Gisela said nothing. She looked coolly back at Stachel.

"All this is simple, Alexandra Gisela Maria von Falkenberg. What I don't understand"—he leaned toward her and she made an effort not to flinch—"is why you didn't leave yourself. Did you really think you could survive this absurd fiction?"

"Herr Stachel, what I have told you is no fiction, but the truth."

Without warning, Stachel slapped her full across the mouth. She cried out and jerked away from him. He leaned closer, his face contorted with fury.

"I am out of patience, dear baroness. You will tell me the American's plans without further dissembling. It is your only chance to see another sunrise, let alone your daughter. I promise you that."

Gisela's answer never came. Müller burst into the room, panting.

"*Herr Direktor.* The comrade colonel—"

"Müller, what are you doing here?" Stachel had turned to face him, furious. "How dare you interrupt me?"

174

Müller flushed but held his ground. He snapped to attention. "*Herr Direktor*, the colonel ordered me to bring you to him. Immediately."

Stachel turned away. "Yes, Müller. Of course. I will be there in a moment. Go."

Müller hesitated, looking fearfully at Stachel. "But . . . the comrade colonel—"

"*Go.* I will be there in good time."

Müller fled, and Stachel leaned close to Gisela again. She sat ramrod straight, disdaining to meet his eyes.

"So we are interrupted, *Liebchen.* But be assured of this: We will catch the Americans and your daughter, and then there will be a real reckoning. And this time, none of your titles or your blue blood will help you a bit." He stroked her silver hair and whispered, "*I* will see to that." His hand continued down to circle her throat, and squeezed. She bit her lip as he squeezed harder. He stood for a second more, applying pressure with his huge hand. Her vision clouded, but still she did not cry out. Then suddenly he released her, and was gone.

Koshka stood by the helicopter door, watching Karl Stachel button his greatcoat and stump across the slippery parking area. He signaled Vanya to start the engines, and the big blades were *whop-whop*ping slowly above them as Stachel puffed to a halt a few feet away.

The Russian narrowed his hypnotic eyes as the rotors gathered speed above them. "Herr Stachel, you have something new to report? Something more than deductions?"

"No, Comrade Colonel, the woman is stubborn. But I know she is lying."

"It does not matter now." Koshka waved a hand to the east. "We will stop them at the Elbe ferry. Müller is already gone. You will follow. And this time, Stachel"—his voice rose above the whining turbines—"this time there will be no mistakes. No mysteriously exploding aircraft, no misdirected searches, no halfhearted efforts. I expect you to be zealous in pursuit of the Americans. Very zealous."

175

Stachel kept his face calm as he absorbed the real meaning of the words. Koshka *knew*. There was no other interpretation. The Russian knew that Stachel was working for his own purposes. He was committed now.

He smiled thinly at the colonel. "Yes, Comrade. I am always zealous in the revolutionary interest. Always."

Koshka ignored the whirlwind of the rotors and pierced Stachel with a look. Finally Koshka, too, smiled and Karl Stachel felt uncontrollable fear stab through him.

"Good, Herr Stachel. I think we understand each other. I now expect you to apprehend this American without further delay. And without, *Herr Direktor*, any damage to the goods. Understand?"

Stachel's mouth moved, but his words were lost in the noise of the blades. Koshka held him a moment more with his eyes, then leaped into the chopper. A few seconds later, the gunship was airborne. Stachel held the flaps of his greatcoat down as the huge rotors whipped the roadside grit into a cyclone.

He watched the chopper angle eastward into the darkness and thought, Yes, Comrade Yuri Andreyevich, we understand each other. And I will be zealous. Perhaps too zealous for you tonight.

Stachel's driver pulled up in the Mercedes. Silently, Stachel slid into the welcome warmth of the interior. The driver looked back.

"Which way, *Herr Direktor*?"

"To the Elbe, Hans. The Havelberg ferry." The driver nodded and slipped the big Mercedes into gear. They slid on the wet, muddy pavement as the tires spun, but Stachel didn't notice. He was congratulating himself on his performance as a subordinate to Koshka. Like a truly *zealous* inferior, he hadn't belabored his superior with needless details. Like the fact that with the help of the younger Koch woman, the American would not need to use the main ferry. And like the fact that she almost certainly knew many roads that Koshka wouldn't.

Such information, he thought, was clearly irrelevant to the Russian colonel. No matter how vital it was to Karl Stachel.

176

He almost chuckled. Thanks to Gisela Koch's transparent treachery, he had stolen another march on Koshka *and* the Americans. It might be all he needed.

20

FOR THE FIRST TEN MINUTES THEY DROVE IN nervous silence. Max was afraid that any minute Johanna would break down and become hysterical. Or maybe whip out her Party membership card and wrest control of the car from him. But she did neither. She simply sat, engulfed by the bucket seat, and stared intently out the windshield at the road unraveling before them. Wilson was still comatose.

Max finally began to use some of the awesome horsepower of the Ford's turbocharged V-8. He lost himself entirely in driving, enjoying all over again the endless fascination of controlling a fast car on a twisting, empty road. His powerful headlights pierced the darkness for half a mile on the straights, and he eased the gas pedal to the floor, savoring the savage lunge when the turbo spun up to working speed.

Johanna's previous experience with automobiles had always been either in plush, whisper-smooth limousines or in the standard East German machines. The raw, urgent power of the big Ford was at first frightening, then exciting to her. She could almost forget their desperate situation in the hypnotic rhythms of Max's driving.

They rolled into another deserted village. Max hauled the Ford down just in time to slide to a tire-squealing stop at a crossroads. He looked at the navigation display, which hadn't been hit by Rudi's bullet. They were in Wende-mark. He turned to her just as she said, "Take the road to the right, toward Havelberg."

He looked up the road. Like the others, deserted. But this one was bigger, with a center stripe, and wide enough for Soviet tanks. A main road.

"Are you sure? We should stay off these big roads—"

"No, no, don't worry. We'll turn off again in four kilo-meters. In Werben. Then we'll go south and cross the Elbe on a little-used ferry. They will almost certainly ex-pect us at the Havelberg ferry if they think we've gone this way."

Max shrugged and turned right. He ignored the speed-limit sign in the little town and floored the accelera-tion pedal. The engine snarled and he corrected the slight fishtailing of the back end that resulted from the sudden increase in power. His mind was somehow made calmer by driving. It had always been so, even when he'd first begun racing. In his first race, with his heart pounding wildly and his throat dry, he'd discovered a new serenity. It was as though keeping two tons of hurtling metal on the ragged edge of destruction was a catalyst to his mind; he could think clearly, ordering his thoughts in the neat, military rows his father loved to use when he was putting his thoughts on paper.

It's too bad, he thought, I can't just drive all my life.

Johanna's warning shout pulled him out of his rever-ie. The turnoff was only just ahead, a poorly marked sec-ondary road. He nearly overshot it, locking up all four wheels and sliding sideways. He jammed the car into re-verse, slammed backward, and, while still rolling, dumped the big chrome shift lever into first and rocketed down the little road. He cursed himself. Being in too much of a hur-ry on these mazelike roads could kill both of them.

Johanna's voice was cold.

"Very impressive, Max, but I hope you didn't leave too much rubber on the road for them to follow us with."

He started to fire back a devastating reply, then real-ized she was right. He couldn't drive as if they were simply outrunning some friends on a Sunday street race. A black streak on the pavement was like a burning arrow pointed their way. He'd have to be far more careful.

At the next turnoff, she warned him well in advance, and he braked to fifty before drifting the car through the left-hander. They were on an even smaller road, half dirt, half gravel. Weeds and debris littered the roadside. He slowed, unsure of the surface. Visibility was poor because of the cramped conditions and the ravines. He switched on the fog lights, and the world in front of them turned black-and-white.

"We should come to a cattle gate soon," Johanna said, "and immediately after that there should be a wooden rail across the road. We will remove it; it's only old Joachim's way of keeping strangers off his ferry."

Max smiled grimly. If this kind of information were necessary to get them back, it was a damned good thing Hansi was along.

They came to the cattle gate, then the wooden rail. Max stopped, jumped out of the car, and slid the rail aside. After he drove through Johanna said, "*Wait.* We must put it back. Otherwise—"

"Yeah, yeah—otherwise the Vopos will know we've been through here. I'll—"

But she was already out and sliding the rail back in place.

Just over the hill they saw the river. In the faint starlight it showed as a featureless black mass about a half mile wide. A hundred yards ahead stood an old building, a ramp, and an ancient flat-bottomed ferry tied to a small jetty. A single light shone in the little building.

They drove down and Johanna said, "Let me handle this. Joachim is an old friend, but even he can get too curious. If he thinks we're breaking the law, he won't hesitate to denounce us to the Vopos." Max nodded and she climbed out of the car.

She disappeared into the building. Max thought about that and began to get nervous. This was the first opportunity she'd had to leave him. If she were working against him, this would be her first chance to telephone, to call for help. . . .

180

Just then Johanna emerged, buttoning her white cardigan against the chill. Her blue print dress whipped around her legs in the wind, and she jumped back in the car. Her bun had unraveled a bit. She reached up and loosened her hair, and it all fell down; long, luxuriant, and fresh-smelling. Her cheeks were red from the cold.

She combed out her hair with her fingers and explained what had happened in the shack.

"Joachim wasn't happy about ferrying us in the cold, but I told him that you were taking me to Berlin for the evening." She grimaced. "He still remembers from twenty years ago that Mother saw Americans, so he's not surprised. I told him you were my chauffeur, that a general was waiting."

Max looked at her. "You lie with great facility, Fräulein Koch." He was amused.

She glared at him. "The stakes are high, Max. And besides"—she softened her look—"in a way it's true."

Joachim stumped out of his shack. He was bundled to the eyebrows in oilcloth and wool, a thick watch cap pulled down over his head. Huge sea boots splattered mud as he trudged up to them. Max had thrown a blanket over Wilson and now rolled down his window. A heavily gloved hand came through, palm up. Max looked at Johanna.

"He wants the fare for the ferry," she said in English. Max dug out his wallet. It seemed years ago that he'd hurriedly stuffed some marks into it, but it had been only that morning. He gave Joachim ten marks. The hand didn't move. He added another ten and it slowly withdrew. He didn't look up at Joachim, and Joachim simply stuffed the money into his nor'easter. He shuffled down the hill to the ferry.

Max eased the big Ford onto the little ferryboat. It took up almost all the available space, so Joachim had to perch on the front fender as he steered the ferry across the river.

Once away from the shore, Max shut off the car engine and the sputtering of the boat's old outboard motor was the only sound. The inky water of the Elbe seemed to suck sounds into itself, just as it seemed to absorb the starlight. The wind shoved them downstream and tilted the boat. Max grew cold at the thought of being in that menacing water. He looked at Johanna.

She was staring up the wide river. In the distance lights glimmered from the endless stream of river barges. The water slapped against the flat sides of the old ferryboat. In the hush of the Ford's cockpit, Wilson's ragged breathing was loud, but Hansi seemed not to notice it. The faint light painted her in creamy colors, accentuating her smooth skin and washing her long hair in shimmering, muted highlights. Her lips were slightly parted as she gazed into the middle distance. Max saw a tiny tear in the corner of her left eye and felt his breath catch. She turned to look at him and smiled faintly at his expression.

"What's wrong, Max?" she asked softly.

Max shook his head and looked out the windshield.

"Oh . . . nothing, I guess. I was just thinking how crazy all this is."

She frowned. "Crazy? How?"

He turned to face her. "Well, just look at the facts. They're crazy enough. We haven't seen each other in twenty years, and within an hour of meeting we're running like scared rabbits from people neither of us knows. *That's* crazy."

Hansi was silent for a moment. When she spoke, her voice cut like steel.

"You're wrong, Max. It's not crazy. At least not any crazier than anything else in the world. And we are not like rabbits; we have free will—we *choose* to run. Besides, the people chasing us—I know them if you do not. They are the scum of the country, soulless little men who take pleasure from the power they have over others. I know them, all right. I know their filthy habits and ugly minds. I have felt their hot breath on my face as they used me like a mindless vessel for their twisted fantasies and I have waited for a day such as this—a day when I would finally be able to escape them." She was breathing hard when she finished.

Max reached over and touched her quivering, clenched fist.

"I'm sorry, Johanna. I keep forgetting that your last twenty years haven't been like mine. It would have been a lot different if . . . if my father could have married Gisela."

She relaxed slightly. "Yes . . . much different. But we shall never know, now. My mother . . . Gisela never recovered from it. Never got over your father. I remember him only as an Ami giant, fierce-looking and strange. But she loved him. She told me everything about him, time and again. Did Eric . . . did he ever speak of her?"

Max watched the sluggish river for a moment before he answered.

"No. After that last day at the castle he never again mentioned her name. Never even talked about the castle."

She was silent a moment, studying him.

"He married again? An American?"

Max nodded. "Yes."

"What is she like, your stepmother?"

"She's years younger than he is—only a little older than me, actually. But built like a movie star, properly obedient, and knows all the right tricks for a company president's wife." His voice was brittle.

"Forgive me, Max, but I don't know so much about American companies. If Eric Moss is a president, does that mean he is its chief?"

Max laughed. It was a harsh bark.

"Chief, hell. He owns the damned thing. Or at least he did, last time I checked. But that was almost five years ago."

Hansi was startled. "You haven't spoken with your own father in five years? Why?"

"It's not easy to explain. Ever since I was a kid, we've had terrible fights over just about everything. The last argument was when he wanted me to work for his company. His goddamned supersecret multimillion-dollar company." He spoke the last words through gritted teeth.

Joachim's outboard droned wearily in the silence that ensued.

"Would that have been so bad, Max?"

He grimaced elaborately. "In a word, yes. Very bad."

183

"But . . . why?"

"Well, because I—that is, he . . . oh, hell. Why do you care about all this, Johanna?"

She moved uneasily in the big bucket seat.

"I didn't mean to pry, Max. It's just that you seem a lot like the way my mother described your father."

He laughed unpleasantly and looked away. "Do I? Maybe that's the problem."

She shrank into her seat. Far away, a river barge sounded its horn. The far shore was coming closer.

"You know, Hansi, in a way we're both victims."

"Why do you say that, Max?"

"Think about it. If it weren't for my father, neither one of us would be here tonight. He refused to believe Gisela when she denied that she was an East German agent. And he refused to let me lead my own life. As a result we're both fugitives. If he hadn't—"

She slapped her hand down hard on the seat. The report echoed loudly in the cockpit and Max jumped.

"*Nonsense,* Max. Can you really believe that? There are always choices open to us. My mother could have done exactly as they told her. Instead she chose to oppose them. And I could have . . . well, many times I had the chance to end my life as a prisoner in the castle. But the price was too high, and in the end, no matter how much I wanted my life to be over, no matter how many times I told myself that it was all for nothing, that no one cared whether I lived or died, I chose not to become like them. You hear, Max? I *chose* not to. Unless you are bound hand and foot, you are never completely a victim. Except, perhaps, of yourself." Her angry, narrowed eyes glinted in the nav-system light.

Stung, Max grew angry, too. "Can you deny that it was my father's affair with Gisela that led the Vopos to regard you as a prisoner? What were your choices after *that?*"

"No. I cannot deny that. But they would have done the same had your father been anyone else from the West. Surely you see that?"

"Maybe," he grunted.

She touched his hand, her anger gone. "You cannot blame your father for everything, Max, just as I can't blame Wolf Koch for my misfortune. Was your life with your father so terrible that you must drag it with you into the present?"

Max laughed humorlessly.

"Exactly the words of the psychiatrist I went to in college, Johanna. He told me I was suffering from a well-known syndrome. He called it the Great-Man Syndrome. According to him, fathers who drive themselves to big achievements usually have two kinds of sons. Those who go crazy trying to overachieve and those who go crazy trying to underachieve. Filial rivalry, he called it. And"—he laughed harshly again—"and you know what he prescribed? He told me to talk to my old man about the problem."

"And did you?"

"Yes. I went home on term break, we took a fishing trip, and I told him all about it."

"What did he say?" Johanna asked cautiously. She could hear the suppressed fury in Max's voice.

Max put both hands on the leather steering wheel and squeezed hard.

"Why, he just laughed. And then he told me to stop wasting time on head doctors."

"That's . . . that's all he said?"

"That's all."

They were silent. The shore was very close. In a few moments they'd be running for their lives again.

Johanna touched his sleeve.

"Max . . . I'm sorry. I thought you were just being—"

"Childish? Immature? Hell, Hansi, so have I, all through the last ten damned years. Sometimes I thought I'd go crazy if I even thought about it. But sometimes—most of the time, really—it's okay. All in perspective—just a little family problem, that's all. Sometimes." He fell silent.

She shivered. Eric Moss was ten thousand miles away

and, for them both, far removed in time. But he had the power to move them.

"Max, I'm cold. Can you turn on the heater?"

Relieved, Max leaned forward to switch on the engine. He was sweating, despite the cold. He hated talking about his father even more than he hated thinking about him.

Joachim nearly jumped into the water when the Ford rumbled to life. He cast a hooded glare at them and sat back down.

All at once the eastern shore of the Elbe was at hand. Max flicked on the headlights to help Joachim steer the boat, and within seconds they were bumping into the rotting wooden ramp on the weed-choked shore. Joachim jumped onto the jetty and tied the boat's lines to a post. He waved Max on vigorously. Max engaged first gear and cautiously edged onto the ramp. The tires spun for a moment and the boat jerked against the restraining line.

A little way up the road, Max coasted to a stop and looked over at Johanna. She was chewing her lip pensively, concentrating on the electronic map on the nav-system CRT. After a moment she glanced at Max and then pointed to the screen.

"Look, Max, this is how we shall go. From here to the center of Potsdam is about eighty kilometers. The fastest way would take us on the main road through Rathenow, but there is a restricted zone there. You know that?"

Max shook his head. Wilson knew, but he was in no condition to tell.

She continued, frowning at the screen as she laid out their route.

"So we must use these roads." She traced the faintest lines on the CRT, the ones that indicated roads barely better than cart tracks. "It will take us longer. The Vopos will probably expect that after they find out that you used Joachim's ferry; they will be sure then that I am helping you. What they will not expect is that we will travel sometimes on farm roads. From *here* to *here,* for instance." She indicated a ten-kilometer stretch between towns with no connection on the map.

Max raised his eyebrows.

"How is it that you know these little tracks and they don't?"

She grimaced. "I may have been born a spy's child, but I was brought up a country baroness' daughter. As a child I got to know every farmer within twenty kilometers, and sometimes, when I thought I would go mad if I spent another minute in that accursed castle or gatehouse, I would make Rudi—or the ones before him—take me for long drives. Usually we would take these tiny dirt roads near the fields. They were . . . they are peaceful, unchanging."

Max glanced at the clock: 1809. Just after six. They had to keep moving. He reached over and gripped her shoulder. She was slumped in her seat, staring out the side window.

"Hansi . . . which way now?"

She blinked. "I'm sorry, Max. But this has been so . . . sudden. I can't get used to it. To the idea that it's all behind me now."

He checked the gauges and said grimly, "Maybe it is. But maybe it isn't. Don't get too emotional yet. I need you." He jerked his thumb over the seat toward Wilson. "*We* need you. And we've still got more than fifty miles to go before Potsdam. And, Hansi . . . even there . . ."

She turned away. "I know. Even there they may not give me asylum. Let's go." She sat rigid in her seat. She looks, thought Max, every inch an aristocrat. And every inch someone he could—no. No time even for the thought. Not now.

He slipped the shift lever into first and gently eased out the clutch. The engine coughed once and then pounded out its beat. He shifted into second smoothly, his eyes searching far down the overgrown road, when a sudden *bang* came from the rear of the car and the wheel was nearly wrenched from his hands. The car tried to slue into the left bank. He knocked the shifter out of gear and gently applied the brakes, steering into the skid. In a moment the car was stopped. They were only inches from the dirt bank.

187

He sat frozen at the wheel. The second he'd heard the sound, he had known the cause. He blinked sweat out of his eyes and quickly reviewed possible solutions.

Johanna released her grip on the grab rail on the dash.

"What happened?" she asked shakily.

"Tire," said Max. "Blown tire. Left rear."

She relaxed. "Oh, then all you must do is mount the—"

"—spare. Wrong. There isn't a spare." In his mind he saw himself heaving the spare tire out with the tools and rifles back in the field where all this had begun. His mind looped back and forth through the scene. If only he'd known. If only he'd—if only. If.

For the first time, Johanna's voice echoed real fear.

"Max . . . without a spare, how can we go on?"

He felt his mind begin to paralyze his body. He had to do something. Anything.

"I don't know," he mumbled. "I just don't know. Maybe there's some way." Before he could be completely immobilized, he jerked open the door and climbed clumsily out.

He stumbled back to the trunk and punched the lock button. It creaked up and the light snapped on. He stared at the green body bag and its dreadful contents. It lay grotesquely twisted around the things he hadn't been able to throw out. The silver helmet and black box lay wedged in a corner. His eyes took in every inch of the feebly lit trunk, scanning it automatically while he stood numbly.

Then he saw it. A large aerosol can jammed behind the body. It took a second for the idea to form, then his hand was digging frantically. He shoved the pilot's body out of the way and held the can up to the light.

The paralysis drained away as he read the label. There was a chance after all. A slim one, but . . .

Quickly he knelt and examined the damaged tire. He found the place, just above the ground, where the big nail had penetrated. He wiggled it and drew it out.

Then he screwed the threaded cap of the aerosol can onto the tire valve. The can hissed and grew cold in his hand. Seconds later, the carcass inflated again. He held the can until it stopped hissing, then unscrewed it. He listened carefully to the tire; there wasn't any telltale leakage. He rocked back on his haunches and thought about his luck. So far, it had been almost incredible. He might easily have thrown out the can with the other things.

Johanna called to him. "*Max.* What's happening?" Her voice was high and nervous.

He threw the empty can into the trunk and jumped back into the car.

"It wasn't punctured?"

He shook his head while he buckled his harness tight.

"No, it was blown, all right. But somehow your guardian angel left us a can of tire sealer. We can go on." He saw her smile and looked a warning at her. "Those things work for only a couple of hours at best. But not at high speeds. So we've got to make it soon, or we won't make it at all."

She nodded, and he gingerly pulled out of the dirt. It was six-fifteen. The full moon was rising. They had lost more precious time. The Vopos could be right behind them.

The skin on Max's neck was crawling as he swung the Ford into the darkened village of Wulkau a few moments later. He drove slowly past the silent houses, his nerves screaming for speed. He held himself in check until they were clear of the town. But when Hansi pointed their way at the crossroads, his foot slammed down on the throttle pedal and the Ford engine bellowed across the dark German countryside.

21

KOSHKA WAITED FOR STACHEL AND MÜLLER AT
the ferry. The helicopter squatted in a small field near the
Havelberg road. The ferry was lit brilliantly by three banks
of floodlights. The ferryboat itself stood at the wharf, the
local traffic still trickling onto it. Four small cars stood on
the decks, and a score of passengers warily watched the
Vopo cars rush up.

Stachel stepped out of his Mercedes as Müller ran up.
Together they walked over to Koshka, who was standing,
blank-faced, with the ferry policeman. Obviously an old
cop, the Vopo had the studied weariness of a man who's
seen it all.

Stachel puffed to a halt a few feet from Koshka and
the guard. When he had regained his breath, he said,
"Well, Comrade Colonel? Have they—"

"No," said Koshka. "Sergeant Dinckel here says that
no car fitting our description has passed through since
dark. He also says that there is a much smaller, older ferry
a few kilometers downriver which they could have used.
Do you know anything about that, Stachel?"

Stachel kept his face composed.

"Of course, Comrade Colonel. However, I did not expect the American—"

190

"There is no time for this, Stachel." To Müller, Koshka said, "You will board this ferry at once and try to intercept the American. He is obviously being aided by the Koch woman, who must have a detailed knowledge of the area." Koshka swung back to Stachel. He was tense as a quivering bowstring. "And you, Stachel, will cross on the smaller ferry. I will patrol with the helicopter a few kilometers on either side of the two ferries and then go across the river. There will not be much traffic tonight; I will check every car I see from the air. And"—he stabbed a long, bony finger at Stachel—"you will *now* call for roadblocks on the highways ahead. They cannot be more than a half hour from us. I have already alerted my troops and military police in the Rathenow area. So they must be between us."

Müller ran off to his car, and Koshka stepped up to Stachel. Koshka was a few inches shorter, but he seemed to loom over the big man. He grabbed a fistful of Stachel's long brown greatcoat. "Stachel, don't ever try anything like this again." His voice was death. He shoved the German away and spun on his heel. In a moment he was in his helicopter, engines whining and the five big rotor blades starting to spin.

Stachel staggered back to his Mercedes. His driver wisely kept his eyes averted and said nothing.

"To Joachim's ferry, and quickly," wheezed Stachel.

There was no more time.

Koshka used the remote control to aim the two big spotlights at the riverside. They flew at about 150 kilometers an hour, tracking along the shore only fifty meters above the black, rushing water. The blaze of the blue-white spots reduced the scenery to a series of stroboscopic images. In the distance appeared the little ferry building with its single bulb, and Koshka motioned to the Ukrainian, Vanya, to investigate. They circled the little shack twice, his lights playing on the weathered wood. The boat was gone.

He pointed to the water. Vanya nodded and the big

gunship moved out across the river. Halfway to the other side, Koshka caught sight of something in the water. He swiveled his lights and illuminated a tiny old ferryboat; a dark figure was seated on one side. It was chugging along very slowly. The man on the boat jumped when the blinding lights struck him and he shielded his eyes. Koshka switched on the radio, called Stachel, and told him to interrogate the boatman. Then he ordered Vanya to head east across the river.

Stachel was waiting when Joachim's little boat *thunk*ed into the ancient jetty. Joachim stared up at the black Mercedes suspiciously. But before he could finish tying up his boat, the Mercedes was on the ramp. A moment later, it was aboard. Stachel's electric window buzzed down and he waved to Joachim.

"Well, Joachim, business is good tonight, I see."

Joachim said nothing.

"Who wants to use your little boat on a cold night like this, eh?"

Joachim tugged at his watch cap and still said nothing.

Stachel's voice turned to ice. "Now, listen, Joachim. I have little time. First you will cast off and take us to the other shore. And on the way you will tell us about those you took over earlier. Understand?"

The old man bobbed his head up and down and untied the boat. He reversed the outboard and they moved out into the Elbe.

By the time they bumped into the east-side jetty, Stachel knew everything. Joachim had thought the Koch woman was simply consorting with Americans. To old Joachim, the events of two decades ago were clearer than those of yesterday, and he well remembered an earlier American visitor to Schloss Falkenberg. To Stachel, however, Joachim's story proved that Johanna Koch was actively helping the American.

Stachel considered the implications. As far as he was concerned, it was a far more serious matter that she defect than that the Americans recapture whatever had been in their A-10. He thought back on the Party functions that he had been to in the Falkenberg castle. With her mother, Johanna had presided over them these last years, coldly and efficiently. And had heard and seen enough . . .

Had heard enough to wreck their apparatus completely. He cursed Wolf Koch. Why had that soft-minded bungler married an aristocrat? And why had he sired such a she-wolf?

Just then the Mercedes whirred to life and his driver pulled onto the road. He stopped and asked for the director's instructions.

Grimly, Stachel told him as he buckled his seat belt. "Straight ahead to Wulkau. And drive as though your life depended on it."

Responding to the gravity of Stachel's mood, the driver nodded and booted the 4.5-liter Mercedes V-8 into full cry.

Koshka watched the road unroll beneath the helicopter and tried to make it agree with the map he was holding. The turbines whined behind him as Vanya held the gunship to a speed of 120 kilometers an hour. They were flying barely above the trees. Koshka would have liked to fly higher to get a longer view, but he was afraid the American—who was proving to be very cagey—would hear him first and so switch off his lights. The only alternative was to fly low.

They came to an intersection. The little road from the ferry crossed a main highway and railroad, then joined a smaller north-south highway near Wulkau. Koshka recognized the major road as one that led directly to the Rathenow military reservation. He ordered Vanya to hover while he oriented himself.

There were three ways the Americans could have gone. Southeast, smack into the arms of his troops. Northeast, away from Potsdam into a barricade fifty kilometers up the main road. Or on a smaller road that went in a generally east-and-south direction. Koshka could check only one at a time. He traced the southernmost route on his map. It wandered across a marshy zone twenty-five kilometers wide, unusually bare of towns and people. The other way twisted and turned through some small villages, foothills, and forests, then rejoined a main highway fifteen kilometers east.

A truck sped north below them, its driver turning his face into the lights of the hovering helicopter. It was a Soviet soldier. He betrayed no surprise at their presence above the crossroads.

Koshka made up his mind. The American could not risk encounters with soldiers. He would steer northeast, away from Rathenow.

The Russian colonel spoke into his microphone and Vanya lifted the chopper up and flew along the northern road.

Six minutes later, Stachel's Mercedes halted at the village crossroads in a shower of gravel. Karl Stachel did not need a road map to tell him where he was, but he faced the same dilemma.

Would the American go south through the restricted zone? Not likely. If he didn't know the danger of that, the Koch woman would.

North? No. She would also know about the Vopo barracks at Kyritz.

That left the two smaller roads. The advantage of the northernmost road would be the little towns that were strung along it. Johanna Koch would have friends in those towns. She was from an old family, respected still in this backward area. Joachim's reluctance to talk reminded him of that.

But that way led away from their goal. They were both desperate to get to Potsdam. The American had a fast car, and they would be willing to gamble on that.

Stachel pulled on his goatee nervously. The seconds ticked by while he struggled with the alternatives. The radio crackled in a burst of static, relaying an unintelligible message.

He made up his mind. He tapped the driver on his shoulder and pointed across the intersection to the southern road. The driver pushed the throttle down hard.

Seven miles away, Max Moss hurled the Ford around a right-hand turn and saw the lights of a roadblock less than a half mile away.

22

THE MOMENT HE SAW THE RED-AND-WHITE POLE across the road, Max killed the lights and slammed into a screaming bootleg turn. He was less practiced than Wilson, but he did well; the car squealed around and in a few heartbeats they were thundering away from the roadblock. His eyes strained to pierce the darkness, relying on his memory and the weak light from the rising moon to guide them. After almost a mile he spotted a break in the marshy ground and low scrub, and dove into it. He reversed the car and they sat without lights a few yards from the road.

He was breathing heavily, Johanna saw. His narrow face was pale and drawn, and his eyes flicked left and right to scan the road, the moor, the sky. He couldn't be much younger than Eric Moss had been when he'd met Gisela, she thought. Except for the too-ready, too-cynical half smile, he seemed much like the man her mother had spoken of. As if reading her thoughts, Max grinned lopsidedly and said, "Well, that tears it. Know any way around the boys up there?"

She shook her head. "This marsh extends for a long way. The only really solid ground is five kilometers on either side of us."

Max looked at the steering wheel, thinking hard. Suddenly a bleak smile appeared on his face.

"Say," he said, "do you think those people up the road are German or Russian?"

Johanna thought hard. She had caught only a glimpse, but . . .

"Russian," she said. "The Vopos don't have gray trucks, and I think I saw a gray truck."

Max nodded.

"Good. Listen, roll down your window and tell me if you hear anything." She did as he asked, and Max reached over to the dashboard and flipped up a toggle switch. A blue light glowed. She looked at him.

"Ready?" he asked. She nodded.

Max squeezed the steering-wheel triggers and spoke softly into the horn-ring microphone. "One, two, three, four, five."

Johanna turned back to him.

"Your voice is coming from outside the car. How—"

"A public-address system. Built into the grille. I don't really know why the car has it, but I'm glad it does. Might give us a chance."

"How?"

"Well, we can't go back and we can't go around. That leaves only the roadblock. And since we're not likely to be able to shoot our way through, we'll have to talk our way through."

She stared at him, uncomprehending.

He chuckled, his eyes glowing in the dim light thrown by the nav map.

"Don't I look like a captured Russian officer to you?"

The captain in command of the Rathenow roadblock had just telephoned about the strange sighting of a few moments before when headlights once again appeared down the road. He hung up quickly and shuffled his men back into position. He checked the barrier and unholstered his Makarov 9-mm pistol.

The headlights drew nearer. The high beams were on, and they couldn't see the car or the driver. The Russian captain wished he'd had time after the alert to collect a powerful searchlight. He held a hand over his eyes and tried to make out the car.

It stopped not fifty meters away. He ordered his troops to cock their weapons. He began to shout through his loudspeaker, but was interrupted by a whistling and crackling from the car.

A man spoke, the sound magnified by a powerful public-address speaker. The man was speaking Russian, the captain heard with shock. He lowered his megaphone and listened.

"Comrades, this is Major Dmitrov. The Americans have captured me. They are holding a gun to my head as I speak to you."

One of the men looked back at the captain, wonderment on his peasant face.

The voice boomed out again. The captain detected a Byelorussian accent.

"They will kill me, Comrades, unless you allow them through. They are desperate men. But they do not know that we can capture them anytime—" The voice broke off. Muffled grunts and thuds came from the loudspeaker. The captain's men raised their weapons.

The voice returned.

"Comrades, let them through. My life is worth nothing, but we may gain much if I am able to personally interrogate them when they are finally captured."

There was a pause. The PA buzzed and cracked again.

"Do not shoot, Comrades. I order it."

The PA clicked off and the car began to inch forward.

The Soviet captain chewed his lip. He had been told to stop the Americans at all costs. The order had been explicit. But that order had said nothing about a captured Russian major. And how could he risk a hostage—especially one who outranked him? The voice had had the tones of command in it. To Russian ears, those tones spoke of high connections, of Party membership and influential friends. The captain was from the rural region of Soviet Georgia. His parents were farmers, and he considered himself lucky to have finally made it to the point where he could even consider successful application to the Party.

He waved the men away from the barricade and ordered them to lower their weapons. He personally lifted the barricade rail, then stepped back and holstered his pistol.

Silently the soldiers watched as the car came into the zone of illumination thrown by their trucks' headlights. The dark-blue paint was muddy and scratched. The captain stared at the interior. The windows, he saw as the car accelerated past their checkpoint, were steamed over, but . . .

But the only passenger was a *woman*.

The Ford's tires spun as Max shifted into second gear. The captain shouted to his men to fire at the car, tearing his pistol from its brown leather holster. A few seconds later, ten Kalashnikov automatic rifles stuttered and his little Makarov barked. But the Ford had disappeared around a kink in the road.

A bullet *spang*ed off the trunk lid just as Max shifted into fourth. They were still accelerating, now doing over a hundred. Johanna sat frozen, her face a mask of fear. When he roared onto a straight, Max flicked off the PA system and the little blue light died. He was quivering. Sweat covered his face, but he was grinning.

Johanna unclenched her hands and said, "If I had known what you were going to do, I probably would have simply surrendered." Her face was ashen. "You are either very brave, Max, or very, very sure of yourself."

Max wiped a hand across his face.

"I wasn't any more sure than you were. But it seemed that we had to do something. We couldn't just wait for them to get us." He kept his eyes on the road, and the speedometer needle hovered at 100. The air screamed past as they raced through the bleak landscape.

Johanna studied him in the darkness. Reflected light showed him tight-lipped, his jaw clenched. His eyes were narrowed, moving restlessly in a cyclic pattern: center of road, left side, right side, dashboard, center of road again.

She felt the car judder as it struck the bumps and holes in the badly surfaced roads.

"Where did you learn to speak Russian so well?"

Max didn't take his eyes off the road.

"Berkeley. I had a professor who had been in the Soviet Army. In fact, his name was Dmitrov before the CIA changed his identity. He taught me a lot more about the language than just how to conjugate the verbs." He fell silent as a series of bends appeared.

"Listen, do you think those people would have more than one roadblock along here?"

She shook her head.

"I don't think so. Not until we come to the junction of the autobahn, the E-fifteen. They will almost certainly have someone there. Why?"

Max glanced in the mirror.

"Because I'm going to have to start driving faster. It seems we've got company."

Johanna whirled and looked out the rear window. Behind them, the sky glowed with the glare of bright headlights.

Stachel listened with incredulity as the Russian captain hesitantly made his report. He peered out of the Mercedes window and, when the Soviet officer had finished, gave him a tongue-lashing that would last him for a long time. Disciplining Russian officers wasn't within his authority, but it made him feel better.

The American was now just slightly ahead of them. His ruse had allowed them through the checkpoint but had also allowed Stachel to close on them. The Mercedes screeched out of the roadblock and accelerated hard down the road.

In less than five minutes they caught a fleeting glimpse of the American's taillights on the horizon. The visibility had become excellent as the night winds cleared away the fog and mist, and the long, flat marsh road stretched with few bends to the junction at Friesack, twenty-five kilometers from the roadblock.

Stachel held on to the back of the seat while the driver hammered the big Mercedes along like a madman. The American had a fast car, thought Karl Stachel, but it had nothing on his special 450 SEL. He looked over the driver's shoulder and saw that they were doing over 240 kilometers an hour. The big black car rocked back and forth under the strain. Slowly the taillights ahead grew brighter.

Max darted a glance at the turboboost gauge. Even at maximum rpm, it was pumping out only five pounds per square inch of pressure. That explained why he could barely top 140. He cursed and remembered the damage to the radio. Rudi's bullet must have continued through the fire wall and ruptured the delicate turbo plumbing in the engine bay. It would take only a small hole for the turbo not to be able to produce the pressure. Since the engine wasn't running hot, Max figured that the leak must be on the exhaust side. He pounded the wheel in frustration, racking his brain for a way to produce more speed. He looked down at the tachometer. They were at 7,500 rpm. He shifted into fifth, then held his breath. The engine rpm dropped and they gained only another two miles an hour. The headlights in his mirror drew closer.

The road was a long, straight line, slightly lighter in the moonlight than the surrounding marsh. He shouted to Johanna over the roaring engine and the tearing wind.

"How far is the road like this?"

She tried desperately to remember. Then, cupping her hands around her mouth, she yelled back, "About fifteen or twenty kilometers, I think."

Max converted the figure in his mind. That meant he had a flat-out race of at least seven miles with whoever was back there. At this speed, no more than four minutes. He knew a junction was a few kilometers farther on, so there were some curves ahead. Curves he might be able to use. But first he had to stay ahead of the car behind him.

They hit a big bump only a fraction of a second after Max saw it in the headlights. The engine screamed in protest as the wheels spun in midair. The Ford lurched and shuddered as they crashed back down. They must have flown fifty feet. Johanna's hands were clamped around the grab rail. Her face was white, eyes wide.

A few seconds later, Max saw the car behind him shoot its lights into the air and then immediately down again. He'd hit the bump, too. They were closer than he'd thought. They had to have at least ten miles an hour on him.

The road was too narrow for a bootleg turn, and there wasn't enough of a shoulder for fancy off-roading. If he so much as dropped a wheel off the road into the soggy marsh, they'd flip instantly. He sweated while the options came and evaporated in his mind. Nothing seemed to be workable. He hunched his shoulders and pushed harder on the gas pedal. And the headlights pursuing him began to illuminate the inside of his car.

Stachel strained to see through the dirty windshield. They had closed to within a hundred or so meters of the American. A thin trail of whitish smoke was emerging from his exhaust pipe.

He saw that it was a Potsdam car. A Ford. Stachel was briefly puzzled. Those Fords were turbocharged, potent vehicles. They had been clocked at over 280 kilometers an hour in chases with his men. And yet this one was being caught. Ah—the white smoke. The engine was not so healthy.

Stachel reached into the door panel and withdrew a 9-mm Stechkin pistol. Balancing against the violent movements of the Mercedes, he screwed a long wooden stock into the grip and slid a twenty-round magazine into the butt.

"Hans," he yelled to his driver. "Pull up as close as you can."

Inexorably, the black Mercedes closed on the Ford's tail. The headlights lit the interior of the American car in a merciless glare. Max thought feverishly about the car behind him. What would they do? There had been no question that the Soviets would have shot them at the roadblock. The articles of the Potsdam agreement were clearly being ignored tonight. Would the occupants of the car behind him try to force him off the road or simply pump bullets into the Ford?

Through gritted teeth, he yelled to Johanna, "Get down, Hansi. They'll probably try to shoot into the gas tank."

She nodded and sank lower into the seat. Its foam and fiberglass would be of little use against bullets. But it helped psychologically.

Max could see now that the car behind him was a late-model Mercedes sedan. Obviously a 450, he thought, and railed at himself for automatically identifying the marque at a time like this. Frantically, he sought a trick that would gain them some space on the road.

The Mercedes was now almost to his rear bumper.

Stachel waited to run his window down until the last second. Then he told the driver to ease to the left slightly, and he touched the window button.

Instantly, the Mercedes was filled with noise and howling wind. The two cars were so close together that they buffeted each other. Stachel had to hold on with one hand while his driver tried to ease up alongside the Ford. Karl inched over to the gaping window and steadied himself. He buckled the seat belt and used the shoulder strap as a grip for his left hand. He laid the stubby barrel of the automatic pistol on his left arm and aimed it out the window. The wind tore at it, nearly wrenching it from his grasp. Finally he was able to hold himself upright and aim. He slowly centered the head of the American driver in the Stechkin's sights.

Max noticed the Mercedes hanging on his left rear fender. They weren't trying to pass him; they were just trying to allow someone in the back seat to draw a bead. Suddenly the scene was familiar.

He was at Daytona. C. W. Highton had rammed his big Mercury right up against Max's Chevy, trying to pull a draft down the long straight. They had been doing better than 190 separately, but the peculiar effects of drafting—

of one car stuck right up the other's ass—added another ten miles an hour to their speed. Max's car had begun to vibrate badly, the engine well into the red zone. In his mirror he'd seen old C.W. grinning. If Max backed off, C.W. would shoot past him at the finish line. If he kept the throttle down, his motor would blow and C.W. could use the longer gearing of his big Merc to slingshot around him.

There had been only one thing to do. A trick nasty enough to have come out of the red dirt of the Arkansas half-mile racetracks.

Max had lifted his foot off the gas pedal frantically and then plunged it down again, simultaneously swerving right.

The effects on his car were minimal. The Chevy bobbed and weaved, then coughed and continued its high-rpm charge for the finish line.

But C.W.'s Mercury had been pulled into the low-pressure zone created by his swerve, and the Merc's front fender had lightly tapped the Chevy's rear quarter panel, causing Max to slide a little more. He corrected that easily, but C.W.'s car had begun a sharp, vicious spin into the guardrail. It was all over in fractions of a second.

The scene flashed through Max's mind. There was no guardrail here, but if he could make the German drop a wheel off the road, the effect would be the same.

He eased the wheel slowly left. The German edged over fractionally, then tightened the space between the two cars. Max noted the maneuver. The guy was good. The question was, had he ever raced on a dusty Southern bullring?

Max jerked the wheel to the right and lifted the gas pedal. The Ford's engine coughed hard and then everything happened at once.

The German tried to correct and just kissed Max's rear fender with his bumper. That threw the Mercedes off the crown of the old road, and the 450 SEL slued completely sideways. The driver overcorrected, spinning the wheel too far. The Mercedes whipped around and began sliding the other way, still traveling at over 120. The Ford stopped fishtailing and Max had just enough time to see what was happening behind him.

The German began a long, slow spin. A shot flashed wildly out the open rear window. The driver was trying desperately to keep the spinning car on the road; he knew what would happen if he fell off it. After nearly completing a full 360-degree spin, the Mercedes had sloughed off almost forty miles an hour. And then the left front tire blew.

The Mercedes plunged immediately backward off the road, still doing eighty. The rear end shot off the embankment and struck the stagnant water of the marsh. The car slowed another thirty miles an hour in less than fifty feet, smashing both occupants rearward. Stachel's finger jerked the trigger of the Stechkin and it fired all nineteen remaining rounds in a staccato burst. Then the Mercedes struck solid ground and it stopped dead, still aimed backward.

Max saw nothing but the Mercedes leaving the road in a whirl of spinning lights. His heart was pounding wildly. Thank you, C.W., wherever you are.

Johanna opened her eyes and looked over at Max. There was a hard, fixed smile on his face. He caught her eye and grinned wider.

"It's nothing," he yelled. "Just a little trick I learned at the University of Daytona."

Her expression matched her puzzlement. Max laughed and gripped the wheel harder.

Karl Stachel regained consciousness slowly. He was tangled in his harness. It was quiet. He opened his eyes painfully and looked around.

They were sitting in the marsh, upright. Acrid smoke filled the car and the dim headlights shone ahead to show that they were facing the road. Stachel was still holding his gun, but the shoulder harness he had been using as an armrest had nearly wrenched his arm from its socket.

He looked at the driver. The man was slumped against the wheel. There was blood all over the front seat and windshield. The driver's window was shattered, the door slippery with blood.

Stachel looked again at his Stechkin. He must have fired when they were spinning. He didn't remember. But he had killed Hans.

He disentangled himself from the seat belt and shoulder harness. The car rocked slightly as he moved. It made oozing sounds. Stachel unlocked his door and tried to open it. It was jammed. He sat back a little way and kicked it. After three tries it popped open.

The water was less than half a meter deep. It hardly reached their hubcaps. Underneath, he could hear the water sizzling as it came into contact with the hot exhaust pipe and engine.

He pulled open the driver's door. The driver fell out, his head an unrecognizable pulp. Stachel tore off the man's jacket and shirt and wiped down the seat and door. He dragged the body away from the car. Before he got in, he listened briefly to the fading snarl of the Ford.

He remembered the black-haired head in his sights.

We are not done yet, clever American.

He turned the key and the engine groaned to life.

Not yet.

23

MÜLLER HAMMERED HIS LITTLE BMW ALONG the autobahn as fast as it could go. The blue police light on his roof whirled and the siren wailed. The drivers of the few cars on the E-15 autobahn saw him from far away and obediently moved over. He slowed as he passed each one, and his assistant played the spotlight over the cars. So far, only frightened East Germans.

Koshka had radioed to order him to the junction a few kilometers ahead. Evidently the Russian colonel hadn't had any luck, either.

The junction appeared out of the gloom and Müller braked to a halt. There were about a dozen cars on either side of the roadblock. A Soviet tank stood on the median, and about fifty Soviet military policemen were inspecting each car. Müller pulled out of the line and rolled slowly up to the barricade. The officer in charge—a major—eyed his car and nodded curtly as Müller got out.

"Any luck?" Müller asked in German.

The officer shook his head.

"We've been here half an hour. Nothing since Captain Zhulov called to report the American had broken through his roadblock."

Müller looked down the dark road that led to the unfortunate captain's barricade.

"That's the only road, Major. If they're still alive, they will come that way."

Müller turned and squinted at the officer.

"Why don't you send a patrol down there?"

The major shook his head.

"First, because I've no orders to. Second, because I don't have enough men."

Müller looked at the soldiers standing around with nothing to do but glare menacingly at the frightened travelers. How many men did the major think he needed to stop a lone American?

Müller pursed his lips. "Hmm. I see your point. However, while we wait for Colonel Koshka I can certainly make a short reconnaissance down the road."

Müller shut off the roof light and drove around the traffic, through the raised barrier and down onto the little road. The autobahn formed an overpass over it. Concrete ramps led in a half cloverleaf to the narrow gravel road below. He looked out into the darkness. There were about five kilometers of gentle curves to Klessen, then a long, winding stretch to Neuwerden.

Müller drove slowly down the road for a couple of kilometers. He rounded a tight curve. Suddenly a black shape emerged from the darkness ahead and roared past him. He was so startled he ran his white BMW off the road, sticking its blunt nose into a weed-covered bank.

Müller cursed and jammed the gearshift into reverse. The lever grated and juddered but wouldn't engage fully. Furious, Müller revved the engine and the gear lever finally chattered into place.

He swung the BMW backward and turned around, the narrow tires squealing. He flipped on the blue light again and screeched off after the now-invisible American.

"Get on the radio and tell them up there what's happening," he told his assistant. The man jerked the microphone off the dash and began calling while Franz Müller drove for all he was worth.

It was just possible that the American could crash through the wooden barricades at the junction. The Russian tank was up above on the autobahn median strip. Only a few soldiers were waiting below. If the Ford suddenly appeared out of the darkness—as it had to him—the tank wouldn't be able to fire soon enough; the Ami could conceivably be through both barricades before the turret could be swiveled around.

The BMW engine whined and rattled as Müller kept his foot to the floor. The radio was blaring a babel of conflicting reports and orders. Ahead, just as he came around the last turn before the straight to the barricade, Müller caught sight of the still-blacked-out Ford just as it smashed the wooden rail to pieces. Soldiers fell to both sides, firing wildly, as the American car swerved under the autobahn and through the other barrier. Müller, sounding his siren to clear them out of his way, drove through the mess of splinters and confused men at more than 120 kilometers an hour. He cleared the other side of the underpass just as the tank fired a 120-mm high-explosive round at the disappearing Ford.

The explosion behind them lifted the rear of the Ford into the air for a moment and sent a shock wave through them, but Max held on and kept his foot down hard. The tank had gotten off a single lucky shot. Any luckier and they would be so much shrapnel.

Max skidded around a turn, and a high bank and trees shielded them from the intersection. He snapped on the lights again. If he hadn't tried blasting through without the lights, that Vopo would have blocked them for sure.

Johanna had bent down and buried her head in her arms on his orders as they approached the barricade. Now she looked up in time to see the lights go on.

"I . . . I didn't think you could do it," she said. Her voice was shaky.

Max blinked the sweat away.

"Neither did I," he said. "Never tried anything like that in my whole life."

She looked up, startled. When he'd explained after getting rid of the Mercedes how he expected to break through the barrier at the junction, she'd thought he'd done it all before. He'd spoken calmly and certainly.

"We've got another one on our tail," he said. "And now they all know exactly where we are. Any ideas?"

She studied the map display.

"We're on the back road to Nauen," she said after a moment. "There are six small villages to pass through in about twenty-five kilometers."

Max thought fast. The distance counter said they were thirty-four air kilometers from the mission. And on this road, say twenty minutes to do the sixteen miles to Nauen. He downshifted and slowed the Ford into a tight hairpin. They slid across some railroad tracks. Max darted a look along the tracks. They went straight for some distance.

"Does the railroad go to Nauen?" he asked.

She frowned. "Yes, I think so."

He stole a glance at the map display. It didn't show railroads.

They slued around another corner. Ahead, he could see the tracks again. He made up his mind.

"Okay," he yelled above the engine roar, "here's what we'll do. Those tracks head straight to Nauen. I'll bet anything on it. And screwing around on this road is only wasting time." He braked hard. "I think the wheel tread of the Ford is too narrow to allow us to straddle the tracks, but we can get one wheel over a rail. It's a good chance that they're all laid on flush cross-ties, so we won't hammer the suspension too badly. When we come to the crossing up there, I'm going to turn onto the tracks. Okay?"

She nodded and clamped both hands on the grab rail.

Then the tracks were just ahead, glinting in the headlights. He slammed on the brakes, gunned the engine hard, spun the wheel, and bounced across the rails. The wheels jerked back and forth for a moment, then settled on either side of the rails. His left wheels were outside the left rail, riding on the roadbed, and his right wheel was between the rails, riding on the cross-ties. The headlights showed the tracks going arrow-straight to the horizon. He accelerated and the car began to bump up and down slightly as the right wheels dug into the dirt between the cross-ties.

He grinned at Johanna.

"Looks like it's going to work. All we need to do now is avoid sidings and switches until we get to Nauen."

She tried hard to remember train trips down these tracks, but her mind was too confused. He interrupted her thoughts.

"While we've got a breather, have a look at Ike. We've taken quite a beating."

She unstrapped herself and examined Wilson while Max kept the car thumping along, half on and half off the tracks at a steady forty miles an hour.

Yuri Koshka heard the news as he was flying down the autobahn. The idiots had let them escape again. It had been so long since anyone had tried to break through a Soviet roadblock in Germany that they'd not expected it. It was clearly the result of too many years of peace.

He spoke with Müller on the radio, getting a fix on their location. They were headed toward Nauen on a slow, twisting road. Koshka smiled. Good. A helicopter could fly straight, whereas a car had to follow the winding path. He told the German to keep after them and signed off.

Vanya tugged on his blue sleeve and pointed at the dashboard. Koshka saw that they were running low on fuel. *Damn.*

"How could this happen?"

Vanya swiveled the mike down in front of his mouth.

"We have been flying for almost three hours, Comrade Colonel. Our endurance—"

"I know about our endurance. How much longer can we fly?"

Vanya pursed his lips. "About ten minutes, Colonel."

Koshka swore under his breath. Just when they were closing—but there was nothing for it. They must land.

"Where can we refuel?"

211

Vanya pointed northeast. "Oranienburg depot is about fifty kilometers that way."

Koshka shook his head. They would have to double back.

"Can we use jet fuel?"

Vanya nodded.

"Good. Then fly to Rathenow. There are short-field interceptors there. We can use their fuel, and it's only twenty kilometers away."

Vanya nodded again and swung the big helicopter around.

Koshka glared at the road below them as Vanya turned back. It's all up to you, Müller. The thought didn't give him comfort.

Müller slammed his BMW to a halt. In front of them stood an old tan Wartburg sedan, a blue light whirling on its roof. Two men stood behind it, pistols leveled. When they saw the car Müller was driving, they lowered their guns and looked puzzled. Müller leaped out.

"What's happening here? Who are you?"

The man on the left said, "Volkspolizei. We were mobilized by the Soviet—"

"And you haven't seen an American car?" Müller interrupted gruffly.

The man shrugged.

"No. That was who we thought you were."

Müller thought furiously. "What district are you from?"

The man flipped open his badge case.

"Nauen," he said.

Müller pounded his fist into his palm. There was no chance the American could have gotten by either of them on this tiny road. The only possibility was that he had turned off somewhere. But where? They couldn't have left the Nauen road. Müller paced nervously back and forth while the others looked on.

There had been no farm roads. No houses. Nothing on the road except railroad tracks. And a car couldn't use . . . . He froze in mid-thought. But, then again, maybe it could.

It was the only possibility.

"Where does the railroad cross the road past here?"

The Nauen Vopo frowned and said, "At Hertefelden. About ten kilometers. But—"

"Never mind." Müller jumped back into his BMW. "Just turn around and go back to Nauen as fast as you can. The Ami has passed us both. He's on the railroad tracks."

The Vopos stared in amazement. Müller jerked the BMW around the Wartburg and headed for the crossing at Hertefelden.

"Is he okay?" Max sounded worried.

Johanna sat back in her seat and raised her voice over the thumping of the tires.

"I don't know. He is very hot and still unconscious."

Max said nothing and looked down the tracks. Ahead, another small town was coming up. He'd already driven through two of them. This one should be the last. He prayed that the station would be as deserted as the others. He'd soon know. It was now only a quarter of a mile away.

Max switched off his lights. The noise of their passing was clue enough. No need to give them a nice, lit-up target. The distant fluorescent station lights twinkled off the steel rails. Max did not slacken his speed. They passed a signal in the open position. At least there were no sidings ahead to tear their wheels apart.

Johanna held her breath as they approached the station. The noise, the pounding, the relentless running, were fraying her nerves. She looked again at Max. He seemed calm. His smile was gone, but he didn't look worried. She envied his composure as her stomach churned.

Just as they were entering the station area the crossties gave way to built-up boarding. Made for the comfort of passengers, it now lifted the Ford onto a stable platform. The sudden cessation of the pounding made them aware of their growling exhaust.

They were at the edge of the platform when a pair of

lights appeared at the far end of the station. Max saw that a road crossed there. Someone was on the tracks, coming right at him.

Müller saw the blacked-out Ford in the light from the station lamps. His mouth set in a grim line and he turned onto the wooden platform bordering the rails. He flipped on his siren and blue light.

Max saw the light go on and a second later heard the siren. So it was a Vopo. He realized instantly what the man was trying to do. There wasn't enough room between the station platforms for a car to turn around in. The German was trying to play chicken with him. Trying to get him to stop. And once he stopped, there would be a hail of machine-gun fire. *Auf Wiederseh'n,* Max Moss and company.

Max knew his only chance lay in making the German flinch and move out of the way. But it seemed unlikely that he would; they had missed him too many times tonight already. The way that guy was barreling down at him, he meant business. Max reached for the headlights and hesitated.

They *did* have a weapon.

He told Johanna to get down again before he floored the gas pedal.

The two cars rushed at each other, both accelerating. The stanchions of the station platform flashed by as Max gained speed.

At two hundred yards, Müller told his assistant to ready the gun.

At one hundred yards, Müller realized the American wasn't going to stop.

At fifty yards, Max snapped on the entire bank of seven high-power headlights.

Müller screamed, blinded. The white BMW plowed off to one side.

Max touched Müller's rear fender with his right front as he flew past. Müller's car jerked from the impact and spun like a toy into the opposite wall of the platform, still doing ninety. The BMW rammed a stanchion head-on and disappeared in a blinding flash.

214

Max slammed on his brakes and slid to a stop on the road crossing. He glanced back at the burning BMW, let out a long, shuddering breath, and looked down at Johanna, who was still covering her face.

He read the sign on the station.

"Welcome to Hertefelden, Fräulein Koch. Time to hit the road."

She looked up, her eyes wide in shock.

Max grinned and gunned the car back onto the highway.

24

"NO LUCK?" JACK MARTIN LOOKED UP AS Aldrich stepped into the room.

He shook his head. "No. No contact at all, Colonel."

Martin said nothing and sat back in his chair. Behind him, a fire snapped and popped in the mission's best fireplace.

Lieutenant Commander Bob Aldrich closed the door to the colonel's office and sat down. His normally cheerful expression was gone.

"How about the Germans? Are they saying anything?"

"Not since we picked up the garbled messages about a break through a couple of their roadblocks. They're still jamming us hard," Aldrich said.

Martin put his hands behind his head and sucked on his pipe. "Russians?" he asked.

"Same thing. A flurry of activity about an hour ago, then routine stuff."

Martin tapped his pipe on an ashtray.

"But those guys are still hanging around at the turn-off."

Aldrich nodded. "Right. Four Vopo cars and one unidentified armored personnel carrier. Czechoslovakian manufacture, but painted green and no insignia. Nobody's been seen to enter or leave it. Type-seven antenna on it, too."

Martin frowned. "Sounds like a command vehicle." He was silent a moment.

"What do you think, Bob?"

Aldrich leaned forward and rested his elbows on his knees.

"I think they're still moving, and pretty close. I think both the Soviets and the Germans have lost them. I think Ike is still rolling."

Martin filled his pipe again.

"Maybe so. But I'd feel a lot better if we'd been able to send an experienced team. Wilson is a fine man, but Moss . . . well, Moss isn't ready for this sort of thing."

Aldrich said nothing. Moss was still wet behind the ears. Saying otherwise would be wasted breath. But at least he was with the best driver in the mission.

Martin broke into his thoughts.

"You know, Bob, even though all the drivers are out, we can still give Ike a little help." His eyes glinted in the firelight. "How about sending a couple of Nubs's boys out on the entry road with the two Cherokees from the garage? Provide a little escort if need be. Maybe even do a little blockbusting."

Aldrich smiled. "Good idea. And I understand a couple of the radio guys have been itching to go to the local taverns. Tonight might be a good time for them to do it. They could start with the ones on either side of the turnoff. And it wouldn't surprise me a bit if they took turns staying in their cars. They might even let us know when Ike shows up, coming one way or the other."

Martin exhaled a cloud of aromatic pipe smoke. It reminded Aldrich of fumes from a burning orange warehouse that had been sprayed with rum. Martin laid his pipe on the desk and looked steadily at Aldrich.

"Do it," he said.

25

JOHANNA COULD SEE THAT MAX WAS BEGINNING to feel the strain. The nervous energy he seemed to thrive on had been exhausted. He blinked often, she saw, struggling hard to keep his vision clear. He needed it to negotiate the serpentine farm roads they had been twisting along for the last twenty minutes.

She was not a worrier by nature, but the closer they got to Potsdam, the more fantastic it seemed to her that they could ever make it. She had a healthy respect for the grim determination of her countrymen. And she knew the Russians never gave up. Besides, although Max almost certainly thought that they were after him, she had a marrow-freezing conviction that now it was her they were really after. She knew too much about the entire East German government, from the Central Committee to its espionage community. Only bits and pieces picked up from her habit of astute listening, but it would be enough. The Western intelligence people could make her pieces fit their jigsaw puzzle. And the Vopos knew that. She shivered.

Max barked a question and she shook her head to clear her tumbling thoughts.

"What, Max?"

Max didn't look over at her. They were speeding through a small town. Max had just passed a lumbering farm truck and the startled driver had nearly sideswiped them.

"I said, what do we do once we're through this village?"

Johanna looked at the map display. The car jounced and lurched. She had to steady herself to study the CRT.

"We will come to a lake—the Trebelsee—and a small town. The road will become a dead end; we'll turn left. The town is Zachow." She had to shout over the racket from the pounding engine.

"And how far is the mission from the village?"

She searched the screen. "The counter says twenty kilometers to the mission, but I can't find it on the map."

Max cursed himself. *Of course.* The inertial navigation system on the Ford wasn't programmed to pinpoint the mission on the map. So even though they knew how far away they were, he'd have to navigate them to Potsdam himself. He struggled to remember the twists and turns Ike had taken at noon. It wasn't easy—Ike had been trying to lose the Vopo tailing them.

"Listen, Hansi. Have you ever been to Potsdam?"

She nodded. "Oh, yes, many times."

"Do you know a new road—two lanes—called the Ulbrichtstrasse? It leaves the city, then goes under an autobahn and—"

"Yes, yes," she cut in excitedly. "It connects with the main road to the Trebelsee. Is the mission on that road?"

"No, but the access road joins the Ulbrichtstrasse at a T-junction. So if we can get to the Ulbrichtstrasse, we can find the mission road."

"Is the mission far from the junction?"

He shook his head. "I think it's about a mile. You can't see it from the main road."

Max fell silent. There would certainly be a roadblock at the junction. They wouldn't take any chances after they'd lost him twice. He pieced together his fragmentary memory of the junction. Fields on one side, forest on the other. He'd have to turn left onto the mission road.

Zachow appeared ahead. A sign warned him to slow to thirty kilometers. He ignored it. His headlights illuminated the village square. An old fountain stood in a small traffic circle. And in front of the circle was a blue Lada, the Soviet version of the Fiat 1500 sedan. It was blacked out. But there were two shadows behind it.

Max stamped on the brake pedal. The Ford's tires howled in protest. He saw a tiny alley leading off to the left. Still braking, Max twisted the wheel and eased up on the brakes, trying to slip into the alley.

He almost made it. The right front fender missed clearing the corner of the old house by an inch. The car smashed into the wall, rending sheet metal and crushing the right-side lights. He cranked the steering wheel the other way and gave the engine full power. The wheels spun on the wet cobblestones and filled the air with blue smoke. The car shoved its nose along the house, then broke free and roared down the little alley. A bullet ricocheted off the road where the Ford had been only a moment before.

Johanna looked on helplessly as Max raged down the alley. Ahead, in the lopsided light from the left headlight, she saw a brick wall twenty feet high. Max didn't slow down. As they rushed toward it she screamed and buried her head in her arms.

At the last second, Max hit the brakes and dove into another alley, on their right. An old moped stood outside a small door, blocking the way. Max set his mouth and smashed into it. It flew into the air and somersaulted over them.

Max kept the throttle down and saw the Trebelsee road ahead. He didn't wait to see if there was any traffic. He burst out from the alley and slid the Ford across the street, sideways. They bounced off a parked Borgward and accelerated down the street. In his mirror he could see the fountain and the Lada, still stationary. Then they disappeared as he rounded a curve. The lake appeared on his right. The road ahead was again empty of traffic.

Max looked down at Johanna. She was still clutching her head, eyes tightly shut. He reached over and laid a hand on her shoulder. She jumped at his touch, then raised her head.

220

"How . . . how did you know?" She was almost incoherent.

Max pointed to a stop sign as they rushed along the lake road.

"You Germans are compulsive about signs. If that alley had been a dead end, there would have been a sign there, don't you think?"

She started to answer, but he stopped her.

"More important is the fact that those guys will have told somebody where we are. I thought we might have been able to stay invisible for a little longer, but . . . " He didn't finish.

Koshka was only a few kilometers from Zachow when he got the call from the men at the square. Then he flipped on his intercom and told Vanya to bring the helicopter over the Trebelsee road at full power. The Ukrainian dipped the gunship's nose, changed rotor-blade pitch, and in a moment they were charging through the night at 270 kilometers an hour.

Koshka calculated on the map how far along the lake road the American would be. If he'd guessed right, in less than two minutes his lights should be visible.

It would soon be over. There was no escape for them this time. The roadblock at the mission turnoff was impregnable. And manned, this time, not by ignorant peasants but by his elite Technical Intelligence troops. Koshka allowed himself a smile. His superiors would be furious at him because of the chaotic way the operation had been handled, but they wouldn't say a thing when they got the vital equipment the American was carrying. Results mattered. Not agreements on paper. Let the diplomats send strongly worded notes. Russia needed the secrets of the A-10. And Russia would get them.

Through the panes of the gunship's cockpit, Koshka watched the lakeshore emerge from the darkness. He motioned to Vanya to gain altitude. The Ukrainian took the Mi-24 up until Koshka waved his hand. They were flying at five hundred meters. Koshka switched on the powerful spotlights under the cockpit and fixed them on the road below. He checked the ammunition feed to the single 30-mm gun in the nose.

The helicopter rose over a small hill. Ahead of them, Koshka saw taillights.

26

STACHEL LEANED ON THE HORN. THE EAR-SPLIT-
ting wail of the compressed-air trumpets joined the ululat-
ing warning of his siren, and the truck finally moved over.
He cursed and pushed the Mercedes' accelerator to the
floor. The wind from the open driver's window was freezing, but Stachel didn't notice it. All he saw was the Potsdam exit ahead.

Wrenching the steering wheel, he shot off the ramp
and past the cars parked at the light below.

He swore again, thinking of how the stupid Russian
captain had taken twenty minutes to drag the Mercedes
out of the marsh and replace a tire. The simpleton was not
content with having let the American through; he had to
waste Karl Stachel's dwindling time by allowing dullard
soldiers to fall all over themselves while they tried to get
his car out of . . .

He shoved the thought away. He had no time for recriminations, satisfying as they might be. He might not
have any time at all. If only the radio still worked.

Koshka no doubt imagined that he, Stachel, had been
eliminated from the chase.

The thought made him smile. He had a hunch.
Koshka would not get the American as easily as he
thought. If he'd used fifty helicopters, perhaps. But alone
. . . Karl Stachel had a feeling for the craftiness of the

American. They'd told him on the autobahn how the American had broken through their checkpoint. And how he'd not only evaded Müller but also managed to kill him. This was no ordinary Yankee. Koshka would find that out soon enough.

He wove through the sparse suburban Potsdam traffic, siren blaring. If he could get to the mission access road, he might have one last chance.

The American would somehow get through Koshka and his men. He would have to. Karl Stachel was betting his life on it.

27

THE ADRENALINE HIGH BEGAN TO FADE, AND MAX
felt the ache in his body return. His arms were leaden, almost too weak to turn the power-assisted steering wheel.
His legs trembled convulsively. A sharp pain in his neck
pulsed with every beat of his heart. He was tired.

Worse still, the car was tired. The wheels shimmied
badly, thrown out of alignment by the violent maneuvers
and the railroad ties. The orange LOW FUEL light kept flick-
ering, then stayed on. A battery connection must have
been nearly severed in one of their collisions because the
voltage output was weakening. The engine, miraculously,
still poured out its lusty power.

The trees along the lake whipped past as Max maintained their speed. The road was nearly straight.

Johanna slumped against the door, eyes closed. The
noise and the night enveloped them, and Max began worrying again.

Mostly he worried about the left rear tire. Chances
were that more evasive driving was ahead. More tire-pun-
ishing slides and stops. So far the sealant had worked well;
the only sign of the differences in pressure in back was a
slight greasiness on right-hand turns as the weight was

transferred to the left tires. But he knew the sealant shouldn't have lasted this long under these conditions. He chewed the insides of his cheeks nervously.

Johanna raised her head.

"Max, should I check Wilson?"

Max said, "Yes. He might need some more anesthetic."

She unbuckled the harness and climbed around in the big bucket seat. She reached back to tighten Wilson's straps and glanced out the back window. The lakeside was quiet. The red glow from the taillights was the only light. She reached down to feel Wilson's cheek. Then she looked up again. She stared hard out the window. The engine noise in the back seat was intense. The car rocked back and forth as they sped down the lakeshore road. She frowned, unsure of why she had looked up again. Something . . .

Then she saw it and her eyes widened. Far behind them, a piece of the landscape was lit up.

"*Max*. There's something coming up behind us."

Max darted a look into the mirror.

"What? Where—"

"Back about a kilometer. You see it? A bright light—"

"Oh, shit. They're using a helicopter on us." He watched in horror as the patch of illuminated road swiftly came up behind them.

"Johanna, get buckled in." He looked back to the front. They were racing through an industrial zone. Big buildings—warehouses—stood along the lakeshore. Ahead, there was an installation jutting out into the lake.

"Do you know what that is?" He pointed.

Johanna strained to see through the streaked windshield.

"I . . . I think it's a storage yard. Where the trains and trucks pick up produce from the river barges." Her voice was barely audible.

Max flicked a look back at the lights. The chopper was closing fast. He glanced at the speedometer. Now down to around 120. It wasn't enough. Even the slowest helicopters could better that easily.

He looked to the left. A maze of train tracks. They couldn't drive over there. It had to be the depot ahead.

"Brace yourself, Hansi. I'm going to break into that place ahead."

She stretched her legs against the fire wall and held on to the grab rail.

The chopper was now almost over them.

Max saw the entrance road to the depot. He held the throttle down as long as he dared, then hit the brakes. The tires shrieked. The car dove onto its nose. Max struggled with the steering wheel. The entrance rushed up to them, and then he let off the brakes. He pulled hard to the right and the car almost spun.

The Ford rocked up on its outside two wheels and Johanna screamed. Max bared his teeth.

"Come on, you son of a bitch, you can . . ." Then they were back on all four wheels and rocketing down the wide entrance to the depot.

Their lights illuminated a chain-link gate. A sleepy guard looked up when he heard the screeching tires. He stared into the glare of the lights, petrified. At the last moment, he jumped aside.

Max rammed the Ford right through the gates. They parted with a groaning crash and suddenly they were inside the depot's marshaling yard.

Koshka yelled, "*Look*, Vanya. Over there—*quickly.*"

The Ukrainian shouted a reply but it was lost in the whine of the turbines and the yammering of the rotors. He swung the big helicopter around to the depot.

Koshka aimed the lights at the Ford below.

"Take it down, Vanya. *Take it down.* We have them now."

They dropped as Vanya trimmed the rotor pitch. The huge helicopter looked like a dragonfly. Koshka sat in front of Vanya in a little bubble. The remote-control handles for the weapons were before him, a pair of handgrips. Vanya looked out through another canopy behind Koshka. This was the most potent gunship helicopter in the world, the Mi-24. NATO called it the Hind-D. Because he loved

227

it, Vanya called it his baby. And pitted against it was a battered American Ford.

Koshka pinned the Ford with the double spotlights. He switched on the external loudspeaker.

"You have no chance. You are *trapped*."

Max felt the air pound down from the big chopper's rotors. It sounded like someone bashing on an empty fifty-gallon oil drum. And felt worse. He slid the Ford around in a controlled spin, using the headlights to find a way out.

Johanna called out, "*Max*. Over there—an open door to a warehouse."

Max didn't hesitate. He slammed the Ford into gear and shot off toward the little door. It was about two hundred yards away.

The Fairmont bucked and heaved on the railroad tracks.

"Hang on, Johanna. We may have to turn away at the last second." Max set his jaw and steered straight for the door.

Vanya followed the Ford without Koshka's saying a word.

He turned off the PA system. All right, he thought. If you need convincing . . .

He squeezed the antitank gun's trigger.

Max almost lost control of the car as Koshka's high-explosive round smashed into the nearby asphalt. The detonation rocked the Ford, nearly overturning it. He held on grimly and drove for the entrance.

"*Vanya*. They're almost there. *More speed*."

The Ukrainian slammed the gunship forward. The big turbojets screamed.

Koshka carefully aimed the gun again.

Just as he was about to squeeze the trigger the blue car burst through the doorway into the huge warehouse.

* * *

228

Max locked up the brakes. He didn't know what was inside, so it was best to go slowly.

"Johanna, look for exits. We've got to find a way out of here. If we stay, they'll surround us."

She caught her breath and started peering around the dark building.

Max stopped and switched off the lights.

"Why did you . . ." she began.

Max pointed upward, and she saw the skylight. Overhead, the piercing spotlights of the Soviet helicopter probed down through it.

Max looked up and down the long, empty building.

The helicopter flew back and forth overhead like an enraged bumblebee. Its downdraft rattled the corrugated steel of the warehouse roof far below.

"This thing must be over two hundred feet long," Max said. He slipped the shifter into gear and crept forward.

Johanna plucked his sleeve.

"Look, Max—over there." She was pointing toward the water.

He stopped. A wharfside door stood open.

He grunted. "Great. Only thing is, it leads nowhere. Just out onto the dock." He kept going.

Koshka aimed the lights down through the translucent plastic of the skylight in frustration.

"*Vanya.* Did you see any exits?"

"No, Comrade Colonel."

"Can you drop down and fly along the walls?"

Vanya hesitated, calculating distances.

"I don't think so, Colonel. The buildings are too close together—"

"Yes, yes, I know," said Koshka. "Well, take it out a way and we'll look at the walls from a distance."

Vanya pulled the helicopter up and swung away.

Max held up his hand.

"Shhh—do you hear that?"

Johanna listened. "What?"

229

"The chopper—it's moving away."

"Are they leaving, Max?"

He shook his head. "No. They must be trying to have a look at the walls. Looking for where we'll come out." He was silent as the banging over their heads diminished.

A glimmer of light caught his eye. It was at the far end of the warehouse. He drove slowly toward it.

"*Damn*—it's a loading-dock gate." In front of them stood a chain-link double gate, about ten feet wide and ten high. Beyond, Max could see a long loading dock. He inched the car forward.

Johanna craned her neck to see. "It looks like it's almost two meters off the ground, Max. If we broke through the gate, could the car withstand a fall from that height? Could *we?*"

Max didn't answer. He was figuring speeds and distances. The dock was about fifty feet long. Obviously, trucks would pull up on either side to be loaded with goods. And Johanna was right; the drop to the pavement from the dock was almost six feet.

The hammering above returned.

They'd have to do it. There was no other way.

But they needed a diversion, something to draw the chopper away long enough for them to get on the road. He grimaced in concentration. Then he grinned.

"*Flares.* We'll use flares."

Johanna said, "What, Max? Flares? But how—"

"Look, here's what we're going to do." He had turned to face her. "In the side pocket of your door there are five flares. Three red, one white, and a yellow, I think. We'll go over to the door by the wharf"—he pointed back through the empty warehouse—"and drop the flares near the door. Just out of direct view from above. That's sure to draw the chopper. When they go over to investigate, we'll break through the dock gate and make a jump for the ground."

She stared at him.

"But . . . what if—"

"No time for ifs, Hansi. It's all we've got. In a minute this place will be swarming with Vopos." He pointed to the door. "Now, dig those flares out. Hold them all in one hand and just tear the strip off one flare. That'll ignite the others. But don't do it until I say to. Ready?"

She nodded.

"Comrade Colonel, shall we call in help?"

Koshka swore violently.

"No, Vanya. We can flush this American. Take us to the north end." Koshka played the lights over the surface of the warehouse below.

"Certainly, Colonel. But . . ."

"But what, Vanya?"

"But why not just shoot into the building?"

"Because we cannot risk destroying the equipment. Any other foolish questions?"

Vanya clamped his lips together and said no more.

Johanna held the flares out the window. She looked nervously at Max.

He was watching the helicopter. It moved to the north end. Once it was there, he turned to Johanna.

"*Now*, Hansi. Pull the strip."

She jerked the friction strip off one flare. It blazed instantly. She dropped it and the others next to the door to the wharf.

"*Hold on.*"

Max fed the turbocharged V-8 full throttle. The tires smoked and they lunged across the empty warehouse floor. Max lined up the Ford's nose with the door ahead.

Johanna buried her head in her arms and took a deep breath.

"*Colonel.* Over there."

"Where?" Koshka's head twisted around.

Vanya stood the chopper on its main rotor and brought them around the edge of the warehouse. "There—ahead. You see it?"

Koshka saw the bright light pouring out of the doorway of the wharf.

231

"Take us out a bit, Vanya, so I can see directly inside."

The pilot pulled away from the warehouse. They hovered alongside the wharf. Koshka strained to see what was producing the light.

"*Closer*, Vanya."

The Mi-24 edged nearer the doorway. The flares poured incandescence out of the opening. Koshka brought the spotlights up and aimed them at the door.

"Move sideways, Vanya. About two meters."

The big helicopter yawed to the left. Koshka struggled to find the source of the light.

Max had only a split second to see that he would have to turn the car hard right after they landed or they'd crash into the silent warehouse opposite. Then they smashed into the dock gate at eighty miles an hour.

The gate sheared in a scream of wrenched metal as two tons of Ford rammed it. The Ford pulled it right out of the wall mounts, dragging it for twenty feet. Then it fell apart and they raced down the dock.

Max hit the brakes just before the end of the concrete dock. The nose pitched down. Then he booted the throttle again and it came up. And they were flying through the air. The engine overrevved violently when the rear wheels left the dock. Max automatically pulled his foot off the throttle. After that everything happened in fractions of seconds.

The Ford crashed to the ground on all four wheels. It staggered as if pounded by a giant fist. The suspension bump stops sheared off and the wheels were driven as far up as the long suspension would allow. Then the belly pan smashed into the ground and the car leaped into the air again. Max gagged and bit his tongue. He just had time to see the wall looming opposite them. He hauled the steering wheel to the right with all his strength and planted his foot on the gas pedal.

The car was flung sideways, still being steered by the momentum of the leap from the dock. The tires were aimed away from the wall, but the speed was so great that they continued toward it.

Three feet away, the left rear tire stopped sliding. It delivered the power of the engine in a sudden burst directly to the ground and the Ford changed its course slightly. A fraction of a second later, the right tire gained a hold and the Ford missed the wall by a foot as it shook itself and shot forward.

Max spun the wheel the other way and they cleared the edge of the wall. He shifted to third gear and pointed the mangled nose at the gate leading to the Ulbricht-strasse.

It, too, burst open before the Ford's mass. And suddenly they were on the lakeside road. Aimed again at Potsdam.

"They're only flares. *Flares,* Vanya. Decoys." Koshka pounded his knee in fury.

"*Quick.* Get some height. They may have escaped through one of the other doors." The engines whined under the load as Vanya pulled back the controller.

Koshka swept the lights around the yard. He saw the tire tracks on the pavement below. And then the twisted gates.

"Vanya, back to the road. *Quickly,* you dolt—every second they pull away from us."

Koshka looked down at the road to Potsdam. He could feel the sweat on his back. A chill went through him as he thought about how easily he'd been duped.

After a few moments Max flicked on his headlights. They were in luck. Three of the seven still worked. He looked over at Johanna.

"Are you okay?" He had had to shout. The muffler had been ripped off. It sounded as if the Indy 500 were being run directly over them.

She wiped her face with the skirt of her dress and smiled back at him.

"I think so. Will the car be all right?"

Max grinned and yelled, "Sure. It's American, remember?"

She smiled in relief.

Max wasn't so sure. The impact had torn off both outside mirrors. The shimmy had become a serious wobble. It was obvious the steering gear was in bad shape.

He looked at the instrument panel. The engine was overheating. Both the oil and water temperatures were climbing rapidly. Even Nubs's reinforced grille couldn't stand repeated use as a battering ram. He had to slow down.

At eighty miles an hour, the needles stabilized. Below that speed, not enough of the cold November air could get through to the radiators. And above it, the beat-up front end made an air dam, keeping the high-speed air out, too.

They seemed to be going agonizingly slowly. Max noticed that Johanna had a huge bruise over her right eye. She looked terrible, he thought, and then imagined what he must look like. Torn blue uniform, filthy hands and face. A specter.

They passed through another village, and suddenly Max began to recognize things. Wilson had left this way. He had just begun to feel they might have a chance after all when the steering wheel began to shake violently. The steering gear *was* breaking up. All he could do was hang on.

He passed a *Gasthaus* he remembered. And then the blazing blue-white spotlights of the helicopter pinned them again.

Max saw that the chopper was still at least a half mile away. He knew they stood no chance as long as it was high above them. A tiny lane appeared ahead and Max dove into it, wrestling fiercely with the steering wheel.

Koshka fired again. The antitank round exploded just behind Max, throwing a fountain of earth and tarmac into the sky. The Ford slued against the far bank of the road.

"Bring it down," shouted Koshka, trying to keep the weaving Ford in his lights. Vanya bit his lip and brought the helicopter right over the Ford. They were skimming the trees now. Koshka was shouting something, but Vanya kept his eyes on the horizon. In the dark night he would need a miracle to see a telephone pole in time to gain altitude.

Max felt the lights as crushing heat. The air turbulence produced by the helicopter plucked at the speeding

Ford. Koshka's voice came from above, magnified and distorted by a PA in the helicopter's belly.

"*Listen,* American. You have no chance to escape. I order you to stop." He spoke in heavily accented English. Max ignored him.

Koshka fired another round ahead of the Ford. Max was through the blast before he had a chance to shield his eyes. Momentarily blind, he steered through the little crater in the road and almost lost control as the wheel tried to wrench itself out of his hands.

Koshka spoke again. His voice echoed across the dark fields.

"You see we can kill you anytime. *Give up.*"

Max saw a churchyard on his right. He waited until the last moment, then twisted the wheel to the right. The Ford lifted onto its outside wheels, staggered drunkenly, then fell back on all four and swerved through the grassy yard.

Koshka watched helplessly. The car could easily out-turn them. He started to speak to Vanya, but the Ukrainian was already standing the helicopter on its rotor, making a full-power turn. Koshka brought his spotlight to bear on the careening car. Within seconds, he was overhead again.

Max knew they were trapped in the churchyard. He yanked on the parking brake and the Ford whipped around. In the wet grass the traction was bad and Max couldn't hold the course. The car slued off the grass and onto a gravel path. Max spun the tires and swung the nose of the car toward the gate ahead. He saw that it was a cemetery gate.

Koshka screamed in fury as Max spun backward beneath them. Vanya turned the chopper as tightly as he dared, feeling the controls shudder in his hands. Koshka swung the lights on the Ford again and saw the cemetery gate ahead. He snapped off a three-round burst and the gatepost exploded into stone fragments.

Max yelled in pain as the bulletproof glass of his windshield cracked under the impact of the stone fragments of the shattered post. He kept the throttle down and the Ford's tires spit rocks as he bulldozed through the debris. Koshka fired another burst and Max lurched off the path to avoid the crater. They were in the cemetery now, the tires churning up dirt and grass.

Vanya tried to follow the weaving Ford. He fixed his eyes on the blue car as it sped through the graveyard, the Ford and the helicopter linked by the blazing beam of Koshka's lights.

Koshka saw that Max had slowed and steadied. He flipped on the loudspeaker again. In his fury, he spoke Russian.

"Little mouse, the cat has you. You have no escape. *Stop.*"

Max swerved the Ford back onto the gravel pathway. The chopper roared around, just outside Max's turning radius. Every bit of Vanya's skill and concentration was focused on the Ford.

Koshka fired again and a piece of the Ford's rear fender flew off.

Max saw the side of the church itself ahead on his left. He accelerated hard. The engine began to vibrate but pumped enough power to leap momentarily to the leading edge of Koshka's merciless lights.

Vanya pushed the gunship forward, eyes fixed on the car. Koshka lined up the 30-mm gun again.

Max came to the corner of the church and jerked up the hand brake, spinning the steering wheel to the left. The Ford slid sideways around the corner in a shower of gravel.

Vanya saw the Ford begin its slide and tried to cut across Max's turn.

Koshka loosed another round and looked up just in time to see the church steeple swinging into view.

He screamed, but it was too late.

Vanya merely stared, uncomprehending, as the ten-ton gunship plowed straight into the ancient stone steeple.

The helicopter exploded instantly, showering pieces of masonry over the churchyard. The car staggered from the shock wave of the explosion, then weaved forward and staggered again as the Ford took a hundred-pound chunk right in its roof.

Max steered through the church gate numbly. He saw that a piece of the rock had penetrated the roof, bending it down in a sharp cone and nearly killing Johanna. But the roll cage had held it. They drove slowly through the cloud of debris down the lane to the main road.

Max looked over at Johanna. There was blood on her face. She looked at him and he saw that blood was trickling from her mouth.

But she smiled in triumph.

28

STACHEL TURNED RIGHT ONTO THE ULBRICHT-
strasse and saw, under the shimmering mercury-vapor
street lamps, a Vopo roadblock. There were two white
BMWs, blue lights whirling atop roofs, and three Vopos
directing traffic. Apparently no one was getting through.

Stachel maneuvered the Mercedes to the head of the
little queue. A uniformed Vopo noticed him and stalked
over.

The man stopped a few paces away and stared at the
car. It was a mess. Mud and dried marsh grass clung to the
car from the door handles down. Weeds were still
wrapped around the axle and suspension. The driver's
door was streaked with dried blood. The window was
missing. The trunk lid was wedged open about five centi-
meters. The Vopo stared at the car in wonderment. Then
he recognized Stachel.

He snapped to attention.

"*Herr Direktor.* We thought . . . that is, they told us—"

"Never mind what they told you." Stachel's cold voice
had silenced him. "Why are you blocking the Ulbrichtstrasse?"

The Vopo leaned closer.

"The Soviets have erected a roadblock near the

American mission road. We were ordered to stop all traffic from this direction. Apparently—"

"Apparently they did not expect me." Stachel scowled. "Open up."

The Vopo hesitated only a moment, then sprang to the front of the car.

"*Klaus.* Clear a way for the director."

He saluted crisply. Stachel jammed the Mercedes into gear and accelerated.

Stachel drove automatically, his mind already examining the possibilities and problems. The Soviets must not get the American. And the American must not get to the mission. Therefore Karl Stachel would have to stop them both.

Obviously Koshka's men hadn't been able to halt the American. Otherwise, there would be no need for a roadblock. He thought over what the Vopo had said. Evidently the Russians were blocking the main road—the Ulbrichtstrasse—and not the mission access road. That meant the block would be erected on the west side of the junction.

The Mercedes skidded on a wet patch that was already freezing, and Stachel forced himself to pay more attention to driving. But he continued to turn the problem over in his head like a jeweler examining a stone.

After ten kilometers he slowed. The mission turnoff was about a kilometer ahead, on the right. He began surveying the roadside terrain, even though he knew it by heart. Forest—deep and dense with undergrowth—lay on the mission side of the Ulbrichtstrasse. It surrounded the mission like a moat to a depth of one kilometer. There were no firebreaks, no tracks or roads through that Stachel knew of. And he knew them all.

On the other side were scattered trees and marshy, unreclaimed fields. There were places where a car could get through, but not near the turnoff. A deep ditch ran next to the road on that side, providing runoff. Its banks were so steep that no car could drive along it.

He rounded a gentle curve, still driving slowly and still deep in thought. Then he saw it. Ahead, about half a kilometer away. The Soviet roadblock.

He killed the lights and pulled the Mercedes over. Reaching into the glove box, he pulled out a pair of high-power binoculars. He got out of the car and focused them on the activity ahead.

They were just setting up the block, he saw. He smiled grimly as he realized they were using the pattern that he himself had developed: an armored personnel carrier in the center of the road, flanked by two sedans on either side. They formed a kind of wedge and ensured that any vehicle—regardless of size—could not batter its way through. It would simply compress the cars and lock them tighter together. He saw that the men were all Russians, in Air Force uniform. He caught the blue-and-silver glint of a lieutenant colonel's shoulder board. They were taking the problem very seriously indeed.

He ignored the cold and leaned against the car, thinking. There was no way the American could get around or through that roadblock. He would need a tank to do it. Or an artillery barrage. He couldn't come to Stachel.

So Stachel had to go to him.

Stachel stroked his goatee as the plan unfolded in scenes falling rapidly before his eyes, like projected transparencies. When the scenes were finished, he ran through them again, critically examining every possible flaw. There were many, he found. The scheme depended on split-second timing, on the American's reflexes, and, finally, on the Russian pattern of instant obedience to authority. He frowned as he counted the loopholes. There were many. But he had to chance them. There was still a possibility he could discredit Koshka.

The cold finally penetrated. He shivered, pulling his bloodstained greatcoat tighter. A lone mercury-vapor lamp stood over the busy Russians in the distance. He heard, faintly, the diesel engine of the armored personnel carrier as it worked into the keystone position in the arrowhead roadblock. The stars glittered like remote diamonds. He wedged his body back into the driver's seat and began reloading his Stechkin. In the stillness, each round snapped into the magazine with a loud metallic sound. Karl Stachel thought, suddenly, that each sounded

240

somehow final. He finished and looked back at the road-block, now completed.

His plan was flawed. It might even, he realized, be simply desperate. The last frantic feint of a cornered man. But it was all he had.

Far away, down the Ulbrichtstrasse and to the west, an orange glow flared and died. Fifteen seconds later, a dull thud followed.

Karl Stachel nodded. Unaccountably, he knew that the distant explosion meant the Ami was still in action. You see, Comrade Colonel Yuri Andreyevich Koshka? He does belong to me.

He turned the key and the Mercedes whined to life.

29

MAX HALTED BRIEFLY AT THE PLACE WHERE THE little church lane joined the main road. He knew they could be only a few miles from the mission now. The final stretch. And it would almost certainly be blocked again somewhere.

His ears were still ringing from the explosion of the helicopter. There were tiny glass splinters stuck all over his body. He slipped the gear lever into neutral and let the engine idle for a moment. Behind them, the debris settled slowly.

Johanna wiped blood off her face. Max studied her for a moment. She had withstood the events of the night as well as he. Perhaps, he had to admit, better than he, because she was merely a helpless passenger whose life depended on the skill of another. And from his ride with Wilson in the afternoon, he knew what that was like.

Wilson. Max had forgotten completely about him. He unbuckled his belt and turned around.

Ike was hanging twisted in the rear-seat straps, which had worked loose again. His eyes were closed. A thin smear of blood covered one cheek. Underneath, dark blood suffused a badly bruised area. His arms were still held tightly by the inflatable splints. Max held a hand to

Ike's throat. A weak, erratic pulse fluttered under his touch. Wilson was in bad shape.

Johanna twisted around to help without saying a word. She gently lifted Ike's head while Max moved him back onto the seat. He pulled the straps tight again and stared wordlessly at Ike's yellowish pallor. It seemed a long time since Max had watched, paralyzed, as Ike had fallen from the wrecked A-10.

Thinking of the A-10 made him start. What about the helmet and Jesus Box? Some of the explosions had been close to the trunk. Max pulled the door handle to get out, but the door opened only half an inch. He leaned his shoulder against the door and shoved. It swung open with a groan. Max stumbled out and walked back to the trunk slowly.

He was amazed at the condition of the car. Jagged holes were ripped in the sheet metal. The roof had been caved in by the huge chunk of masonry. Only Nubs's roll cage had kept them alive. The tires were slashed and torn, but they still contained air. He knelt and examined the left rear tire. It was barely inflated. A piece of wire stuck out of the sidewall, a souvenir of their gate-breaking. Only the sealant inside the tire had saved it from going flat. But it wouldn't last much longer.

Max stood painfully and saw that the trunk had somehow missed all the mayhem. The bumper had been ripped off somewhere, and both taillights were blown out. The trunk lid was twisted. He punched the button and tried to lift it, but it didn't move. He shrugged. At least nothing would fall out. When he climbed back in the car, Johanna said, "How is it? Can we go on?"

Max smiled thinly. His face was covered with dirt, making his teeth unnaturally bright.

"Sure. After all, they can't stop *us*." He had meant to make a wry comment, the kind of snappy patter that heroes always make in the movies. But his smile wouldn't work when he spoke. He was just too tired.

Johanna looked steadily at him and touched his hand.

"You're right, Max. They can't." His heart caught as

he realized she was serious. She had misunderstood his mocking.

He didn't have the strength to fire a witty reply. All he could do was nod.

"Are you ready?" he asked.

She shook her head. Surprised, he took his hand off the shift lever. "Why not?"

She leaned quickly across the center console and kissed him. He noticed there was a faint odor of lilacs around her.

She leaned back in her seat. Her eyes were serious.

"Whatever happens, Max, it was worth it. Thank you." He sat speechless. The snappy patter was over. He suddenly smiled. The smile was broad, spontaneous, and genuine. A smile of happiness.

"Yeah," he said in English. "You're damned right. It was worth it."

Then he snicked the gear lever into first and turned onto the main road. The road home.

Max drove carefully. His mind had been cleared. He felt calm. Still weak, but calm. His main concerns now were the car and the roadblock he knew would be ahead.

The engine was overheating badly. Max turned the heater full up to circulate as much coolant as possible, but the needle stayed high, touching the red zone. Every time he accelerated hard the needle snapped into the red. If he cruised steadily and didn't try to gain speed quickly, they might not cook the motor.

Only two headlights were working now. The dash panel lights flickered on and off, too. The fuel needle registered empty. That meant, Max figured, they had about five miles of fuel left. Maybe ten at the most.

He accelerated slowly through the dark night. The engine vibrated as the rpm climbed. A reek of hot oil and burned air came through the vents. Max and Johanna were sweating profusely.

Max now recognized the countryside. He didn't need much light. Even at the Trebelsee crossroads, the Ulbrichtstrasse at this point was a lonely road. A few taverns were set into the forest on their left, and in the distance, on their right, lonely lights on the moors identified the hardy farmers who waged grim war with the marshland. A steep drainage ditch followed the road.

A few miles from the churchyard, they streaked by a little tavern. Max saw as he passed that one of the three cars parked in front was Air Force blue. He caught a glimpse of someone sitting in it, and considered stopping, but the memory of the Russian Lada back in Zachow kept his throttle foot down.

The American major in the tavern parking lot watched Max go by. The Recovery car was battered almost beyond recognition, trailing a sizable smoke screen.

The major squeezed the transmit button on the radio microphone he held in his hand.

"Kettledrum, this is Trumpet. Figaro. Repeat, Figaro."

He snapped the microphone back onto the dashboard and started the car, simultaneously leaning on the horn. In a moment another American came running out of the tavern. He was followed by the curious stares of the few locals out drinking on this cold night.

He jumped into the car, panting.

"He go by?"

The major's jaw was set. "Just now. He'll be getting to the roadblock in a few minutes. I hope Nubs's boys are on the mission road."

The other man buckled his seat belt as the major switched on the lights and turned onto the road.

"I still don't see how Ike's going to get through that roadblock."

The major's expression didn't change.

"I don't either, right now. But from the looks of that car, the Russians have been playing rough. And two can play at that game."

The other man looked again at the pair of M-16 automatic rifles on the back seat.

30

MAX SAW THE ROADBLOCK AND HIS HEART SANK.
He lifted his foot and the engine coughed and slowed.
Two hundred yards from the blunt nose of the armored
personnel carrier, he stopped the Ford.

He had time to see that there was no way around the
wedged vehicles before a blinding light stabbed out from
the tanklike personnel carrier.

The web of cracks in the windshield caught the dazzling beam and diffused it. Behind it, Max and Johanna
squinted and held up their hands to cover their eyes.

No sounds came from the roadblock. No hailing, no
threats. Everyone knew what was happening. There was
no need for wasted words.

Max looked out to the right. The ten-foot ditch, then
a wasteland. The Ford would either be flipped on the
ditch wall or be sunk to its fenders in marsh.

He looked left. Thick, impenetrable forest grew right
to the edge of the road.

The V-8 stuttered. It was overheating. The oil stink
got worse.

Still shielding her eyes, Johanna looked over at Max.
He saw the question in her eyes and shook his head.

"No. There's no way around. I'm sure the mission road is just behind them, right by that light pole. But I don't know how we can get through."

Max looked in his rearview mirror. To go back was to extend their time before capture. That was all. If the pursuing Lada didn't get them, a helicopter or another roadblock would.

On the other side of the Russians, Karl Stachel watched as the searchlight flared into life. He couldn't see the American car, but he knew it had to be there.

It was time.

He turned on his headlights, as well as the high beams and fog lights.

He clamped the little rotating blue beacon onto the roof. The beacon *thunk*ed and then stuck magnetically. The wire ran into the dashboard. He flipped a switch and the light began whirling.

He slipped the oblong plastic gear lever into DRIVE and booted the Mercedes forward. A second later, his wailing siren ripped through the night.

The Soviets turned toward him. Their faces were white in the glare of his powerful lights. As he closed with the back of the roadblock he saw a hatch pop open on the armored personnel carrier and a man's head appear. Stachel kept accelerating as he recognized the lieutenant colonel.

The Russians heard the moan of the fuel-injected Mercedes engine and looked nervously at one another. They saw the whirling beacon and began to shuffle away from their posts. The colonel barked an order. Uneasily, they stood in place. The American car was ignored.

Stachel waited until the very last moment to slam on the Mercedes' powerful disc brakes. He slid on smoking tires to within ten feet of the armored personnel carrier's steel tailgate.

He sat with the beacon whirling and the siren wailing.

No one moved for ten heartbeats. Then the Soviet colonel ordered a soldier over to Stachel's car. The officer could see that it was an official German Mercedes, but the glare concealed Stachel.

Uncertainly, the soldier advanced on Stachel.

He stopped a few paces from the window and looked inside.

Stachel favored the young Russian soldier with a cold stare. In his best official Russian he said, "Tell your commander to report to me."

The soldier gulped and turned to look at the colonel. The Russian officer stared back coolly.

The soldier looked back at Stachel and cleared his throat uneasily.

"Your pardon, Comrade, but who shall I say—"

"Director Karl Stachel of the Military Intelligence Liaison Division. I am in command of this operation."

The soldier stood to attention and saluted. The colonel scowled and called to the soldier, "Borzov, who is it?"

The soldier ran through Stachel's lights to the colonel. Above the noise of the siren, he gave the colonel Stachel's message.

Stachel watched impassively. He sat motionless behind the wheel of the Mercedes while the light threw strobe-like blue flashes across the scene. The colonel looked into the glare for a moment, then disappeared down the hatch. A second later, he jumped out the rear door of the APC. He stood for a moment, then pulled his tunic straight and walked slowly over to Stachel.

"You claim to be Director Stachel?" His voice was cold.

Stachel turned his head slowly to stare up at the Russian.

"I do not claim to be he, I *am* he." Stachel flipped his badge case open on the windowsill.

The Russian's eyes flicked to the case, then back to Stachel. Their eyes locked for a long second. Then the Russian blinked. He stepped back slightly.

"Yes. We thought you dead, Comrade Stachel. Colonel Koshka—"

"Ah, yes. Where is the colonel?" Stachel's voice was flat.

The other man hesitated. "We ... we don't know, Comrade Director. He was in a helicopter, trailing the American."

Stachel smiled.

"Ah. And the American is out there. So Comrade Koshka must be gone. So there is no question about my authority, then, is there?"

The Russian hesitated again. "Colonel Koshka assigned me to the command of the roadblock."

Stachel nodded. "Obviously a good choice. But since I am here now, I am in command. You dispute this?"

The Russian bit his lip. He could not deny that the German had legal control of the apparatus for capturing Americans.

The wailing siren continued. Its rising and falling howl made the Russian soldiers nervous. They began to edge away from the Mercedes.

Finally the colonel nodded stiffly to Stachel. "Correct, Comrade Director. You are in command. Your orders?"

Stachel pointed at the personnel carrier.

"You will remove this vehicle. I will then approach the Americans and speak to them. They are desperate men. They could easily destroy themselves and their cargo. And above all we must have their cargo intact."

The colonel stared at Stachel.

"You wish to break the roadblock?"

Stachel frowned. "Do I have to repeat myself, Comrade Colonel?"

The colonel stiffened. "No, Comrade Director. But if we break the roadblock, the Americans have a chance to escape."

Stachel leaned out the window slightly. He bared his teeth. "Colonel, I promise you the Americans will not escape."

The Russian saw the madness in Stachel's eyes and backed away. He waved to the driver of the APC, who was watching curiously.

"*Sergeant.* You will move the personnel carrier out of the roadblock."

The driver stared for a second, then started the diesel

engine. Gears crunched and the twelve-ton vehicle slowly rolled forward. A thick trail of smoke emerged from its exhaust, following its movement to the side of the road. The spotlight winked out.

The colonel looked down at Stachel.

"Should we fire on them if they try to break through, Comrade Director?"

Stachel slipped the Mercedes into gear and shook his head. He fixed the colonel with a stare and said, "No matter what happens, Colonel, you will not fire. The cargo is not to be risked. Understand?"

Before he could answer, Stachel laid a streak of rubber on the ground and sped toward the American car.

Max watched in amazement as the armored car moved aside. Behind, he saw the headlights of another car. A blue beacon spun atop it. Across the two hundred yards, he could hear the siren. Then he recognized the pattern of lights. The car was a Mercedes. *They were coming out to get him.*

Johanna sat frozen. Her hands lay limp in her lap. Max saw the nose of the Mercedes rise upward and knew the car had started for him. He engaged first gear and let the clutch out slowly. The Ford inched forward.

The Mercedes continued straight at them. Now one hundred yards away, it continued accelerating. Max knew it wouldn't slow down.

He waited until it was half that distance away, then mashed the throttle down. The Ford engine instantly responded and the car shot forward. The Mercedes was aimed right at them. Max sawed at the wheel and the Ford lurched to the right.

Stachel tried to correct, but he was too late. The black Mercedes screamed past the Ford, missing it by inches. He wrenched the steering wheel around, and the Mercedes rocked sideways to a stop.

Max slowed after Stachel passed him. He watched as the Mercedes wallowed to a halt behind. Then his eyes flicked to the roadblock. There was still a hole ahead. Savagely, he jammed the gearshift home and punched the gas pedal. The Ford shuddered as the battered engine roared again. The tires smoked, and the Ford lunged forward.

Stachel watched in horror. Then he whipped the Mercedes around and shot after Max.

Max saw the startled faces of the Russians scatter before the onrushing cars. The German's headlights filled the Ford's interior with bright light.

Max shifted into second gear just as he roared through the roadblock. The Russian colonel swore and raised his pistol. He jumped onto the deck of the APC and aimed at Max's car.

Just before he squeezed the trigger, a burst of automatic-rifle fire, richocheting along the personnel carrier's flanks, made him flinch. He spun around and saw another American car a hundred yards away. A man was aiming an M-16 out the window right at him.

Stachel, too, burst through the roadblock. The Russian officer ignored him, staring at the blue car. Before he could speak, the American with the M-16 yelled to him, "Hold your fire, Ivan. We're playing this one by the book."

The Russian jammed his pistol back in its holster and twisted around to watch the disappearing cars.

Max didn't take time to wonder at having made it through the roadblock. All he cared about was the Ford. The Mercedes could still stop him. Even one foot outside the mission gate was East Germany. He had to make it through the gate.

He pitched the Ford through the left-hand turn under the streetlight. The car coughed once, twice, and then continued. The fuel was draining away from the pickup in the tank.

He shifted into fourth gear once the car stopped sliding. The temperature needle was in the red zone and still climbing.

Stachel appeared in Max's mirror. Max looked down the road. No place for tricks. Just a gentle curve to the left, then the mission gate, a mile ahead. He winced as the oil-pressure gauge flashed a red light at him.

Stachel held on to the shaking Mercedes steering

wheel with his right hand. With the left, he worked the Stechkin machine pistol out over the blood-rimmed windowsill. He gained rapidly on the American.

Max pushed the throttle pedal all the way down. He saw the Mercedes closing. He started weaving across the road.

Stachel fired a burst and the bullets flashed past on Max's right. The German cursed and fired again. One bullet whined off the bulletproof glass of the Ford's back window. Another thudded into the trunk. Max slued back to the right.

Stachel held the gun out the window and pulled the trigger again. The American was right in front of him. He could not miss.

The gun clicked emptily. Stachel screamed in frustration and threw the gun out the window. He pushed harder on the Mercedes' accelerator pedal.

Max saw the mission gate far ahead. Then he saw the Jeep Cherokees. One on the right, one on the left. They were standing at right angles to the road, blacked out. As he watched, puzzled, they moved onto the road.

Their timing was perfect. Max jerked the Ford to the left around the one entering the road from the right, then spun the wheel and slalomed around the other. They were forming a blockade of their own—a mobile chicane.

Stachel didn't see the Jeeps until he was almost on them. He watched Max shoot around the first. He twisted the Mercedes steering wheel hard to the left and barely missed the huge four-wheel-drive vehicle. The second time he wasn't so lucky.

The Mercedes leaned heavily on its right side as Stachel desperately wrenched the car around to avoid the Jeep on the left. His left front fender smashed into the Jeep's massive bumper winch.

The Mercedes slid out of control. Stachel hung on to the wheel. The left fender was ripped off, the headlight gone. The car flung itself sideways down the road, doing over a hundred. Stachel looked wildly around, then jerked the wheel into the slide. The Mercedes sloughed off

252

speed, the wheels gained traction, and suddenly it was facing forward again.

Stachel saw the Ford come into view. He had only one thought in his mind. The Mercedes stabilized. Stachel took aim on the American.

Max looked up. The mission gate was a quarter of a mile away. He knew the engine was done for. But maybe ... He pressed with all his strength on the accelerator pedal. The Ford began to gather more speed.

Stachel was still gaining.

Max steered for the open gate.

The Ford speedometer registered 110. The water- and oil-temperature needles were pegged.

Max looked in the mirror. Stachel was almost on his bumper. The German swung out to the left. He was going to try to ram the Ford off the road. Max held the throttle down.

The engine was being overrevved. Max tried to shift into top gear, but the lever stuck. The V-8 was turning at over ten thousand rpm. The engine note rose to an ear-splitting crescendo.

Stachel smiled grimly. An eighth of a mile from the gate, he knew the American could never make it. Max's car was pouring out dense smoke. Stachel pulled the Mercedes to the left and eased up to Max's blown-out tail-lights.

Johanna looked at Max hopelessly. She covered her face with her hands. Max worked the wheel, but the shuddering steering mechanism wouldn't respond.

Stachel's mangled front end touched Max's left rear fender.

The German shouted in triumph and started to turn the wheel to the right. He was going to force the Ford off the road.

Max finally freed the gear lever. He slipped it out of fourth and desperately tried to jam it into top gear. It hung up in neutral and, free of the load, the engine revved to fifteen thousand rpm.

There was a deafening explosion. The Ford's cockpit

instantly filled with smoke. Oil burst from the seams of the blown engine.

Stachel saw the flames shoot out from underneath the Ford. He didn't see the oil.

The Ford V-8 pumped seven quarts of boiling oil onto the pavement in less than a second, lowering the coefficient of friction between the Mercedes tires and the road surface in the same amount of time to nearly zero.

Stachel felt his car begin to slide to the left. He spun the steering wheel both ways. But the car was being steered by the laws of physics.

The Mercedes hurtled sideways for forty feet. Then the front wheels encountered dry road and the car stood up on its outside tire. Still hurtling at over a hundred, the Mercedes pitched drunkenly vertical and flew through the air, standing on its nose. The rear end was just beginning to topple over when the car slammed into the densely packed trees. Karl Stachel's agonized cry was cut off by the instantaneous rupture and explosion of the gas tank. The Mercedes kept going, cutting a flaming swath through the upper branches of the forest. It finally stopped and hung, burning, twenty feet off the ground.

Max had seen nothing. The instant the Ford's engine had blown, the car had begun to slide on its own oil. The steering wheel gave no resistance when Max spun it desperately. The acrid smoke choked and blinded him. He coughed and struggled for control of the car.

The massive stone pillars of the gate loomed a hundred feet in front of him. Max sawed at the wheel. The Ford whipped back and forth.

Max let go of the wheel. He covered his eyes.

The Fairmont was a four-thousand-pound freewheeling unguided missile. It wobbled straight through the gate, then immediately began spinning.

Johanna screamed.

The Ford struck the six-inch-high row of stones around the circular grassy area in front of the mission. The right-side tires hit first. Both blew out instantly. The Ford's momentum carried it up and over on its side. It

254

smashed the flagpole to kindling in mid-roll across the grass. And kept rolling.

The automatic fire extinguishers cut in as it began its second roll, still traveling fast. It flipped across the other side of the grass, crashed down on its wheels, and bounced into the air.

The Ford came down on its blown right-side tires and tilted far over as if to roll again. Teetering on the twisted rims, it rocked gently for a moment, then fell back over onto all four wheels.

It rested on the driveway directly in front of the mission's doorway. It uttered one last groan, and the right-side suspension broke off.

Max sat stunned. His ears rang. He tried to focus his eyes.

He saw running people converge on his smoking car.

He saw Nubs Pierce appear next to his door.

He watched as Nubs looked up and down the car.

He heard Nubs speak.

"Jesus H. Christ, boy. Where'd you learn to drive like *that?*"

He watched Nubs grin and spit Red Man at the ground.

And then he passed out.

31

"SERGEANT MAXWELL T. MOSS, PLEASE STAND and face the court." The general's voice was as cold as the snow that blanketed the mission's lawns outside.

Max scraped his chair back over the Turkish carpet and stood up. He tugged down the tails of his dress-blue blouse and looked across the ten feet to the three officers of the court of inquiry. In the center sat an Army major general, the vice commander of Berlin Command. On his left, Colonel Jack Martin, the mission chief. And on his right, an Air Force brigadier general from Supreme Headquarters, Allied Powers Europe. All three regarded Max soberly.

The Army general was president of the inquiry. He picked up a piece of paper and said, "Sergeant Moss, you have heard the statements made over the last two days regarding the subject of this court of inquiry. Before the court rules, do you have any closing statements?"

Max stood painfully erect. A week had elapsed since the recovery of the A-10 equipment and pilot. He'd spent two of the seven days they'd allowed him in a Berlin hospital, resting and undergoing extensive observation. Then a few days back at the mission to prepare for this hearing.

He hadn't been surprised when Colonel Martin told him he would be subjected to an inquisition. The only place the hero gets a stack of medals, the girl, and the money by tearing up the rule book is in the movies. The military lived by rules. And the delicate balancing act of the semisecret missions demanded strict, almost ruthless adherence to the peculiar rules governing their existence.

The old grandfather clock ticked noisily in the hush of the room. Aside from the three officers of the court, only he, his counsel, and a recorder were present. No formal prosecution was involved; the court simply called witnesses to testify on the subject at hand.

He thought over what had gone on in the old baron's study the last two days. Outside, the rain had turned to snow. Now Nubs had the Jeeps on the roads all the time, and the fast Fords slithered awkwardly over ice-covered roads.

And, inside, he had heard the enormity of his deed recalled in the dispassionate words of professional military men, diplomatic people, and members of what the military euphemistically termed "the other side." In other words, the Russians.

The Soviet general had made it crystal clear in Oxonian English that in first allowing Johanna Koch to defect to the West by way of a mission vehicle and then in giving her asylum, the United States had outraged the letter and spirit of the agreement made in 1947. Max had listened, fascinated, as the corpulent Russian had indicted first him, then the mission's officers, and finally the entire command structure of NATO in his impassioned diatribe. He threatened, blustered, shook his fists, and climaxed his three-hour speech with dire warnings of impending doom if the damage to Soviet-American friendship were not repaired.

The president of the court broke into Max's thoughts. "Well, Sergeant Moss?"

Max glanced down at his counsel. Lieutenant Commander Aldrich had offered his services. He had been helpful and encouraging. Now he did not look at Max. It was up to him. He looked back at the general, his green eyes devoid of humor.

257

"You've already heard my testimony. I believed on the road—as I believe now—that if I hadn't allowed Fräulein Koch to accompany me to the mission, I never would have made it over the Elbe. And I guess that means my only defense is that to me getting Captain McCulloch's body and the Jesus Box back here was more important than the provisions of the agreement. Maybe if Wilson hadn't shot Rudi, it would have been different. I don't know."

He paused. They were all looking at him intently. The soft clicking of the recorder's machine stopped when he did.

"But I do know that if I were in the same position again, I'd have to do the same things."

He paused again. His palms were wet and his heart was pounding hard. He looked steadily at each officer of the court. Then he continued.

"That's all."

He sat down. The silence continued for a moment.

The Army major general spoke again, slowly.

"Commander Aldrich, do you have anything to add?"

Aldrich stood.

"No, sir. I believe Sergeant Moss has stated his position more eloquently than I could." He sat down.

The general nodded. "Then the court will retire to consider its findings. There will be a half-hour recess." He snapped a gavel block down and they all stood up.

Aldrich touched Max's shoulder as he was turning to leave.

"Max, there's a visitor in the dining room for you."

Max looked at the Navy man. "Thanks, but I'm not sure I'm feeling like—"

"You'll want to see this one, Max," Aldrich said. "It's a major general."

Max shook his head.

"No offense, but there's already enough brass around here to polish. I really don't feel up to it now."

His stomach was turning over about once every thirty seconds. He felt worse now than at any time during his frantic race to the mission.

Aldrich was insistent.

"Sorry, Max. If you make me, I'll damn well order you to see him. As your counselor and as your superior." Max was surprised at his tone. Aldrich had seemed the most even-tempered of men, the least likely to pull rank.

Max smiled sourly.

"Okay. Let's go."

Aldrich shook his head.

"No. This one's all yours. I'll meet you back here in twenty minutes."

Max shrugged and walked across the empty study to the dining-room doors. He was only slightly curious about the purpose of the major general's visit. He had learned to expect intense interest from brass hats in the mission.

He swung the door open and saw, across the elegant dining room, a man in an Army major general's uniform. He was standing at the tall windows, looking out at the little lake behind the mission. It was beginning to freeze along the edge, the ice so thin that Max had watched it crack as he jogged along the shore that morning.

Max closed the door, making sure it clicked.

The general began to turn around. Max noticed he was leaning heavily on a cane.

The general faced him, and Max knew that, to identify the man, he didn't need to read the nameplate on his right breast or examine the six rows of ribbons below the combat infantry badge and the master blaster's parachute wings.

It was Major General Eric Moss.

His father.

For a long moment neither man spoke. They examined each other from across the room.

Max saw a man aged far beyond the five years that had passed since they'd last met. The black hair was now white and thinning. Liver spots dotted his cheeks and hands like freckles. The left side of his face seemed slacker than the right. The brilliant green eyes were dulled. He had lost weight and, somehow, height; the spotless green uniform hung on him badly. He was still ramrod straight, but he leaned on the gold-headed ebony cane. His hawk's nose still jutted forward like a ship's ram, and his jawline was as unsullied by slack jowls as ever. But the animating energy that had made Eric Moss the center of attention wherever he went was just ... gone. He looked alert, proud, stiff-necked, and still every inch the Eric Moss who would never accept that he could not impose his own order on the chaos around him. But the lightning bottled up inside was gone.

Eric Moss saw a different son from the one he had last known, too. In the thirty seconds they stared wordlessly at each other, he saw not a truculent boy, gifted with intelligence and wit but recklessly rebellious, but a stranger in his son's grown body. A man who stood as erect as he, who looked steadily across a room and held his eyes.

They were strangers.

Max broke the silence. He smiled the half smile that always leaped to his lips when he confronted his father. "Well, General, I don't know whether to shake your hand or salute."

Eric Moss scowled. His consistent, immediate reaction to their meetings.

When he spoke, his voice startled Max. It had lost its crisp edges. Had become slightly slurred.

"Let's not begin that way, Max. It's time-wasting and pointless. And I have only another fifteen minutes here."

"Certainly. We'll skip the pleasantries. Exactly why are you here?" The smile was fixed on Max's face.

Eric Moss walked slowly toward him, moving his left leg stiffly.

"The spooks wanted me to verify Johanna's identity and story. As usual, when Uncle called for me in Army green, I went."

"Makes sense, at least if you're a major general. But she's in Berlin. Why're you *here?*"

"Why do you think, dammit? When I found out you were the one who'd taken her out, what'd you expect me to do?" In anger his voice regained some of its lost power.

Max shook his head. "Whatever you want, I guess. What surprises me is that you'd want to be here. Not that you're here."

Eric pulled a chair away from the highly polished walnut dining table and sat down heavily.

"I don't have the stamina for this anymore, Max. Look—somebody ought to thank you for pulling Johanna out. Gisela . . . Gisela can't do it, so I am. And, besides, I wanted to see you. After all, it's been almost five years."

Max's bitter smile faded.

"Yes, it has. Well, you're welcome. I'm sure you know I couldn't have made it without her. So she really pulled me out. And I'm also sure you know about that, too."

"I know what she thinks. She thinks she owes her life to you. And from what Jack Martin tells me, she does."

"That's not the way I see it. I just drove the damned car. She got us back."

Eric Moss shook his head. "It doesn't matter. The important thing is that she's safe. And so . . . so are you."

"Not quite. Didn't Jack Martin also tell you about the court of inquiry? In fifteen minutes I'll probably find myself recommended for a court-martial. I don't think of that as particularly safe, do you?"

Eric Moss stood again. He walked over to Max and looked him in the eye. He seemed to grow three inches.

"I've never been any good at getting through to you. I hope I succeed this time. If you'd use your damned head, you'd know that this whole show is only for the record. The Russians would have made this a full-fledged international incident if they'd wanted to. But they know and we know what went on over the border. And, maybe more important, the A-10 scared the hell out of them. They won't risk anything for another year—at least until they find out more about our biocybernetic capabilities. So your hide is as safe as if you were in a nursery. Which is where, frankly, you'll belong if you don't stop this bullshit." He was breathing heavily. A slight trickle of saliva formed at the left side of his mouth.

Max backed away.

"How do you know so much about all this?"

His father smiled contemptuously at him. "What exactly do you think Moss Electronics does? But I guess you needn't answer that. You never actually took the time to

261

learn, did you? Just another cog in the military-industrial complex. I believe that's how you characterized the company."

Max glared back.

"Well, that's what it is, isn't it? Without your Pentagon contracts, you'd fold in a second."

"So what? Where would you be without *your* Pentagon contract, *Sergeant?* Look at the clothes you're wearing. I don't have any idea what impelled you to join the Air Force, and even less about why you reenlisted. But I'll tell you this. You're playing in a serious game, Max. You're not a kid anymore. You can't just go home if you get tired of playing with the big boys. You've had a little taste of the realities of life out here, and you had better learn from it. Of course, you didn't have to come all the way over here to find out"—he waved his cane toward the window—"you could have done it just as well in your own backyard." He stopped talking and looked away.

"Naturally," he continued, "that would have been possible if you actually cared. But you didn't, did you, Max? Always too busy hating me, blaming me for your failures."

"You made it easy enough," Max said quietly.

Eric nodded. "No doubt you're right. No doubt I failed pretty comprehensively in some important ways." He narrowed his eyes. "But that's in the past, Max. I can't undo those things, and neither can you. What counts is what you do next."

Max smiled grimly and pointed to the two silver stars on his father's shoulder. "I always thought that you figured these were what counted."

Eric knocked his hand away, his eyes blazing.

"Of course. The power to change things comes only with personal power. I've always believed that. But these uniforms"—he grabbed Max's tunic and then released it—"these don't mean a damned thing unless there's something inside them. Don't you know that by now?"

Max's eyes glinted.

"Yes, Major General Moss, I believe after four years of active duty, and after eighteen years of dependent duty,

I do know that what's inside the uniform counts. Unfortunately, so far most of what I've seen inside them is horseshit."

Suddenly the ebony cane was behind his ear. His father stood very close. His voice was a hoarse whisper.

"I came down here to pay my respects—my belated respects—to a son who'd done something extraordinary. I'd been told by reliable men that he was himself something extraordinary." He paused, breathing hard. His eyes burned like green fire. "Instead of finding that son—the son who made me proud of him for the first time when he took the oath four years ago—I've found someone—no, some*thing*—entirely different." He eased the pressure of the cane on Max's head and turned away.

Facing the windows, he said, "I'll always be waiting to welcome that extraordinary son home. But the conceited, hypocritical whiner that my son once was will never be welcome." He turned slowly to face Max.

"I hope that's clear enough." His voice was weary.

Max felt paralyzed. The air in the dining room had grown cold.

"Yes." It was all he could say.

His father looked at him for a second more, then gathered his cap and overcoat from the table. He walked to the opposite door and turned back to Max.

He looked across the gulf between them for a long time. When he spoke, his words seemed cast in lead.

"I didn't want it to be like this, Max." He began to speak again, then jerked open the door and walked out, leaning on his cane.

The last Max saw of him was his board-straight back.

Max stood motionless for a long while. How had it happened? They had not seen each other in five years, and in ten minutes the old battle lines were drawn.

They had both changed. Max knew it and his father knew it. Eric Moss had obviously suffered a great deal. The marks of a severe stroke were plain. And the rusting away of the sharp edge of command that he had always had must have been as great a blow as the convulsion in

263

the brain that had given him the slack face and limp.

But the old patterns, the old arguments, had prevailed.

A light knock on the door ended his paralysis. The door opened, and Aldrich looked in. He betrayed no surprise that General Moss was gone.

"Time, Max."

Max turned slowly and followed Aldrich back to the study. The officers filed in and everyone sat down.

The Army general rapped the gavel.

"This court of inquiry is back in session. Sergeant Moss, please stand and face the court."

Max stood again. Curiously, he felt nothing. It was like a play he was watching. He was a spectator.

The general looked impassively at him, then spoke. His voice was clear and controlled.

"Sergeant Moss, it is the opinion of this court that on November 1, 1982, you did knowingly violate the terms of the agreement between the United States and the Soviet Union which specifies conduct of military personnel of the United States Military Liaison Group in Potsdam, East Germany. In so doing, you endangered good relations between the two nations and jeopardized the successful accomplishment of the entire mission of the group." He paused. Max began to feel light-headed.

"Under the circumstances, the Uniform Code of Military Justice requires that one of two actions be taken. One, that you be charged with dereliction of duty and sent before a court-martial, or, two, that you receive an Article Fifteen punishment."

Max's throat tightened.

"It is the unanimous judgment of this court of inquiry that you receive punishment under the guidelines of Article Fifteen of the Uniform Code.

"Sergeant Maxwell T. Moss, you are hereby reprimanded. This court is dismissed."

Max stood, stunned. The Army general's gavel crashed in his ears like a cannon. Then they were all around him, smiling and talking at once. Aldrich stood up and grabbed his hand, beaming. They were all congratulating him and apologizing. He caught only snatches of what they were saying.

"... damned Russians knew better than to push their luck, Max, but demanded that we at least have an inquest ... "

" ... understand, just for form's sake, there was no option ... "

He nodded and smiled. Someone broke out the whiskey. The room began to fill with other mission people, noise, and smoke.

His father had been right. The whole ordeal had been a show for the Russians. Nothing more. An Article Fifteen reprimand was the sort of thing you got for being late to work.

Colonel Martin took Max aside. His keen gray eyes pierced Max's confusion.

"I hope you understand, Max. It was necessary. Another part of the game."

The game. Max smiled and nodded. The colonel slapped him on the back and went back to the party, which was rapidly becoming more boisterous. Max watched the men laughing and drinking. It was as though a valve had opened. He realized they weren't celebrating his being cleared of charges. That had been a foregone conclusion to everyone but him. No, they were celebrating a victory.

His victory. In the game. He thought about it. Wilson in the hospital. Hansi Koch being interrogated ruthlessly, and with every interrogation coming closer to final escape. And Captain McCulloch in Arlington Cemetery. Without his Jesus Box. That was already being examined somewhere in a secret laboratory. He smiled. Maybe even at one of his father's laboratories.

Someone shoved a glass of beer in Max's hand and slapped him on the back again. He walked over to the window.

He watched the snow piling up in little drifts around the mansion's columns. It was getting deeper.

Eric Moss had said he hadn't wanted their meeting to

end that way today. Max sipped at his cold beer. He thought of Christie. And then of Johanna and Gisela.

Maybe, he thought, maybe someday it wouldn't end the way it had today. He turned back to the room as another burst of laughter broke out.

Someday. But not today.

He drained his glass and joined the party.

Outside, the hush of the snowfall was split by the rolling bellow of a Ford engine.

32

"NO ONE SEEMS TO BE HERE." THE YOUNG VOPO
trooper in front of the door looked back at the officer. The
lieutenant was standing in the snow a few feet away,
frowning up at the chimneys. No smoke hung over them.

"Open it, Wechsler," the lieutenant said. He glanced
around to make sure his men had covered all the exits.
Grim-lipped troopers stood at each window, Kalashnikovs
at the ready.

Wechsler cautiously turned the doorknob. It moved
easily. He shoved the door halfway open and aimed his
automatic rifle down the silent hallway. Nothing moved.
He looked back at the the officer.

The lieutenant unholstered his pistol and elbowed
past the trooper into the hall. He strode forward a few
paces and halted. It was as cold in the house as it was outside. He motioned to Wechsler and two others to enter.
He waved them into the rooms that stood on either side of
the hall.

"No one here," said Wechsler.

"Not in here, either, Comrade Lieutenant. If she's
here—"

"She's here, all right," said the lieutenant. "Berlin is
sure of that. Keep looking."

The Vopos shrugged and tramped upstairs. The officer opened the door to the drawing room and looked
around. It was empty. Cold ashes coated the fire grate. A

voice came from upstairs. "Nobody up here, either, sir." The lieutenant shut the drawing-room door and turned to the hallway. Pursing his lips, he stood a moment in thought.

"Well, we'd better check the castle. Get the men." Wechsler saluted and ran outside.

Fifteen minutes later, the lieutenant's platoon spread out over the Schloss Falkenberg grounds, the men trudging through the ankle-deep snow. The officer took five men and unlocked the castle's massive main door. The snow all around the entry was virgin white.

"If she's inside, Comrade Lieutenant, she's been here for a long time," said a sergeant, pointing at the undisturbed snow. The lieutenant said nothing but indicated they should search the silent rooms.

Their footsteps had ceased to ring on the cold stone of the floors and stairs when he found her. She sat at the head of an ancient, scarred table in the great hall. He knew immediately she was dead. She sat like a wax statue, clothed in white. Her long silver hair hung to her shoulders, a baroness' tiara on her brow. Her features were frozen in agony, hands like talons clutching the arms of the chair. A single cup lay on its side before her.

The lieutenant stood at the end of the table for long minutes, pistol in hand. Finally, he slid the Makarov back into its holster and slowly approached her, mesmerized by the expression on her face. As he drew nearer he saw that through the pain of the poison, another, almost ineffable expression was etched indelibly on her bloodless face. The moment before he forced her eyelids down to cover the dulled blue eyes, he knew what it was, and it chilled him to the marrow.

It was triumph. Gisela Koch had finally escaped.

EPILOGUE
1983

THE BELL TINKLED ON HIS SHOP DOOR, AND THE proprietor of the tiny newspaper stall off Trafalgar Square looked up from his *Daily Mirror*. He rolled the Woodbine around in his yellowed lips and watched the big man struggle through the door.

He was obviously an American. Green Alpine hat with silly feather, knee-length Harbor Master raincoat more suited to California drizzle than London snow, red polyester trousers, and wet Hush Puppies.

He was also a GI, the proprietor saw. The man's fat, cheerful face was dominated by a big red nose and juglike ears. A white-sidewall regulation haircut disappeared into the hat. And the eyes were wary.

Gustav Hornak blew on his hands. Even in the little shop it was cold. He pointed to a magazine in the far corner of the big rack behind the stall owner.

"I see you have *Dog World* from America. Do you also carry *Cat Fancy*?"

The proprietor narrowed his already squinting eyes. He looked closer at the American and nodded.

"Right, mate. Got it here somewhere. You a fancier?"

Hornak smiled. "Yes, I love cats."

271

The shopkeeper folded his newspaper and bent low behind the counter top. Then he straightened, holding a German cat magazine. "Then I expect you'd like this one, eh?"

Hornak flipped through it.

"Yes, I think so." He paid the man and stuffed the magazine into his raincoat.

He waved as he went out the door. The proprietor squinted at the ten-pound note through the Woodbine smoke and smiled.

"Cheerio, mate."

Hornak waited until he got back to his little cottage near Bentwaters to open the magazine. He'd spent the rest of the afternoon in London in tourist fashion, sightseeing. All the way back home on the train, he had had to suppress the urge to look at the magazine. Finally, late in the evening, he sat down at his glass-topped desk.

He carefully opened the magazine and turned to page 34. There was a headline with a bold exclamation mark. He got out a strong magnifier and studied the period under the vertical mark. After moving around his high-intensity desk lamp, he found a small, shiny spot among the paper fibers and clotted ink.

Hornak took a small plastic box from a drawer. Inside were an eyedropper, a vial of colorless fluid, tweezers, and a stack of microscope slides. He dropped a tiny blob of the fluid on the shiny spot and waited a moment. Then he used the eyedropper to transfer the fluid to a slide.

A microscope stood on his desk, ostensibly for use in his stamp-collecting hobby. He slid the glass under the lens and focused. After some time writing appeared beneath his eyepiece. It was, as he had expected, in code.

He copied the coded message in grease pencil onto his glass desk top.

He studied it for a moment, then began the process of decoding.

Twenty minutes later, the message was scrawled across his desk in grease pencil. He read it slowly.

*   *   *

URGENTLY REQUIRE FLIGHT PLANS FOR USAF NORWE-
GIAN WINTER EXERCISE SNOWBALL. HIGHEST PRIOR-
ITY TO A-10 FILE.

He read the words again, savoring the nuances. Then
he wiped the glass clean.